The
Misperception

by

NICOLE PYLAND

The Misperception

Holiday Series Book #5

Paisley Hill cared about one thing – she was building her company from the ground up without accepting any money from her wealthy family to do it. That was important to Paisley, and she took her job as a consultant seriously, wanting to help companies grow and get more efficient because of her ideas. The one thing Paisley hadn't cared much about in years, was a relationship. She'd been fine with casual dates and hookups every now and then, but Paisley had watched several of her close friends find love this year, and she tried to push the loneliness and fear of losing her friends to love out of her mind.

Trinity Pascal had an idea one day, told her best friend about it, and now, years later, they were trying to establish their new company with money from investors. Trinity loved problem-solving and brainstorming, but she wasn't much of a fan of the day-to-day business stuff. When her business-partner-and-best-friend suggests they bring in a consultant to help, Trinity is more than surprised to see her old high school bully, Paisley Hill, walk into the building.

While Trinity definitely remembers Paisley, Paisley doesn't seem to know who Trinity is, at first. As they navigate their work relationship, and things clearly start to move from beyond work-only, both women have to decide if they're ready for something that might just be the real thing – right in time for Paisley's nosy mother to invite Trinity to the family Thanksgiving dinner.

To contact the author or for any additional information, visit: **https://nicolepyland.com**

BY THE AUTHOR

Chicago Series:

- Introduction – Fresh Start

- Book #1 – The Best Lines

- Book #2 – Just Tell Her

- Book #3 – Love Walked into The Lantern

- Series Finale – What Happened After

San Francisco Series:

- Book #1 – Checking the Right Box

- Book #2 – Macon's Heart

- Book #3 – This Above All

- Series Finale – What Happened After

Tahoe Series:

- Book #1 – Keep Tahoe Blue

- Book #2 – Time of Day

- Book #3 – The Perfect View

- Book #4 – Begin Again

- Series Finale – What Happened After

Boston Series:

- Book #1 – Let Go
- Book #2 – The Right Fit
- Book #3 – All Good Plans
- Book #4 – Around the World
- Series Finale – What Happened After

Sports Series:

- Book #1 – Always More
- Book #2 – A Shot at Gold
- Book #3 – The Unexpected Dream
- Book #4 – Finding a Keeper

Celebrities Series:

- Book #1 – No After You
- Book #2 – All the Love Songs
- Book #3 – Midnight Tradition
- Book #4 – Path Forward
- Series Finale – What Happened After

Holiday Series:

- Book #1 – The Writing on the Wall

- Book #2 – The Block Party

- Book #3 – The Fireworks

- Book #4 – The Sweet Escape

- Book #5 – The Misperception

- Book #6 – The Wait is Over

- Series Finale – What Happened After

Stand-alone books:

- The Fire

- The Disappeared

- The Moments

- Reality Check

- Love Forged

- The Show Must Go On

- The Meet Cute Café

- Pride Festival

CONTENTS

CHAPTER 1

The party was winding down already, and Paisley was exhausted. On top of that, she had to leave for a new client tomorrow, so she should be getting home. After taking one last look into Carmen's backyard and at one of the coolest haunted houses Paisley had ever been to, she turned to go. Repeatedly, she had told herself that she didn't want what her friends had – at least, not yet. She'd been working on building her company for years, and as the owner and only employee, if she didn't put in the effort, no one else would. That meant traveling a lot and working practically all the time, but Paisley continued to tell herself that it would be worth it. One day, it would be worth it.

She'd set out to prove to herself – and to her family probably, too – that she could do this on her own, without their money or their help. They weren't bad people, but she'd had that silver spoon in her mouth since she was a zygote, and while it came with its definite perks, it also came with certain assumptions about her. Paisley hated those assumptions. It was fine to her that Aria lived mostly off her family money, and that Weston had used her family money to support her writing career until it took off, but Paisley had been damn determined to not let that be her situation. She was in a good place now. She could afford to hire two to three people right now if she wanted, but the money she saved on payroll – and the taxes that came with it – would help her later when she was finally ready to expand.

Paisley had grand plans for her business, and she'd see them through even if it meant leaving a Halloween-slash-birthday-party behind alone while now four out of their group of six friends from college had girlfriends, and they were making plans for their futures. Weston and Annie had been together since around Valentine's Day officially, but probably even before that; Talon and Emerson had been together for pretty much just as long, too; and while Aria and London had reconnected only in July, they already lived together. Now, Eleanor had Carmen, and although they were still relatively new, Paisley could tell her friend was happier than she'd ever been – Carmen might just be the one for Ellie. That, besides Paisley herself, left just Scarlet, who was still in the closet with her family and was shy and had a hard time talking to women she found attractive. Paisley didn't have that problem and was out and proud as a bisexual, but meeting men *or* women wasn't easy since she was always on the move. Sexual encounters would have to suffice for now, and she would get to the rest later. In her thirties, she'd focus on settling down at least a little. She would have an office by then with a few employees and could maybe travel only for the major clients and be home for dinner with the person she'd fallen for. Yeah, it could wait. She didn't need what they had now. It was fine.

"Even Janet found someone," Paisley muttered to herself, though, when she pulled into the driveway of her house and waited for the garage door to open. "The girl couldn't hold her liquor on the boat and spewed everywhere, but apparently, Mariah is into that kind of thing."

Mariah and Carmen were London's friends that had just tagged along initially but were now part of the group. Janet had been Carmen's date at first, but now was maybe Mariah's girlfriend? Paisley wasn't sure how that turned out, but she'd overheard them tonight calling each other *"baby"* and *"honey"* and talking about meeting up with someone later to have some fun. She didn't think Mariah was into drugs, so *"fun"* likely meant sex. She'd have to get the download on that from one of the others later, though, because she needed to get some sleep before she drove to her client location.

Of course, she had to finish packing first. By this point, packing her bag was a science. Paisley never knew exactly how long she'd be gone for, so she usually packed a carry-on and a larger bag, but this time, the client's location was close enough for her to decide to drive, so she could bring whatever she wanted. Paisley decided to bring an extra bag and a few more business suits than usual, because she could, and hung them in her garment bags over the closet so they wouldn't wrinkle overnight. Then, she pulled out her laptop and checked the directions for the drive, making sure she'd leave at the right time to avoid traffic. She wasn't meeting the client tomorrow, so she could leave a little later and take the four-hour drive around midday, arrive at dinnertime, and pick something up on the way to the hotel before settling in for the night.

After that, she remembered that she'd be staying in a modest business hotel for however long, and in her home, she had a very nice rain shower and a jacuzzi tub. Paisley stripped and waited for the water to fill in the tub before adding just a few bubbles. Any more, and they'd overflow, thanks to the jets. She climbed inside and let those jets relax her body for a while. Then, she rinsed in the shower and climbed back into bed naked after drying off, choosing to enjoy her very nice silk sheets one last night before enduring the barely-there-thread-count hotel sheets. The silk felt amazing on her skin, and for whatever reason, that had Paisley thinking about something.

She should be falling asleep. It was the middle of the night already, and she needed to drive tomorrow. Still, she grunted because now that it was in her mind to do it, she knew she wouldn't be able to sleep without it. Paisley rolled over and reached inside her drawer. Pulling out the vibrator, she turned it on, testing the charge and the strength, which she needed because she got off faster when it was all the way on high. Paisley slipped it beneath the blanket and top sheet as she spread her legs.

"One, and then sleep," she told herself.

She pressed the vibrator to her clit, wanting to come fast so she could get to sleep. When Paisley closed her eyes, she instantly had a fantasy in mind that she knew would get her there quickly.

She was in an upscale hotel bar. There was a woman there, leaning into her, whispering something into Paisley's ear.

"I want you to get us a room, take me upstairs, and fuck me all night long," the imaginary woman with green eyes and blonde hair pinned back said.

"Oh, yeah?" Paisley said back with a smirk.

She pictured herself turning to face the woman more. Her hand slipped between the woman's thighs under the table, and the woman spread her legs for her, letting Paisley move her hand to her sex, which Paisley cupped.

"Yes," the woman said.

"Yes to what I'm doing, or yes to the room?"

"Both," the woman said very clearly in Paisley's fantasy.

Paisley's clit was already close, but she didn't want to come yet.

"Shit," she said to herself, moving the vibrator to the side to drag it out.

"Your panties are soaked," Paisley noted. "Did I do that to you?"

"You're doing that to me," the woman replied, pressing Paisley's hand into her sex harder. "God, I'm going to come spontaneously if you don't touch me."

"I'd love to see that," Paisley said into her ear, but she used her finger to flick at the woman's clit, earning a gasp. "You're hard for me, baby."

"Yes," the woman said.

"If I let you come here, can you be quiet?" she asked softly.

"Yes," the woman replied.

Paisley moved the fabric aside and slicked a finger through the woman's wetness. Then, she moved her hand out from under the skirt and held it in front of the woman's mouth. Not wasting any time, the woman leaned forward, took it into her mouth, and sucked it.

"Fuck," Paisley let out, needing to come now.

She moved the vibrator back to her clit and pressed it hard until she came, letting it remain there for a few more seconds before she pulled it away.

"Fuck," she muttered again, covering her face with her free hand. "Fuck."

She needed another one; Paisley could tell. Her clit had somehow just been activated, and she now needed to come again before sleep. She'd have to revisit the woman with green eyes and blonde hair again and fuck her in the bar in front of other imaginary people. Then, she'd be able to finally get some rest. So, she did. After that, she tossed the vibrator onto the blanket, knowing she'd wash it tomorrow and pack it along with its charger, because she'd forgotten to do so before anyway. She rolled onto her side, feeling finally ready for sleep, and closed her eyes, seeing green ones and blonde hair in her dreams.

***

"I thought you were coming for Sunday dinner," her mom said.

"I was going to, but I decided to drive up today instead of Monday morning super early, Mom," Paisley replied as she focused on the road. "I'm already driving there."

"Honey, you're allowed to take a weekend off, or even just a day. You work way too hard. Where is that staff you told us you were going to hire?"

"Well, I haven't hired them yet," she said into the phone, which was connected through her car, leaving her hands-free to drive.

"And why not?"

"Because I don't have time to hire them."

"I know you're smarter than that," her mom remarked.

"Mom, I'll hire people eventually, okay? It's just easier if I do things myself right now."

"Didn't you go to a party last night?"

"Yes. Why?"

"When did you get home? Should you even be driving? I assume you drank."

Paisley laughed and said, "Mom, I'm twenty-nine; I don't exactly party how I did in college."

"Oh, yeah? How exactly *did* you party in college, Paisley Jane Hill?"

"Mom," Paisley said, laughing. "I had one drink, ate food, and waited long enough before I drove home. I'm fine."

"Whatever you say," her mom replied. "So, no Sunday dinner this week. What about next week?"

"You know how it is when I'm with a client. I'm there all the time, basically living there."

"So, that's a no?"

"Mom, I'm doing the best I can here."

"Well, what about Thanksgiving?"

"What about it?" she asked.

"Paisley Jane, your mother is asking if you'll be home for Thanksgiving."

"Oh, I don't know yet."

"What do you mean, you don't know?! You're not working on Thanksgiving, Paisley."

"I mean, I honestly don't know yet, Mom. That's a Thursday, and it's a four-hour drive one way. I don't know if I'll come back for Thanksgiving only to have to drive right back if we're working that Friday."

"This client doesn't take the Friday off?"

"Black Friday isn't a national holiday, Mom." Paisley laughed. "I'll have to find out from them what they do and see about my schedule."

"We can fly you home."

"What?"

"The jet. We can send the jet for you, and you'd be here in thirty minutes. It can take you back after dinner."

"Mom, I love you. Can you just let me figure out how this client is going to be? You know sometimes they don't have their shit–" Paisley stopped. "*Stuff* together."

"I thought you were twenty-nine years old. You can't say bad words in front of your mother?" the woman joked.

"Have you met *my* mother?" Paisley laughed.

"Yes, she's a gem of a woman and wants to see her daughter once in a blue moon. Besides, James Lofton will possibly be there with his parents."

"James Lofton?"

"Mr. and Mrs. Lofton's son," her mom explained.

"Well, obviously." Paisley rolled her eyes. "Wait... Mom, are you trying to set me up with him?"

"No. He'll just be here, and he's single. You're single as far as I know."

"I don't even really remember him all that well," Paisley said.

"That's because you're never here," her mom retorted matter-of-factly before adding, "And just so you know that I'm very accepting of your bisexuality, I wanted to tell you that Alexia Weaver will also be here."

"Mom, I don't need you to set me up on dates. I *definitely* don't need you to set me up on Thanksgiving dates."

"Alexia just got her Ph. D.," her mom didn't give up. "And James is a music producer, I think."

"Music producer?"

"He lives in New York, so he's only in town for the holidays. Anyway, they're both single."

"Well, I don't even know if I can make it, so... Can you not make any promises, okay?"

"Fine." The woman sighed. "You let me know as soon as you do, Paisley Jane – I need to work out the place settings before the day everyone gets here."

"Yes, Ma'am."

"I love you, honey."

"I love you, too, Mom."

CHAPTER 2

"I'm so confused right now, Trin. We talked about this," Vidal said.

"I know, but it's a lot of money," Trinity replied. "And I'm worried they'll make recommendations we don't want to actually do, and we've then wasted that money."

"This company comes highly recommended; I did my research. There were calls and contract negotiations."

"Did you really vet them, though? Or did you just google? Sometimes, you just google."

"Hey! Me googling random things and falling into the black hole that is social media helped us figure out that we had a real idea here, that that idea could be turned into an actual business, and that we'd make money." Vidal shrugged a shoulder. "Well, eventually, anyway."

"If we're looking to make real money, we need to spend less," Trinity replied.

"My dear business partner and best friend," Vidal began, placing a hand on Trinity's shoulder. "I love you like a sister, I do, but this is the right call. We had the initial round of manufacturing in the Philippines – that saved us a ton of money. Shipping costs were a bitch, and *personally*, I'd like to *not* have to deal with customs on that scale ever again – I'm hoping we'll have a Director of Operations or something hired by then so that I don't have to – but, nonetheless, we're okay. This consultant is expensive, yes, but they'll help us figure out how to do what we want to do here, in the US, which was important to both of us. We wanted our product to be made in the USA, right?"

"Yes, but I'm just worried–"

"I know, and I get it. I like it; you help keep me grounded when I want to make extravagant business plans we're not ready for. But this is a consultant – she'll help us figure this out."

"*She'll?*"

"Yeah, the consultant is the owner of the company. She's got amazing reviews and references that I *did* vet. I would've involved you more in the process, but you seemed okay with the idea."

"I am." Trinity sighed and pushed a flyaway behind her ear. "I just worry it's too soon."

"When should it be, then? After we've already built everything out here and then have to change it all or fix it?" Vidal argued. "If we start this now, we can build out the right way," she reasoned.

"You're assuming this person will tell us the right way," Trinity remarked.

"Whatever she suggests – it's still our call, and we'll make it together, okay?" Vidal sat behind her desk in the office they shared.

"Fine. I guess I just wish I wasn't out sick for like a week; seems like a lot happened while I was out."

"You had strep – I wasn't letting you in the office, sorry. We may only have two full-time employees here, but if we're all out for a week, the business stops functioning."

"I know, but I could have worked from home, done some of the research for you." Trinity sat down at her own desk.

"You were barely conscious," Vidal said, laughing. "Thank God you had Claudia there to take care of you, because I love you, but both of us can't be out."

"Well, there was the help when I was sick, and then there was the cheating. Since the cheating came first, I'm guessing taking care of me was out of guilt more than anything," Trinity noted. "So, there's that."

"Yeah, she sucks. Sorry about that," Vidal replied. "I have a date tonight," she added. "Want me to see if he has an attractive, successful, gay sister, cousin, or friend from the office for you? Only if it goes well, that is. If he's a dud,

I'm not interested in being connected to him through you after."

Trinity laughed and said, "No, I'm good. Thanks, though. Just tell me you didn't meet the guy on Tinder," she added.

"Better than Grindr," Vidal joked.

Trinity laughed again and was very thankful for her best friend in the world.

"Hey, what's the name of the consultant that's coming?" she asked.

"Their info is in your email," Vidal replied.

"It is?"

"When you were out, since I knew you'd try to work, I moved everything from your inbox into a folder and automatically had it marked as read so you wouldn't get a bunch of notifications."

"Genius," Trinity said. "Also, you suck."

Vidal laughed and said, "You got better fast, didn't you?"

To check her email, Trinity opened her laptop, which was an old MacBook Pro she'd had for the past few years. Initially, she and Vidal had both splurged when they'd had this crazy idea and got the computers they needed, after neither of them having anything new since they'd gone to college. They'd used these laptops to create their Kickstarter campaign, marketing videos, and other content that they then launched and prayed. When people started funding it, they'd met their goal well before the deadline. Now, it was years later, and they were still here. They were far from becoming profitable yet, but they were well on their way. Thankfully, they had gotten an influx of investor cash this year that helped them get an office and two US employees. The rest of the team was small but in the Philippines. When she and Vidal had dreamt up this business, though, they'd wanted the product to be made in the US to help provide jobs and keep everything as local as possible while they tried to expand their reach globally.

That wasn't well-received by the investor, who'd given them a little less money than they'd wanted because of it, but they'd understood. Other countries gave them cheaper alternatives for manufacturing and hiring, but since it was important to both of them to keep their business as US-based as they could manage, they had decided to take the risk and go at the pace their cash allowed. Of course, it meant that both of them basically lived on ramen, despite being in their late twenties, but if that was what it took, they were both up for it. Trinity opened her email and went to the folder she found there that Vidal had called, "DO NOT READ: YOU ARE SICK, ASSHOLE," and laughed.

"Really?" she said.

"What?"

"The title of this folder."

"Oh, yeah," Vidal laughed as she put on her red-rimmed UV-blocker glasses to help with the headaches from the computer screen. "I'm hilarious."

"Yeah, real funny," Trinity replied sarcastically.

Then, she clicked into it. She went through some of the more basic emails, replied when needed, and then saw the one she assumed Vidal was referring to when it appeared in the reading pane. Then, her breath caught.

"Um…" she said to no one in particular.

"Yes, Trinity? Something you'd like to say to the rest of the office?"

"No," Trinity replied.

There was a picture in the upper right-hand corner of the email, which was actually showing a preview of a PDF document they'd been sent from the consultant, and that picture was of Paisley Jane Hill. Her friends in boarding school got to call her PJ. Trinity hadn't been one of her friends. She'd been the kid lucky enough to get to go to the exclusive Vermont boarding school for the rich and famous. She'd been the one with rented skis on the rare occasions she was invited to a birthday party in the winter, when everyone else had their own, custom-built skis, and those skis came along with private coaches and exclusive gear. It didn't matter anyway – Trinity had preferred hot chocolate in the lodge to actual skiing. So, she'd stopped renting skis in her junior year to save the money.

Paisley Hill had been the popular girl, one of the richest at the school thanks to her family basically being of Mayflower blood. Hell, one of them probably signed the Declaration of Independence or something. Paisley was the student government president every single year, skied like she could have been an Olympian had she practiced hard enough, played field hockey in the spring and summer, and also managed to date boys from the boys' school across town. Trinity remembered looking out her window one night as the snow started to fall for the first time that year, and she watched as Paisley got into the car of one of those boys to go out on a date. Trinity hadn't wanted to go out with that boy – or, really, any boy, for that matter – and she'd hated the fact that she'd wanted to go out with Paisley because Paisley had *not* been nice to her.

PJ had been a little bitch, if she was being honest, and Trinity was definitely honest. She was also a hell of a lot more confident now than she was as a teenager, when Paisley made comments about how her uniforms never looked new, being a little tattered along the hems from repeated washing, or how Trinity couldn't play any sport well in gym class and usually ended up getting picked last because of it. Yeah, *PJ* had been a bit of a bully to Trinity, and a few others possibly, too. Trinity had wanted to hate her – and she *should* have probably hated her – but she couldn't hate her back then, and she wasn't sure she'd ever be able to hate her because Paisley Hill had also been her first crush. She was the girl that helped Trinity realize she liked girls, to begin with, and Trinity had to watch Paisley go off with boys, hang out with the popular girls at school, and walk past her without so much as a smile in Trinity's direction.

Boarding school had been her mother's idea. When her mom had gotten a job at the boys' school across town, that gave Trinity the chance to go to the girls' school for a – well, a deeply discounted price. Her mom had been the one to suggest she live in the dorm because they'd save money that way. Her mom could live in faculty housing at the boys' school, Trinity could live at the girls' school in a tiny room she shared with a different roommate every year to promote getting to know one another, and they could still see each other on the weekends. Her dorm was included in that discount, and her mom got to stay in faculty housing for free. It worked for them, but Trinity would have preferred just going to the local public school and saving herself some of the bullying.

Trinity studied Paisley's picture. Yes, it was really her. And she'd, of course, grown up to be drop-dead gorgeous. Trinity's blonde hair, on the other hand, was a little on the stringy side most days, and she felt like she still had teen acne flare-ups that were supposed to be long gone by now. Trinity still felt relatively attractive, but when her now ex-girlfriend, Claudia, had cheated on her with someone who was younger and a lot hotter than Trinity felt she was, that was a real kick to the confidence for a woman who liked to eat ice cream out of the tub on a regular basis and hated the gym. The workout apps were better for Trinity, but she'd probably tried them all and hadn't ever been able to develop a routine, and well, ice cream was damn delicious, and she liked it too much to give it up or even eat it in moderation.

Paisley's hair was the same rare auburn shade it had been back in school. Maybe it was even prettier now as it framed her face in the photo. Paisley's eyes were green like her own, but they were lighter, too, and Trinity remembered how they'd change colors depending on the light. She'd had to stop staring repeatedly, or she'd risk being found out, but on the days they had to give presentations in class, Trinity had had an excuse to stare into Paisley's eyes and watch how gracefully she stood up at the front of the room with the confidence of the debate team captain and someone who was going places. Trinity was lucky if she could get through a presentation without saying, "Um…" fifty times and without tripping over her own feet. Things had changed for her in that department since then, which was nice. She'd gotten better at public speaking in college and now had no issues standing in front of employees or investors to make her case on something for the business. Maybe going to that school and dealing with Paisley and her gaggle of friends had helped her become who she was today – a business owner who had confidence in what she was doing at work. Now, if that confidence just extended to her personal life, things would really be moving in the right direction.

"Are you sure we can't reconsider this?" Trinity asked.

"Trin, she's literally on her way here. I think she actually got in yesterday so that she could be here this morning. The contract is signed. We'd be out at least some of the money. What's wrong here, exactly?"

"Nothing," Trinity replied.

"Yeah, right. Did you even read her stuff? She sent a bunch of info on what she does, how she does it, who she's worked with, and it's good."

"Not yet," Trinity said.

Just busy picturing her as my high school crush and bully, she thought to herself but didn't voice.

She sighed and clicked to open one of the other attached documents so she could read through it because she had to for work, but her heart began racing when she realized that Paisley Jane Hill, PJ to her friends, would be arriving at her office later that day.

CHAPTER 3

"So, that's really a thing?" Paisley asked.

"Yes, it's really a thing. Is that so hard to believe?" Eleanor asked.

"That you get to have sex *every day* with your girlfriend because Carmen likes to start the day off with an orgasm? Yeah, that's hard for me to believe. When I was with Grace, I was lucky if we had sex twice a month. With Tucker, he'd be up for it just about any time, but we were twenty-four, and I had more energy then. Plus, he only made me…" Paisley looked around as she walked around the corner. "You know, once every few times."

"Is that why you ended it after a couple of months? Bad sex?"

"No, work. That's why it ended with everyone, so it's just better not to try at all."

"Then, you'll never get morning sex with a girlfriend, or a boyfriend every day. This morning was mind-blowing."

"Stop trying to make me jealous; it's working." Paisley laughed as she checked her Apple watch for the time. "I'm five minutes early, actually. Tell me more."

"It's just different when you love someone, you know? Now that we've said that, it's like everything is amplified."

"But you can't keep up the every-single-day thing forever, right? I know it's her thing to get off every morning, but sex every single morning? Seems like it might get… tedious after a while."

"She made me come twice in the shower this morning. I cannot see *that* getting tedious. And that was before we went to the kitchen for coffee. Let's just say… we christened the counter."

"Her place or yours? I've eaten at your counter, Ellie."

"Hers." Eleanor laughed. "And I'm staying at my place

tonight. She's staying at hers, so she'll have to get herself going in the morning."

"Why?"

"Why what?" Eleanor asked.

"Why are you staying at your place?" Paisley clarified.

"We just felt like we should spend a night apart. We really haven't, and I don't want to crowd her."

"Did she *say* you were crowding her?"

"No, but when she opens, she wakes up super early and needs to head out pretty much right away to get to the bakery on time and get things in the oven. When I'm staying at her place, she's typically later than she should be. They have a big catering order that she and Mariah need to work on together tomorrow anyway, so I figured it was a good idea to let her sleep and get there on time."

"That's a valid reason. But, El, if she's not telling you that she needs space, don't assume she does, okay? You two are new, and she's getting daily kitchen counter sex, so I'm pretty sure she wants to wake up next to you."

Eleanor laughed and said, "I know. I know. So, where are you this time?"

"Doesn't really matter, does it? Some small-ish city with an even smaller warehouse district. That's where I'll be working and practically living for the next few weeks. Well, that, and the three-star business hotel I moved into last night after checking into and out of the hotel I *had* booked because there were holes in the blanket on the bed, and I found two carpet stains. I'm pretty sure one of them was blood, Eleanor. I have no idea what crime scene I would have witnessed had I had a black light with me."

"Hotels should give you one of those at check-in. 'Here's your key, your breakfast coupons, a brochure about the sights in the area, and here's your complimentary black light. If you see something, say something, and we'll bring the bleach.'"

Paisley laughed and said, "I checked into a better place, but the bartender actually put a bowl of nuts in front of me that he'd taken from another customer and slid over the bar in my direction, like I'm going to eat from the same bowl as a stranger."

"They still put nuts out at bars? I thought they did pretzels now because of peanut allergies."

"I get the impression this town is about ten years behind everywhere else in the world. I actually saw an Obama sign in the window of one of these warehouses when I got out of my car. It was from 2008, totally faded from the sun, but I could still make it out."

"Do they still have CDs?" Eleanor asked, laughing.

"No idea. I'll hit a store tonight and let you know, but now I have to run."

"I'm going to the bakery, anyway, to check out my girlfriend's ass *and* get a coffee and probably a cupcake."

"Talk to you later," Paisley replied, hanging up the phone to then look up at the large metal numbers on the building indicating she'd arrived at her destination.

She slipped her phone into its slot in her bag and opened the front door.

"Can you hold that for me?" someone said from behind her.

Paisley turned to see a woman with blonde hair pulled back into a ponytail. She was wearing a pair of jeans and a T-shirt that said, "Not today," and had a picture of a cat sleeping on it. Paisley was dressed in a steel-gray business suit with a white button-down under it that she'd ironed that morning.

"Sure," Paisley replied.

The woman looked at her with a glare, and Paisley wasn't sure what that was about since she'd just agreed to hold the door for her.

"Wait," Paisley added after thinking for a second. "I don't know if I should let you in. Do you work here? Sorry, this isn't my building. I don't know what the policy is on guests."

The woman shook her head and said, "Yeah, I work

here. And sorry our small-ish city with an even smaller warehouse district isn't up to par. I hope the hotel puts pretzels out tonight for you instead of peanuts. I can call over for you and make sure you get a fresh bowl. Jim Bob, the owner, owes me a favor."

"Sorry?" Paisley asked, taken aback as she closed the door without going inside. "Were you listening in to my phone conversation?"

"I've been walking behind you for the whole block. Hard *not* to hear some of it."

"Have I done something to offend you? I was talking to my friend. It was a private conversation. Are you the town's mayor or something?"

"No, I'm your new client," the woman replied, pulling the door open herself. "This is *my* office. After you, Miss Hill."

Paisley swallowed hard as if she'd just been scolded. That was a feeling she hadn't experienced in a while. She followed the woman in the T-shirt inside the warehouse, and after the woman closed the door behind them, she walked on without Paisley.

"Are you coming or not?" she asked.

Paisley was about thirty seconds away from turning around, getting back into her car, and driving to the hotel to get her stuff and check out. She'd never been greeted by a client like this before, and there was nothing in her contract about being treated like *this*. She couldn't risk pissing this person off even more, and she *definitely* couldn't risk the negative review if she just disappeared. This woman wasn't the woman she'd talked to on the phone; her voice was deeper and a little huskier, and damn it if Paisley didn't find it sexy. Paisley gritted her teeth, pushed that last thought out of her mind, and followed the woman who felt a little familiar to her, although she had no idea why.

The building was a warehouse that had definitely seen better days. Many of the windows lining the top of the structure were broken and covered with plastic and tape. Paisley looked around and found an old assembly line that someone appeared to be working on. The tracks would be used to move finished products from one place to another and likely, end up in shipping. The man twisting a screwdriver looked up and waved at Paisley, offering her a smile.

"Hey, Trin," he said.

"Hey, Will," the woman replied, waving at him. "How's it coming along?"

"Oh, fine," he said. "Should have this up and running within the next week. Then, we'll run some tests to check out the work and make sure it'll do what you need it to do."

Paisley had been watching the man who was talking to the woman in front of her and hadn't been paying attention. Apparently, the woman had stopped walking.

"Hey!" she exclaimed when Paisley bumped into her.

"Oh, shit. Sorry," Paisley said, backing up and closing her eyes for a second because she'd just cursed in front of a client.

"It's this way," the woman said, looking even more annoyed now.

Great. Just great, Paisley thought to herself. They walked farther past a few empty offices that lined the outer part of the building, and the woman opened a heavy white door that squeaked as she did.

"This way," she said again. "Vidal is down the hall on the right." She motioned for Paisley to walk through the door.

"You're not coming?"

"I'm going to go grab us all some coffees," the woman replied. "The walk I took didn't give me the stress relief I needed, unfortunately. Going to hit the local coffee place and try to let the caffeine help instead. It's not Starbucks, but it's not swill, either. So, do you want anything?" she asked Paisley.

"Oh, I had coffee at the hotel. Thank you, though."

Paisley *really* wanted another cup of coffee. Initially, she'd expected them to have some at the office, but she wasn't counting on that anymore. She also wasn't going to ask this woman, who clearly hated her, to buy her *anything* right now.

"Tell Vidal I'll be right back. You can get started without me, though," the woman replied.

Then, she turned around and walked back through the warehouse.

"Paisley?"

Paisley turned to see Vidal, the person she'd talked to about what was needed, the contract, and more with. She smiled at her gratefully because she knew Vidal would at least be civil. The woman she'd just literally bumped into must be Vidal's business partner. Paisley normally did much more research before accepting a new client, but this time, she'd been busier than normal, and she'd let the research slide. On top of that, the said business partner had been out sick when they'd talked about how this would work. Maybe she was still recovering and felt terrible, so she was taking it out on Paisley. Yeah, that must be it. Paisley would give her the benefit of the doubt and hope for the best.

"Vidal, how *are* you?" she asked, putting her professional face back on and walking toward her.

"Did I see you with Trin?"

"Yes. Well, I think so," Paisley said as she heard the door slam behind her. "Is that your business partner?"

"Yeah. She went on a walk to clear her head, and I thought she'd be back by the time you got here. Where did she go?"

"She said she was going to get you guys some coffee," Paisley said, holding her hand out to shake Vidal's.

"Oh, great. We're not exactly all the way set up yet. I splurged on a fancy machine for the office yesterday, but Trin doesn't know yet, so please don't tell on me. It should arrive tomorrow, so we won't have to keep going to the place down the street every day." She shook Paisley's hand.

"No problem," Paisley said. "Can I ask you a quick question before we get started?"

"Of course," Vidal replied, tossing her long, thin braids behind her shoulders.

"Does *Trin* want me here?"

"Why do you ask?"

"No reason. Just curious since she wasn't involved in the contract and talks."

"She does. She's just been a little out of the loop with strep throat, but she's good with the whole thing, I promise."

Paisley nodded.

"Okay," Vidal continued. "We've got you set up in your own office. Trin and I work in the same one because it's just easier right now. There are three inside this part of the building. The ones out there will be for the warehouse people we eventually hire." She motioned for Paisley to walk with her.

Paisley followed and stopped when they arrived at an open door.

"It's not a corner office with a view, but we thought you'd like to have a desk and, you know, at least a chair to sit in."

"It's great. Thank you," Paisley replied. "And where is your office?"

"Right next door," Vidal said. "But we're usually in one of the other ones if we're working on logistics, though. We turned that into a small conference room for now."

"Mind if I get set up in there, and we get started whenever she gets back?"

"Sounds good to me. I have a few calls to return anyway."

"Great." Paisley nodded and carried her stuff to the room Vidal identified as her temporary office space, placing her bag on the round table.

Then, she took a deep breath. *This* was going to be fun.

CHAPTER 4

Trinity carried the coffee tray, including the four cups she had in it in one hand and then another cup in her other hand.

They'd offered her two trays, but she'd been an idiot and had said, "No, I've got it."

Now, she carried a hot coffee in a hand that may or may not be on actual fire and had an iced coffee, that could be used to quell the burning on the inside of her palm, sitting perfectly in the tray. As she walked down a busy sidewalk, Trinity couldn't see a single way to get that relief while still holding on to the hot coffee. She'd been fired up already when she'd gotten to the coffee place, so she hadn't exactly wanted to order Paisley Hill a cup of coffee, but she wasn't an asshole, either, so she'd gotten one for Vidal, one for herself, one for Will, one for Chad, and one for Paisley. PJ got the black coffee; the others all got what Trinity knew they liked. She'd at least grabbed some sugar and a few of those creamers and had those in her pockets. *Her mother would be so proud*, she thought to herself sarcastically.

She had needed the breather. Seeing Paisley again after all these years had hit her harder than she'd thought it would. After realizing who Vidal had hired, Trinity had needed a long walk to clear her head, and then her head got all foggy again because there was fucking PJ Hill looking sexy as hell in her business suit, talking trash about Trinity's town. Yes, Trinity had eavesdropped, but she'd started to walk slower, at least toward the middle there. She'd heard some of what Paisley had said, but not every single word. That was at least good, right?

Now, she stood in front of the door to the warehouse.

It was a solid white door, just like the inside one, and had cracked paint all over the place and rust on the hinges. She needed to get it looking better than this, but that was a low priority. Right now, she needed to figure out how to open it while holding on to all of her drinks first.

"I'll be right back. Just need to–"

The door opened abruptly, and Trinity made a move backward to avoid it, but unfortunately, it got her left foot as it flew open, and that meant the tray of coffee she'd carried so carefully all the way here hit the sidewalk and splashed the liquid everywhere, including all over her jeans and shoes. Some even managed to hit her shirt, and a few wet spots made it to her face. Trinity wiped her cheek and looked up, fully prepared to see Vidal or Will – since Chad wouldn't be in for another few minutes, at least – and, instead, she saw Paisley Hill.

"Oh, my God," Paisley said, covering her mouth with both hands when she saw what she'd just done.

Trinity glared. She knew she was doing it, too. It was a total and complete angry stare that, in her opinion, Paisley Hill deserved. First, she bagged on Trinity's town. Now, she was spilling the coffee Trinity had brought for everyone. Oh, well, not everyone – Paisley's coffee, she'd managed to hold on to.

"Here," Trinity said, holding out the hot coffee. "This is yours."

"I am so sorry. There's no window on the door or next to it. I didn't know you–"

"Cream or sugar?" Trinity asked, pulling both from her pockets.

"What?" Paisley asked.

"Do you take cream or–" She held her hand out. "Never mind. Here."

Paisley took the sugar and creamers from her and then took the coffee, relieving Trinity's hand from the heat.

"I can't believe I did this. Let me help you get cleaned up. Is there a restroom inside?"

"You think we don't have a bathroom?" Trinity asked, looking down at the mess.

"What? No. I just mean that I'll help you get cleaned up there. I have a stain remover stick in my bag. I can–"

"You think a Tide stick is going to help *this*?" she said, pulling at her jeans by the pockets.

"I meant for your shirt," Paisley said a little more softly. "There are only a few coffee spots. I can get those out for you and pay for dry cleaning or new shoes; whatever you need."

"I need to go home and change," Trinity stated. "I have my very own washer and dryer because those weren't invented in the last ten years." She referenced Paisley's comment from earlier about the town being outdated.

"Will you please let me–"

"Paisley, no. I've got it." Trinity held her hands up. "Just go inside, please. Can you let Vidal know where I went?"

"Of course," Paisley said. "I really am sorry, and I'll pay for–"

"I don't need your money, Paisley Hill."

She pressed her hand to her front pocket, feeling her car keys there. Then, she bent down to pick up the litter.

"I've got that," Paisley interjected.

"Fine," Trinity replied, not wanting to argue anymore.

She turned and walked down the street, trying to control her annoyance. Then, she got into her car and drove to her apartment that, luckily, wasn't all that far away. Unlocking her apartment door, she was surprised to see Claudia sitting on the sofa in her living room.

"What the fuck?"

"Hey, baby," Claudia said.

"Not your *baby* anymore. What are you doing here, Claudia?"

"I was just leaving you a letter I wrote." She held up an envelope. "And I saw your car pull into the lot, so I thought I'd sit, and maybe we could talk instead. Wait. What happened to you?" she asked, pointing to Trinity's pants.

"Coffee spill. I'm just here to change." She walked briskly toward her bedroom. "And we don't have anything to talk about."

"If you won't hear me out, will you at least read the letter?" Claudia asked, following Trinity into the room.

"Why would I do that?" Trinity pulled a new T-shirt from the drawer, closed it, and grabbed another pair of jeans from the drawer below it.

"Because I love you."

"No, you don't," Trinity replied, kicking off her soaked tennis shoes and rifling through her closet for another pair.

"I love you, and that scared me, so I made a mistake."

Trinity sat on her bed and removed her sopping wet socks, throwing them into the hamper.

"It scared you that you loved me?"

"Yes. I'm twenty-three, Trinity. I'm in grad school. I wasn't supposed to find someone and fall in love yet. I was supposed to finish grad school, find a job in the field I want, and then maybe meet someone once I was settled where I want to end up."

"Well, sorry I ever said hello, then," Trinity replied, removing her T-shirt and dropping it into the hamper, too, before slipping her new one on.

"Trin, that's not what I mean, and you know it." Claudia sat down on the bed just as Trinity stood and began unbuttoning her jeans.

"Claudia, I can't do this with you. I'm only here to change my clothes. I have to get back to work, where a girl I went to high school with will probably manage to kick me in the crotch next or something."

"What?"

"Nothing," Trinity replied, lowering her jeans to the floor. "Look, it's over. I'm not trying to be a jerk here. I'm having a really bad day and wasn't expecting to see you at my place in the middle of the day."

"I know. I really was just dropping off the letter, I promise."

Trinity looked down at her underwear, making sure it was dry, and noting that it was, slipped into a new pair of jeans.

"I believe you about that. I just don't know that I can trust you again, Claud."

"It happened once," Claudia said, giving her pleading eyes. "Once, and it won't happen again. I'll make it up to you however you want, Trin."

"You slept with someone, and it wasn't just once. It was one *night*, Claudia. You told me it was one night, and you stayed over. You had sex with her over and over again; you knew what you were doing. You probably even thought about me before she reached over and tried to start round number three, and you still did it. That's the part that gets me. I can picture you thinking about your girlfriend, asleep alone in her own bed, while you fucked another woman and she fucked you over and over again. Plus, she's in your grad program; you see her every day. Hell, you probably spend more time with her than you do with me because I'm so busy at work."

"I don't love her, Trinity. I love you," Claudia said, reaching out to take Trinity's hand.

Trinity moved hers so that she couldn't.

"I can't." She shook her head slowly. "Maybe it's just too raw still, but I can't think about us being together like that again without thinking of you being with her. I *know* her, Claudia. I went to that party thing. You introduced the two of us, and now all I can think is that I shook the hand of the woman who slept with my girlfriend." Trinity sat down on her bed. "She went down on you. She had her hands all over you." Trinity shook her head. "You say you love me… How would you feel if someone touched me like that?"

Claudia sighed and said, "Awful."

"I have to get back to work." Trinity stood, walked to

the dresser, and pulled out fresh socks, putting them on while standing because she couldn't sit down next to Claudia on the bed again.

"I'm sorry," Claudia said, hanging her head. "I'm so sorry."

"I know. Me too. But, Claudia, it's over, okay?" She slipped her feet into her shoes, tightening the laces.

"What if we just take some time apart?"

"No," Trinity replied. "I don't want to take time apart. I want you to be able to be happy with someone – or not, if you want to be single right now. I want *me* to be able to find someone I can trust because I can't trust you anymore." She stood up straight. "Claudia, I need my key back."

Claudia looked at her then and said, "Will you at least read my letter?"

Trinity hated seeing the sad expression on her ex-girlfriend's face, so she nodded.

"I'll read it when I get off work, okay?"

"Will you call me after?"

"I can't promise that," Trinity said. "I really do have to go; I'm not trying to brush you off. We have a consultant there, and I need to get back."

"Can I keep your key until after you read the letter?" the woman asked, standing up.

"Claudia…" she said. Then, she reached inside her pocket for her own keys and removed the one for Claudia's apartment. "Here. I should have given this back to you the day I found out, but I was–"

"Crying," Claudia interrupted. "You were crying, and I did that to you." She pulled her keys out of her own pocket and found Trinity's. "I will never stop being sorry, you know?"

"I don't need that from you, Claudia. I don't want you to feel bad. I just want to…"

"Move on," Claudia finished for her and handed Trinity her key. "I'll go."

"Thank you," Trinity said softly.

"Yeah," Claudia replied.

She left Trinity's room, and a few seconds later, Trinity heard the sound of the door closing softly behind her. Trinity then sat on her bed again and flopped back on it. She and Claudia hadn't even gotten to the point in their relationship when they'd said they loved each other. The first time Trinity had heard it from the woman had been when she'd found out about the cheating. Trinity hadn't been prepared to say it back; things were still so new with them. Claudia was also younger than her and newly out to her family and at school, while Trinity was so busy trying to grow her company and hadn't planned on a relationship at all when they'd met. Maybe it was just poor timing for both of them. Either way, she'd shaken the hand of the woman who had fucked her now ex-girlfriend, and she could still see the woman's smirk when closing her eyes – like she'd won something – and Trinity had lost it.

"Today fucking sucks."

She sat back up, put her game face on, and stood. Time to get back to work.

CHAPTER 5

It was November 4th. Paisley had been counting the days because Trinity had been annoying and angry for all of them. She also hated that it clouded her judgment of this particular job because Vidal was wonderful. She hadn't yet spent time with the two full-time employees, but they'd been cordial to her. Trinity, on the other hand, had been aloof, at best, with her, and when she was talking to Paisley about the job, she still had an attitude. Paisley knew their introduction hadn't been great, but she'd been on the phone joking with one of her best friends; she didn't mean it. Well, she did, but not in a way that should matter. The woman must really love this town if she was still angry with Paisley about it. The coffee incident hadn't helped, and Paisley was still cursing herself for not opening the door a little before pushing it all the way open. She'd done so every time now, but not that one time when Trinity had been standing there with four cups of coffee on a tray that then crashed to the ground.

Paisley had gone to the coffee place that day herself and picked them all up new coffees to help make up for it, and when Trinity had returned, she'd seemed tempered somehow and took the coffee with a soft, "Thank you," making Paisley feel a little bit better, but that had been about it. From there on, it had been mildly better, but not by much.

"So, she's just a bitch?" Aria asked.

Paisley pressed the phone between her shoulder and cheek as she reached for her suit jacket.

"I don't know. Maybe she just has a problem with me. I said some stuff on the phone with Ellie that I probably shouldn't have."

"But you were on the phone with your friend, and it's not like you bad-mouthed your client," Aria argued.

"Babe, we've got to go," London said.

"Am I on speaker?" Paisley rolled her eyes.

"Yup. Say hi."

"Hi, London."

"Hey, Paisley," London said back. "Sorry, we have an appointment we're running late for."

"She needs a passport," Aria added. "Someone got one a while ago and then managed to lose it in her many moves this year, so now we have to go get her a new one."

"I said I was sorry," London replied.

"I've got to go anyway," Paisley said.

"Just remember: you're there to work. Right? Not to make friends."

"I've got enough of those," Paisley remarked.

"And we're already a lot of work," Aria joked. "Just get through this job and move on to the next one. That's a benefit of your job: you don't have to see the same people every day; you just move on to the next client."

"There's something off about her, though, Aria."

"What?"

"I can't put my finger on it, but she's familiar to me somehow."

"Did you sleep with her?!" London half-yelled from somewhere far away, making Aria laugh much closer to the phone.

"No, I would remember that. Trust me."

"Oh, she's hot, then?" Aria asked.

"She's attractive, yes. When she's not scowling at me, that is."

"Some women enjoy a good scowl," London noted.

"Are you one of them?" Aria asked.

"Okay. While you two start with your foreplay, I need

to find my other shoe so that I can get to the office. I can't be late. I think she might burn me in effigy if I show up even one minute after the agreed-upon time."

"Does she already have a voodoo doll that looks like you?"

Paisley laughed at her friend's joke and replied, "Probably."

"Good luck," Aria told her.

"Thanks," she said, hanging up and dressing quickly before checking the clock.

The hotel wasn't that far from the office, and she was okay on time, but as Paisley grabbed her stuff, she decided to risk being just a few minutes late in the hopes she'd get credit for a gesture. Thirty minutes later, she pulled up to the warehouse with a box in one hand and a bag in another. She pulled the door open and headed inside, head on a swivel because she didn't want to risk bumping into Trinity again.

Will was working on the machinery again, so she gave him a smile and a nod, holding up the easily identifiable box. He gave her a thumbs-up back. Paisley made her way to the inside of the administration building, where she saw Trinity and Vidal sitting at the small table in the little alcove they used as a kitchen or breakroom.

"I hope it's okay… I brought donuts, and since you now have a coffeemaker in here, I thought I'd just bring a bag of espresso and one of regular coffee for you guys." She placed the bag on the table next to the box.

"You didn't have to do that," Vidal said, smiling up at her.

"I wanted to," Paisley replied.

"Thank you."

"I saw Will out there and gave him the heads-up, but I didn't see Chad."

"He's got a newborn at home, so he usually helps his wife in the morning and comes in a little later," Trinity replied.

There was no anger or annoyance in her tone, but she also didn't appear to be happy at Paisley's gesture.

"I bet he could use the coffee, then," Paisley noted, smiling at her.

"Yeah," Trinity said.

Vidal opened the box, took out a chocolate-glazed donut, and said, "Thank you. My favorite."

"You're welcome. Trinity, do you want a jelly one? Those usually go fast," Paisley offered.

"Not much of a donut person, but maybe later."

Paisley just nodded and said, "Well, shall we get started?"

"We're just going over a few things based on what we all talked about yesterday. We can meet you in there," Vidal replied.

"Sounds great."

Paisley walked toward the small conference room, dropped her bag on the table, pulled out her computer, and got to work on where they'd left off yesterday – discussing possible software solutions to gain production efficiencies and automate as much as they could. Her phone rang. She glanced at the readout and noticed it was one of her clients that she'd worked with a few times now.

"Gavin, hello," she said, smiling into the phone.

"Paisley, how have you been?"

"Great. You?"

"Great as well. Listen, I know you're always booked up in advance, but I was hoping you could squeeze in some work if I sent it your way."

"What is it?"

"A good friend of mine is expanding into a few markets and wanted to figure out the best way to do that without a bunch of staff overhead. I told him you'd helped us with something similar. It likely would just be a few days of work. You might be able to do it remotely, too."

"Oh, sure. You can send him my way. Happy to talk to him about it," she replied.

"Great. He's in a bit of a hurry to get moving... I hope that won't be a problem."

"It shouldn't be. I'm with a client right now, but if it's simple enough, like you say, I can work on it in the evenings for him. The more info he can send me up front, the faster I can get my recommendations over to him."

"I'll have him email you," Gavin said.

"I look forward to working with him," Paisley replied, grateful for referral business.

Then, she looked up and saw Trinity standing in the open doorway. Gavin said his goodbyes. Paisley said hers. The call ended, and Trinity was still staring at her.

"Hi," Paisley said with a smile.

"Aren't we paying you a lot of money to be with *us* right now?" Trinity asked, crossing her arms over her chest.

"I don't bill for any time I spend with other clients when I'm on the job, but I do get calls I have to take from past clients and potential ones. It won't ever interfere with what I'm working on for you, and I only take them when we're not in meetings."

"Still," Trinity replied, shrugging. "We're working right now."

Paisley sighed and asked, "Can you close the door, please?"

Trinity looked surprised but closed it all the same.

"I know we didn't get off on the best of terms," Paisley began. "I apologize for saying what I said about the town. I travel a lot for work, all over the country, and I don't mean to be insensitive, but I've seen a million towns that look like this one, and I was talking to my friend. We have inside jokes between us, and you overheard that. I've apologized, but I don't think I deserve to be treated like this over that. I know the coffee thing happened, and I've apologized for that, too. It was a genuine accident that I'm trying to make up for by bringing donuts and coffee and offering to pay for your dry cleaning, and – hell, the gas it took you to drive back to your apartment if that–"

"I told you, I don't need your money," Trinity stated, sitting down across from her.

"It's not about the money; it's a gesture. I've tried to apologize, but that hasn't worked. I don't punch a clock; I'm not paid by the hour or by the minute. I'll work on stuff for you guys tonight and probably every night while I'm working with you. I put in the time. I'm here to help you guys accomplish your business goals. You and I don't have to be friends, but I'd like it if we could at least be cordial to each other." Paisley closed her laptop. "I designed the software you're going to review today. It's meant to help you manufacture your product faster and smoother with a simple flow. There are other options, and we'll review them, too, but the one I designed is the best, and I have references to back that up. I'm a one-woman show here, Trinity. I design the software, I'm the consultant, the salesperson, I'm in charge of marketing, and I'm the account manager. I don't have an assistant to take calls for me. I could get one, but I prefer to do it myself now. I've busted my ass trying to make this company great. I've done it all on my own, with no investors and no staff. You and I aren't all that different. We're just two women trying to make a company they're proud of."

Trinity nodded and said, "I didn't know that."

"You didn't ask, either," Paisley said. "And that's fine. I don't usually lay all of that out for my clients. I'm here to work, and I won't take calls from other clients while I'm here in your office anymore; I'll return them when I get back to my hotel. That's fair."

"When you say you've built it all on your own and didn't take money, what do you mean?" Trinity asked.

"I mean, I started it after graduation on my own."

"No. Like, family help?"

"Family help?" Paisley asked, confused as to where that question came from.

"Yeah. I mean… Did your family not help? Vidal's family gave us a little start-up cash."

"Oh, no. I don't take money from my family. I mean, they have it; I just…" Paisley shook her head at herself. "I don't know why I just said that. I just wanted to do something on my own."

Trinity nodded.

"Can I ask *you* something now?" Paisley asked.

"Sure."

"Why do you care?"

Trinity seemed to think about how best to respond, but before she could, the door opened, and Vidal walked in with a donut in hand.

"These are great, but I will be on a sugar high for the next twenty minutes. You've both been warned," she joked as she sat down.

"Maybe I should go get one, after all," Trinity said, standing. "And then, we can get started."

"Will took a jelly, and you know Chad loves those, so grab the last one if you want it," Vidal suggested.

"Paisley?" Trinity said.

"Yeah?"

"Do you want a donut?"

"No, thank you," Paisley said with a soft smile.

Was this progress?

CHAPTER 6

"So… With this, we'll be able to automate that whole part of the process?" Vidal asked.

"Yes," Paisley replied. "The goal of the software is to make it as simple as possible. We launched it last year after I'd spent years recommending different systems to other clients where I kept seeing gaps that needed addressing."

"We? I thought you designed it," Trinity said, taking a drink of her lukewarm coffee.

Did she sound like an asshole? She hadn't meant to sound like an asshole. Paisley had told her that *she'd* designed the software, so Trinity was curious about who the *we* was in that sentence and not trying to sound accusatory.

"I did," Paisley replied. "But I'm not a software developer. I have a friend, Scarlet. She's an analyst, but she develops on the side and is really talented. We worked on it together, and she did all the hard work, honestly. I kind of just got to tell her what I needed, and she made it happen."

Trinity nodded and watched as Paisley smiled at her. She wasn't sure she'd ever received a smile from Paisley in high school. God, that felt like so long ago. She'd been skinny, and her face had been dotted with pimples that never seemed to go away. Trinity had kept cheap concealer in business. She'd spent most of the allowance her mother had given her on the stuff along with other makeup to try to hide the blemishes because the other girls at school didn't seem to have the same problem. While the acne had mainly cleared up, and she only dealt with a little of it now, every time a pimple appeared on her skin, she was right back in high school trying to cover it up with concealer, hoping no one would notice.

"And we're not obligated to buy it," Vidal said.

"No, of course. I'll present the other two options I've reviewed and think would be good for you, too, in just as much detail. I'm not here to push my software on you; I'm here to help you become even more successful."

"We're not successful at all yet," Trinity replied.

"Your Kickstarter campaign was funded well before the deadline, your initial batch of products came in on time and just a little over budget – which is a modern miracle, and from what I've seen, you had very few negative reviews. The thing actually worked right the first time. Do you know how rare that is?" Paisley asked her. "Most situations like yours either don't get funded at all or go all the way to the deadline. They take at least twice as long as they promise and come in way over budget, so they start offering more rewards to try to bring in more cash to actually do what they set out to do in the first place."

"You did your research," Trinity noted, surprised as she held Paisley's still gorgeous green eyes.

"Not as much as I would have liked, but Vidal and I spoke at length to make sure I was the right person for this job."

Paisley held on to her own, darker green ones, and something passed between them, but Trinity wasn't sure what it was, so she just looked away.

"Anyway… It's lunchtime, and I'm starving," Vidal said, clearing her throat. "How about we hit up the little bistro over on Crenshaw?"

"That sounds great. Can we walk?" Paisley asked. "I could do for some air, and we could talk on the way there."

"It's two blocks away."

"Perfect," Paisley said, closing her laptop.

Trinity looked at Paisley's green button-down that matched the woman's eyes. The top button was undone. She couldn't see anything of consequence, but the thought of unbuttoning the next button and maybe getting a glance at the pale skin beneath caused Trinity to clear her own throat.

"I'm going to skip lunch," she said. "I've got a lot of work to do."

"Yeah, we'll be doing it as we walk there," Vidal argued, closing her own laptop.

"Can you just bring me something back? Whatever you're getting is fine," she said, standing up. "I'm going to work in the office for a bit."

Trinity had been staring at Paisley too much already today and had way too many thoughts about how pretty Paisley had been in high school, along with how gorgeous the woman was today – and checking out her boobs wasn't just unprofessional, it was also dangerous.

"Sure, but I'm getting a sandwich with oil and vinegar on it, so prepare yourself. If you eat in the office, it's going to stink, and you hate vinegar."

"You hate vinegar?" Paisley asked.

"No, I don't," Trinity replied. "She just gets it all the time, and we share an office. Get me mustard, please. No vinegar."

"Okay. Boring mustard it is," Vidal replied. "Paisley, are you a boring mustard kind of woman?"

Paisley met Trinity's eyes and said, "I don't think mustard is boring at all."

Trinity swallowed. Then, she turned and walked briskly into her office. She could *not* still have a crush on this woman. Everything Paisley was saying was somehow turning into an innuendo in her head. What the hell was going on? *She'd been talking about mustard, not you, dumbass,* she thought to herself.

"Hey."

"What?" Trinity turned around, surprised to see Paisley standing in the open doorway of her office as if she'd heard her thoughts.

"I can skip lunch if *I'm* the reason you don't want to go."

Trinity sighed internally and said, "No, it's not you. I just want to catch up on email, so I'd be bad company."

"Okay. If you're sure," Paisley said.

"Yeah. Thanks."

"Since Vidal isn't much for boring mustard, are you a yellow mustard kind of woman, or should I make sure she gets you Dijon or spicy stuff?" Paisley asked.

Trinity couldn't stop her smile and said, "Which one are *you* getting?"

"Depends on the sandwich." Paisley shrugged a shoulder.

"For me too," she said.

"On the side, and I ask for all three mustard varieties for you?"

"Not only does that seem excessive, you're expecting our outdated town to have three kinds of mustard," she joked.

"I guess you're right," Paisley said. "They have regular old mustard, don't they?"

"Yeah... And it's in one of those big containers that you have to pump. Are you able to handle that without breaking a nail?"

Paisley held up both of her hands and said, "I don't really have fingernails." She wiggled her fingers and showed Trinity her clear nail polish and short, neatly trimmed nails. "So, I think I'm good."

Paisley turned and left the room.

"Jesus," Trinity said, breathless, sitting down in her chair. "What the fuck?"

She watched minutes later as Vidal and Paisley left. Then, she picked up her phone and dialed, hoping she'd answer.

"Hey, long time no talk, stranger," Kelly said.

"I know. Sorry. I've been crazy busy."

"Yeah, me too. I have a two-year-old, a nine-month-old, and I'm working on a doctorate. What's your excuse?"

"I own a company, and its new," Trinity said.

"I guess that'll work," the woman replied, chuckling. "What's up?"

"Can you talk?"

"Yeah. The kids are napping, and I have a whole twenty or so minutes to myself right now. What's up?"

"Something totally unexpected happened this week."

"Like Claudia went back in time, decided not to cheat on you, and you got married?"

"No, that's over," Trinity replied. "She *did* try to get back together with me. She wrote a letter."

"A letter? She's, like, twenty-three. Don't they just text?"

"We're not that much older than that, so you might want to not argue that point. You text me constantly."

"I have two children, and I'm working on a Ph. D. What's her excuse?"

"I get it; you're busy." Trinity laughed. "Anyway, I read it."

"And?"

"And she says she loves me. She tried calling last night."

"It was two and a half months, Trinity."

"I know."

"Did you love her?"

"No," Trinity replied. "I liked her, and I thought I could love her one day, but I wasn't exactly about to say it when I found out she'd slept with someone else."

"Are you thinking about taking her back?" Kelly asked.

"No, I texted her that it really is over. I mean, I don't even have time for a relationship anyway."

"So, that's the unexpected thing?"

"No, the unexpected thing is PJ Hill," Trinity replied.

"Huh?" Kelly asked.

"PJ Hill. Paisley Jane Hill."

"I'm sorry. Is that a new TV show? Because if it doesn't have a cartoon dog in it, I haven't seen it."

"Kelly, PJ from school."

"School?" Kelly said as if she were trying to place the name. "Oh, shit. PJ from boarding school?"

"Yes."

"Okay. What about her?"

"She's here," Trinity explained. "She's the consultant that Vidal hired to help us figure out how to expand and optimize. She got here on Monday."

Kelly laughed and said, "PJ Hill is your consultant?"

"Yes."

"Whoa. Small world," Kelly said. "Didn't she use to pick on you at lunch?"

"Yes. One of her lackeys tripped me once."

"You dropped your tray; I remember that."

"Paisley just watched," Trinity added.

"You ate in the bathroom for a week after that. I remember going in there to check on you a couple of times, trying to convince you to go back to the cafeteria."

"You were my only friend."

"I wasn't your only friend," Kelly replied.

"Yes, you were."

"Well, we were roomies. Roomies have each other's backs, right?"

Kelly had been her roommate sophomore year, and she'd been the only person that actually made any real attempt to get to know Trinity. While they were from completely different worlds, and Kelly already had a husband and two kids while Trinity had chosen to focus on her career, they did their best to remain in touch with each other. Usually, it was with sporadic texts, but every now and then, they actually got to talk on the phone for more than three minutes.

"What do I do?" Trinity asked her.

"About what?" Kelly replied.

"Paisley."

"What about her?"

"She's here."

"Yeah, I got that part." Kelly paused. "Wait. Are you, like, regressing back to high school? That happens to people sometimes. You're not that teenage girl anymore, Trin.

You're not shy. You're confident. You're a business owner. You have a degree from an Ivy League university. I would have said that you have a hot girlfriend, too, but–"

"Well, thanks for the pep talk," Trinity said, laughing to herself. "I want to be so angry with her, and I want to stare at her boobs at the same time. I *did* stare at her boobs, actually."

Kelly laughed and said, "Are they still looking good?"

"Yes, of course, they are," Trinity stated. "What is wrong with me? I had a crush on my own bully, and now that she's here and still looks hot, I'm crushing on her again. She doesn't just still look hot; she looks hotter. It's like she grew into herself or something."

"So did you," Kelly remarked. "If I were at all inclined to sleep with a woman, I'd be totally into you."

"Don't make it weird."

"Not trying to, but you're hot, girl. You came out of your shell. You've got those rare green eyes rocking and–"

"Not so rare – Paisley has green eyes, too."

"Oh, shit. I don't think I ever paid enough attention to know that."

"I did," Trinity replied, leaning back in her office chair. "And hers are better than mine."

"No, they're not. Stop that. You're gorgeous. I can look her up online and tell you that she's gorgeous, too, but that wouldn't make you any less gorgeous, Trin. Don't compare the old version of you to the new version of PJ Hill."

Trinity took a deep breath and said, "I was really mean to her when she first got here."

"Well, she *did* probably deserve that," Kelly argued.

"Not really," Trinity replied. "She doesn't know who I am."

"What do you mean?"

"I mean, she doesn't remember me. Why would she? She never really even looked my way unless she or one of her friends was saying or doing something mean."

"But you told her who you are, right?" Kelly asked.

"No. Why would I do that?"

"So, she just thinks you're being a straight-up bitch for no reason, then?"

"Probably."

"Trin, this is your business – you can't be petty right now. If she's there to help you, you can't be mean to her just because she was an asshole in school. That was years ago. We were all kids back then anyway. Don't be stupid."

"It's just like my initial instinct; I can't control it," Trinity said.

"Well, work on it because if you're a dick to her, she might not want to stick around to help."

"I actually think we were flirting earlier," she blurted.

"Wait," Kelly said. "I'm confused here. Now, there's *flirting*?"

"I don't know. I was probably reading into it."

"What did you say? What did *she* say?"

"We were talking about mustard," Trinity replied.

"You were flirting over mustard?" Kelly asked.

"No, we were talking about it."

"And that's how people flirt now? I've been married since after college, so you'll have to forgive me."

"It's not just that... She showed me her fingernails."

Kelly laughed and said, "I am so confused. I'm also very tired. Maybe I'm just too tired to get what's happening here."

Trinity saw Will walking down the hall toward her, likely with an update on the warehouse they'd rented because it had come with old machinery that they would refurbish and use. She liked working with Will the most right now. The guy could fix just about anything, and he had all sorts of cool ideas to try to make what they have work for the modern-day packing and shipping process. Trinity enjoyed spending her time trying to draw processes on a notepad with Will, who would then point out what could work and what wouldn't while giving her his thoughts, too.

"I have to go. One of my employees is coming," she

said to Kelly.

"But you'll text me later? Explaining the mustard and fingernails? I'm living vicariously here. The last time my husband attempted to flirt with me, there were breast pumps involved."

Trinity laughed and said, "Yes."

"Hey, Trin?"

"Yeah?"

"You're a badass, babe. Just be yourself. You have nothing to prove to PJ Hill."

"Yeah, okay," she said with a soft smile and hung up. "Hey, Will. What's up?" she asked as he arrived.

"I'm going under the machine. Want to get dirty with me?"

She laughed at him and said, "Hell, yeah."

CHAPTER 7

"Hey, Mom," Paisley said into the phone.

"Have you figured it out yet?"

"Figured *what* out?" she asked, climbing out of her car.

"Paisley, I'm talking about Thanksgiving."

"Mom, I've been working non-stop since I got here."

"You act like that's a good thing," her mother said. "You know you don't have to work yourself to the bone. You can hire the people you need, and if you need a loan, Dad and I can—"

"I don't need your money," Paisley said and thought back to Trinity saying that to her a couple of times this past week.

"You keep saying that, and then you tell me you can't take national holidays off work to have dinner with your family."

"And the two people you're setting me up with at the same time," Paisley reminded. "Am I supposed to talk to Alexia during hors d'oeuvres and then James during the salad course? Do I then decide who to marry after dessert? Is there a presentation or something? Do I have to look at their bank statements? Present one of them with a few cows as my dowry? Do I get a rose and have to hand it to one of them?"

"You're being dramatic," her mother said. "We always invite people for the holidays."

"And you happened to choose a single guy and a single gal for me this year?"

"You're going to be thirty next year, Paisley."

Paisley walked toward the restaurant and pulled open the door.

45

"So?"

"So, it's time to at least try a real relationship that lasts more than a month or two."

"Mom, I'm about to have dinner with a client. I have to go. I'll let you know about Thanksgiving as soon as *I* know, okay?"

That was a lie. Paisley wasn't having dinner with any client. She was just done with this conversation. She let her mom go and headed to the bar, where she sat at a stool and reached for a menu that was stuck between two napkin holders. The restaurant was typical of towns like this. It was a chain placed in a strip mall next to all the other chains, and she'd probably visit all of them during her time here. She was getting tired of the shrimp cocktails, fried green beans, potato skins, burgers with fries, chicken Caesar salads, and the molten chocolate cakes, but it was the best she could get, and she didn't like spending money she didn't need to at any of the better restaurants in town.

"Paisley?" someone said.

Paisley turned and saw Trinity standing there, wearing the same thing she'd worn to work that day. There was some dirt, or maybe a grease spot on her shirt by the collar that hadn't been there before lunch, but Paisley had spotted it later and wondered how she'd gotten it. Thankfully, at least Paisley hadn't been the one to put it there.

"Oh, hi. What are you doing here?" she asked.

"Um… dinner," Trinity replied and pointed to the menu Paisley was holding. "I didn't feel like cooking."

"I was just going to get something to go, so I'll–"

"You don't have to," Trinity interrupted. "I mean, if you're just saying that because *I* showed up – you don't have to. I was going to sit at the bar instead of taking up a booth since I'm by myself, but I can grab a table or something."

"Do you want to–" Paisley stopped. "Do you want to grab a table together?"

Trinity looked at her, considering her proposition for a moment, and Paisley could swear that her eyes darkened a bit. Maybe she hadn't been imagining the flirting from earlier, after all. She'd thought that maybe Trinity had been a little nicer after their chat, and that when they'd talked about mustard, they hadn't actually been talking about mustard. Paisley had not said anything, of course, because Trinity was a client, but she had felt a little like they'd turned a corner after she had explained way too much about herself to Trinity. She'd let the flirting go on too far as it was, though, and had been hoping that Trinity hadn't thought of it since Paisley had handed her a sandwich and their hands had brushed for a second. That had been a long second that gave Paisley a slight shock, if she were being honest, but she needed to push those thoughts out of her mind.

"Okay," Trinity agreed.

"Are you sure? You don't really like me all that much," Paisley said, now second-guessing the invitation she'd just given.

She should eat alone, return to her room to work, have a basic solo orgasm, a terrible shower in the low-pressure water, and then get to sleep. She should *not* be having dinner with a woman she was working for that she'd flirted with earlier.

Trinity sighed and said, "You really have no idea who I am, do you?"

That question threw Paisley out of her thoughts about how good Trinity looked in graphic T-shirts.

"What do you mean?"

"Let's get a table," Trinity stated, turning around and motioning for Paisley to join her. "And alcohol – one of those massive margaritas meant for, like, four people. That's just for me, though. You get whatever *you* want."

Paisley put the menu back between the napkin holders and followed her to the hostess, who then found them a two-person booth in the corner of the bar and handed them both menus. When the bartender walked over to them and tossed out two coasters, Trinity ordered that giant margarita, looking exhausted and also a little nervous.

"White wine?" Paisley said, assuming they only had a house white of which he would just bring her whatever was the most expensive to increase his tip later.

Either way, Paisley didn't really care. The bartender nodded and walked back to the bar. When Paisley then met Trinity's eyes, Trinity quickly looked away.

"My name is Trinity Pascal," she spoke after a moment.

"Yeah, I know that," Paisley said. "Should I recognize the Pascal name? Is your family acquainted with mine?"

"No way." Trinity laughed and picked up the cutlery wrapped in a napkin. "At no point would my mom and your parents ever *voluntarily* interact. I guess they could have bumped into each other if we were in any of the same activities or something, but I doubt your parents would have given my mom the time of day back then."

"Back then? What are you–" Paisley's breath caught in her lungs. She cupped her hand to her mouth. "Oh."

"Yeah. I had a lot more acne back then, and probably weighed more than I do now. I also grew a couple of inches after graduation."

"Trinity Pascal," Paisley replied.

"That's me," she said.

"Boarding school."

"Yes."

Paisley had about a thousand flashbacks all at once. None of them were particularly good. Most of them had nothing to do with Trinity Pascal, but there were a few of them in there where Trinity wasn't treated very nicely, and it might have been Paisley's fault. There was a cafeteria tray incident that Paisley had just watched. There was gym class where Paisley knocked Trinity over in a game of basketball that Paisley hadn't wanted to play, to begin with. There was Trinity staring at her in class, where Paisley would scowl back if she noticed. Trinity would blush and look away.

"Why didn't you say anything?"

"I don't know. I guess I thought you'd put two and

two together eventually. I gave you more credit than I should have, huh?"

The blender behind the bar started up, likely making Trinity's margarita. Paisley turned to the sound, distracted by it, but also *needing* that distraction.

"You don't need my money," Paisley said softly.

"Huh?"

"Your mom worked at the boys' school, didn't she?"

Trinity nodded.

"So, you were on scholarship back then, and you want to make sure I know you don't need my money."

"I've not processed seeing you again well," Trinity replied. "Can you blame me? You didn't make high school the best experience in the world for me."

Paisley looked down and said, "You're right."

"When did you lose the PJ?"

"What?"

"You used to go by PJ."

"Oh, wow. No one has called me that in years."

"No?"

"No. I hated my first name when I was younger, so I went by PJ, but Paisley is more professional. Pais is what my friends call me now."

"Pais," Trinity said as if trying it on for size.

"I *am* sorry, you know? I took out my own crap on others when I was an angsty teenager. I don't mean that to sound like an excuse. It's just–"

"Your own crap? What crap did *you* have?" Trinity asked as if in disbelief.

Paisley was taken aback by that and replied, "We all have crap, Trinity. We all especially have crap when we're teenagers and have raging hormones, peer pressure, parental pressure, and the worries about where we'll go to college. And just because we pretend we're not going through it, doesn't mean we aren't."

Trinity nodded as their drinks were brought to the table.

"Are you ready to order?"

"Actually, can we have another minute?" Trinity asked him.

The guy nodded and walked away.

"What were you going through?" Trinity asked her.

"Considering I treated you like crap, I think I should probably just leave it at that and let you yell at me if you need to or slap me if you feel like that would help," Paisley said.

Trinity pulled the margarita that was bigger than her head toward herself and said, "I don't need to yell at you. I *definitely* don't need to slap you. You weren't *that* bad, I guess."

"I didn't stop it when things were, though."

"I remember you standing there in the girls' locker room while your friends laughed at me," Trinity said.

Paisley pulled the wineglass toward herself and took a gulp, not a sip, but a gulp.

"I'm sorry. I should have been stronger back then."

"So, why weren't you?" Trinity took a drink of her margarita.

Paisley sighed and said, "I suppose, for the same reasons we all have our weak moments. I mean, not all of us have the same reasons; I don't know what I'm saying right now."

Trinity took another drink and said, "Want to hear something that's *really* messed up?"

Paisley laughed and said, "Okay, I guess."

"I had such a major crush on you back then." Trinity laughed softly and rolled her eyes at herself.

"What?" Paisley asked with a small smile.

"I know… Who crushes on their bully?"

Paisley dropped the smile and asked, "I was your bully?"

She'd never thought of herself as a bully. She hadn't been the *nicest* girl to everyone in school, but she'd never considered that to someone else, she might have been a bully. Paisley thought back and tried to replay every moment of high school. Trinity had mainly been on her periphery, at best. Had she actually bullied someone?

"I don't know," Trinity replied, interrupting her thoughts. "It felt that way to me, but you didn't actually *do* most of it. Your friends did sometimes, and you were kind of in charge of them, and you just never stepped in. So, I guess that means you had henchmen, and they did all the dirty work. I assumed you'd told them or encouraged it since it didn't look like you ever stopped it."

"I'm sorry, Trinity," Paisley said. "I'm sorry, I don't know what else to say. I'm kind of stunned."

"I'd moved past all of that, and then I found out *you* were our new consultant."

"I probably should have recognized your name, but–"

"You barely remember me at all, right?" Trinity noted.

"If it makes you feel any better," Paisley went to reply, "I don't remember most of the people from boarding school. I don't talk to anyone from that time in my life, really. I put it all behind me, too, I guess."

"Why?" Trinity asked.

"I went to college, made new friends there, and tried to build a business on my own without taking money from my parents, so high school no longer seemed to have any relevance in my life. I didn't even go to the ten-year reunion. And I was the senior class president – I was supposed to organize it. I had the VP do it instead and said I was working and couldn't go."

"I didn't go, either," Trinity said with a nod just as the bartender approached them again.

"We're not quite ready yet," Paisley said. "Sorry. Can we maybe just get…" She looked at Trinity. "Appetizer?"

"Pretzel bites are good here."

"Yeah, those," Paisley said to the bartender.

"Mustard or beer cheese?" he asked.

Paisley and Trinity looked at each other with wide eyes. Then, they both burst into laughter. Neither answered his question, at first. Finally, Trinity told him to bring both. Paisley sipped on her wine again, looked down, and realized it was almost finished already. She needed to drink it slower.

"Junior year, I figured something out about myself," Paisley blurted after the bartender walked away.

"What's that?" Trinity asked.

"Well, I had a boyfriend from the boys' school."

"Oh, trust me, I remember that."

"Really? You *do*?" Paisley asked.

"Major crush on you, remember? Big. Huge." Trinity said, laughing. "And as a baby gay who had a crush on the most popular girl in school, I knew you had a boyfriend."

"You're gay?" Paisley asked.

"What about me crushing on–"

"That's just a crush," Paisley argued.

"Okay. Fine. It was more than a crush." Trinity took another long drink from her margarita. "I was into you, despite the fact that you weren't very nice to me."

Paisley smiled and thought about the flirting from earlier. So, maybe she'd been right, after all.

"I had a crush on a girl," Paisley said. "No, it wasn't a crush; I really liked her. She worked at the ski resort."

Trinity looked surprised as she continued to suck on the straw that came with her giant frozen drink.

"So, *that's* what I was going through," Paisley added. "I was in love with a girl while I was dating a boy."

"In love?" Trinity asked.

"Straight up in love. First love kind of thing. She ran the ski lifts some days, and I always tried to ski on the days she worked."

"Paisley Jane Hill is gay?" Trinity said.

"No, I'm bi," Paisley replied. "Still confusing as hell when you like a girl for the first time. I wondered if I *was* gay. When she and I…"

Trinity's cheeks were now flushed either from the alcohol or from the topic of conversation.

"When you what?" she asked, teasing Paisley now.

"For the first time…" Paisley did not elaborate. "I knew I definitely liked girls."

"But guys, too?"

"Yeah. Obviously, the junior-year boyfriend and I ended, but I know I'm attracted to guys as well. I had a boyfriend for many years in college. That was mainly because of my parents, though. He was someone they thought I should marry, but we were both with other people during the relationship since we knew it wasn't going to last."

"Wait. What about the girl from the ski resort?" Trinity asked.

"Oh," Paisley said. "She graduated college and went back home." She shrugged.

"College!"

The bartender, who was still behind the bar, looked over upon hearing Trinity's outburst.

"Yeah?"

"You hooked up with a college senior when you were a high school junior?"

"Yes." Paisley finished her wine.

"You really *did* have it all, didn't you?" Trinity laughed.

"Yeah. Yeah."

"Another wine?" Trinity asked.

"No, I'm stealing some of this margarita." She reached for Trinity's straw, taking it out of her hand, and moved it to her side of the giant glass, taking a long drink.

Trinity just watched her.

CHAPTER 8

Trinity woke up with a bit of a hangover, but not the worst one she'd ever experienced. They'd nearly finished that margarita together, shared the pretzel bites, laughing like drunk idiots over the mustard that came with them, and then they left without eating an actual dinner because it had gotten so late. They'd grabbed a shared ride together, with Trinity dropping Paisley off at her hotel and then going home. Now, she needed to pick her car up from the restaurant before going into the office. She also needed a shower and ibuprofen with a very large side of coffee.

In the shower, she placed her face directly under the spray, hoping it would help her wake up. She hadn't slept well the night before. The restaurant had closed at eleven, and she'd been back home by midnight, but she hadn't been able to stop thinking about Paisley Hill all night. She finally fell asleep around three or four, but the few hours she'd gotten would have to be enough to get her through the day. Trinity was certain Paisley would show up today looking perfect and completely unaffected while wearing one of those wrinkle-free business suits, like always. Her hair would probably be pinned back, and she'd hold a pen to her lips a few times, drawing attention to her full lips. Trinity looked down and realized her hand had moved on its own accord to between her legs.

"Oh, come on," she said to herself. "She's not *that* hot." She moved her fingertip over her clit, gasped, and added, "Yes, yes, she is."

She rubbed slow circles and pictured Paisley on top of her desk, legs spread, with her own face between them, and that was enough to get her there. Then, she rolled her eyes at herself and got out of the shower.

***

"I have a lunch date today," Vidal said.

"You do?" Trinity asked as she checked her email.

"He's picking me up at one."

"Is this the date from the other night?" Trinity asked.

"Yes, so I need you to take Paisley to lunch."

"Why?" Trinity looked over at her.

"Because she's our guest, and I know your mother raised you better than that, Trinity."

"She's our consultant, not our guest."

"She's both," Vidal replied. "I'm not sure what your deal is with her, but she's making great recommendations and probably saving us money in the long term. So, take her to lunch, buy it for her, put it on the company, and act like a business owner who has her crap together," she said. "Hi, Paisley."

Trinity glanced to the door, finding Paisley standing there, looking a little unsure of something.

"Hi. I just met with Will, and I think we're good for now."

"Great. I'm going to head out for lunch, but Trinity, here, is going to take you out."

"That's okay," Paisley said. "I can always just order something in."

"Nonsense," Vidal said, standing up with her purse. "Take her to the Cantonese place. It's great."

Trinity nodded, and Vidal left the office. Then, Paisley took a few steps into it.

"You don't have to take me to lunch. I'm a grown woman; I can find my own food," Paisley told her.

"I don't mind," Trinity said.

"Didn't seem like that a minute ago," Paisley noted.

"You heard?"

"Yeah…"

The woman looked down for a second, and damn it, if that shyness wasn't also hot.

"That wasn't about you," Trinity said. "I'm hungover. I don't really want to do much of anything."

"You too, huh?" Paisley gave her a small smile.

"Want to order in something sloppy and hope it soaks up whatever it needs to soak up so that we can start feeling better?" Trinity asked.

Paisley laughed and said, "Yes, that sounds good to me."

Trinity picked up her phone and opened her app.

"I'm thinking burgers with lots of cheese and maybe bacon. Chili cheese fries on the side?"

***

Forty minutes later, they had that greasy, sloppy food in the conference room and had both taken their first bites.

"Thank God for this," Paisley said, taking a drink of her water. "I didn't really even drink that much."

"We finished a margarita made for four people and only ate pretzel bites," Trinity remarked.

"I had a granola bar when I got back to the hotel," Paisley said.

Trinity laughed and said, "Granola bars are not hang-over cures."

"I haven't been hungover in a while."

"Me neither."

"So, that's not a usual thing for you?" Paisley asked.

"No," she replied. "I really was just going to sit at the bar alone, order a beer and a burger, eat it, and then go home."

"Me too," Paisley said. "Well, back to my hotel," she added.

Trinity ate a fry and decided to say something.

"Hey, I think it's really cool that you do this on your

own. Not that you need my–" She stopped talking when Paisley looked up at her. "I just mean that it's cool that you're doing this whole thing without the support of your family."

"They support me just fine." Paisley chuckled a little. "They *wish* I'd take their money, and I keep refusing, but they're very supportive."

"What about the bi thing?" Trinity asked.

"The bi *thing*?" Paisley laughed a little harder.

Trinity laughed as well before saying, "What? What else should I have said?"

"Should I call *your* thing a gay thing?"

Trinity laughed into the bottle of water she'd almost finished and said, "No idea. I'm not the most PC person in the world, in case you haven't noticed. I assume you were sent to etiquette classes and had a tutor who explained how *not* to put your foot in your mouth."

"Yes, exactly. There's a whole rich kid course," Paisley joked. "They start us young, too."

Trinity smiled and rolled her eyes at Paisley's joke.

"But, to answer your question," Paisley began, "they're supportive. They're annoying, but they're supportive."

"Annoying?"

"My mom tries to set me up with people all the time. She's always careful, too, so if she brings up a guy she thinks I might like one time, the next time, it's a woman."

"Really?" Trinity chuckled.

"Yeah, and I love her for that, but it's also a lot. She thinks that because I'm almost thirty, I'm withering away on the vine. I mean, my boobs still look fine, right?"

"What?" Trinity said, swallowing and intentionally not looking down at Paisley's boobs. She then cleared her throat and said, "She's worried about grandchildren, isn't she?"

"Probably, but I'm not even sure I want kids. I mean, who has the energy?"

"My friend Kelly has two already," Trinity replied.

"She's our age?"

"Yeah, you might remember her. She's the only person I still talk to from school. Kelly Benson?"

Paisley took a bite of her burger, getting grease all over her hands, and this was a far cry from the prim and proper PJ Hill that Trinity had known back then. Trinity liked this new side of her.

"The name sounds familiar, but I don't know that I remember her, specifically."

"Well, she got married after college. Now, she has two kids, and it's like her whole life revolves around them. Cool for some people, but not what *I* want."

Paisley nodded and said, "None for you?"

"I can't imagine finding the time. I mean, I'm almost thirty, too. We're just starting to get this thing working here, and I know Vidal wants a husband and kids, so someone needs to be here to hold down the fort. By the time I'll come up for air, I'll be in my mid-fifties already and going through menopause."

"You could adopt a teenager then, give them a loving home," Paisley suggested with a playful smile on her face.

"I didn't like *me* as a teenager," Trinity argued. "I definitely don't think I should *raise* one."

"Hey, you ordered in?" Vidal said, entering the room.

"Yeah, Trinity introduced me to the best burgers in town," Paisley said.

"And the cheapest," Vidal replied. "You bought her diner food?" The woman turned to face Trinity.

"No, it's what *I* wanted," Paisley replied. "She *did* buy, though."

Trinity laughed silently and said, "How did your date go?"

"So good. We're going to dinner tonight," Vidal said, sitting down next to Trinity and helping herself to her fries.

"Did you stare at him with heart-eyes the whole time and skip actual eating?" Trinity asked.

"No, I just wanted to steal your fries because I knew it would annoy you."

"Oh, I didn't know that." Paisley reached over and, despite having her own fries, stole two of Trinity's, winking at her. "This is fun."

Trinity gave her a playful glare, and Paisley winked at her again. Trinity recalled touching herself in her shower that morning and had to clear her throat yet again. Now, she was picturing Paisley winking at her for an entirely different reason.

"So, lunch date and dinner in the same day?" Trinity prompted.

"Yes." Vidal turned to Paisley then. "Can we be incredibly unprofessional for a minute?"

"I don't think you need my permission for that," Paisley replied.

"I'm *so* going to have sex tonight," Vidal blurted.

Trinity and Paisley laughed. Vidal stood up and stole another fry.

"Anyway, back to work. I'll grab my computer and be right back in." She left the room.

"What are *you* doing for dinner tonight?" Paisley asked.

Trinity finished her burger and looked up, surprised.

"If you're not doing anything, maybe *we* could do something."

Trinity swallowed and said, "Dinner?"

"Or not," Paisley said, closing the container her food had come in.

"No, I can do dinner," Trinity replied.

Paisley just nodded.

***

"We're going to dinner," Trinity said into the phone.

"*Who's* going to dinner?" Kelly asked.

Trinity turned around in a circle, making sure Paisley wasn't anywhere on the sidewalk to overhear her.

"Paisley and me," Trinity replied.

"You're going to dinner with PJ Hill?"

"She goes by Paisley now."

"Oh, I'm so *very* sorry. Lady Paisley of the Hill family," Kelly teased.

"She asked me to go to dinner, Kelly."

"Like a date?"

"No. Just dinner," Trinity replied.

"Are you freaking out because you think she's going to knock your food off a tray again? Take her to a nice place where you don't walk down a line with a tray, Trin."

"It's not a date. I'm not *taking* her anywhere."

"But you're going to dinner with her?"

"Yes."

"Why?"

"I don't know. She asked."

"You could have said no," Kelly argued.

"I didn't want to."

"Oh, no. Are you regressing again?"

"What? No, she's actually–" Trinity turned in a circle again. "She's actually nice now."

"Well, I'd hope so. We're not in high school anymore."

"What do I do?"

"Go to dinner with her."

Trinity turned just in time to see Paisley turn the corner as she walked toward her car.

"I've got to go. She's driving, and she just left the office."

"Have fun," Kelly said.

Trinity hung up and smiled as Paisley approached.

"Are you ready?"

"Yeah. All good." She nodded. "I was thinking about the Cuban place."

"This town has a Cuban place?" Paisley teased.

"Come on." Trinity laughed.

CHAPTER 9

"Hey," Talon said.

"Hey. Got a minute?" Paisley asked.

"Yeah. Emerson's here, and we're about to do some online house-hunting, but yeah."

"Oh, never mind, then."

"Is everything okay?"

"Yeah, everything's fine. I was just calling to say hi."

"You never call to say hi."

"I sometimes call to say hi."

"Okay. We'll go with that." There was a voice from Talon's side of the call, and Talon added, "Emerson just grabbed her computer."

"I'll call you later, then," Paisley said.

"Are you sure?"

"Yeah, I'm sure."

"I can talk for a few–"

"No, it's fine. I'll call you back later."

"Okay. Have a good night, Pais."

Paisley looked at her list of favorites in her phone. She had her parents and her five friends. She wasn't about to call her mother, who would only ask her about Thanksgiving again. So, another friend would have to keep her occupied. She'd had dinner with Trinity at the Cuban place, and they'd had fun. Surprisingly, they'd had *a lot* of fun. They hadn't had much to drink this time, given their experience the previous night and because Paisley had driven, and when she'd taken Trinity back to the office to get her *own* car, they'd

said an awkward goodbye that had her doing a lot of thinking.

"Hey, Scar," Paisley said, needing to talk about that
goodbye with someone.

"Oh, hey. What's up?"

"Are you free?"

"Aren't I always?" Scarlet asked.

Paisley should have called her single friend first.

"What's up?" Scarlet repeated.

"Something weird is going on."

"Weird?"

"I ran into someone I used to know. Well, sort of used
to know, but not really."

"At work?" Scarlet asked.

"Yeah, it's my client, actually."

"Oh, hold on," Scarlet said. Then, there was a pause.
"That was my mom."

"Do you need to take it?"

"It was a text." Scarlet sighed. "I'm having a hard time
talking to my parents, and it's getting worse. It's like having
this big secret between us only makes me feel like *everything*
I'm telling them is a lie."

"Sorry, Scar," Paisley said.

"I'm going to come out," Scarlet replied.

Paisley rolled her eyes as she flopped back onto the
hotel bed. She'd heard this before. She'd heard it over and
over again. Scarlet was a broken record when it came to telling her parents that she was gay.

"When?"

"I think the next time I see them."

"Okay. That sounds good."

"I mean, I have to, right? I go back and forth about it
because it's not like I've ever really had a reason to tell, so I
can maybe keep it to myself for a while longer."

"Scar, can we maybe talk about *my* thing?" Paisley
asked.

"Oh, yeah. I'm sorry," Scarlet said, sighing again.

Paisley knew that sigh. It was Scarlet's deep-thinking sigh. She wasn't going to get anywhere with Scarlet tonight.

"On second thought, I'm tired. I think I'm just going to get some sleep," Paisley told her.

"No, I'm sorry. Tell me all about this person you ran into."

"It's okay. Really, I'm running on empty anyway. I'll call you tomorrow night, okay?"

"Shit. Pais, I'm sorry."

"Scarlet, you have nothing to be sorry about. I'll talk to you later."

"Yeah, okay," Scarlet said, sounding disappointed.

Paisley stared at the cottage-cheese ceiling above her head. She wasn't tired. Well, she was – she was exhausted, but she wasn't going to sleep anytime soon. When she'd dropped Trinity off at her car, there had been a moment. It was so brief; Paisley was still wondering if it had happened at all. Trinity had unbuckled her seatbelt and had leaned just a little in Paisley's direction as if their dinner had been a date and they were saying goodnight in Paisley's car.

She knew she could call Weston or Aria or Ellie, but they were probably all with their girlfriends, and Paisley wasn't in the mood to hear more about how Annie and Weston were both about to become published authors, how London and Aria were planning their trip to Italy, and how Ellie and Carmen were having amazing daily sex. So, she picked up her phone and searched her contacts.

"PJ?"

"Really?" Paisley said, laughing. "I thought I told you tonight not to call me PJ."

"You did. I chose to ignore you," Trinity replied.

"Then, I'll only respond to Paisley from now on."

"What if I *never* call you that?"

"What *else* will you call me?" Paisley asked, looking down and noticing her hand was on the waistband of the black slacks she still wore from work.

"PJ; we've been over this," Trinity replied.

"What are you doing right now?" Paisley asked.

"I just got home. Why?"

"Do you want to grab a drink with me?"

"Tonight?" Trinity questioned.

"I'm exhausted, but I don't think I can sleep yet." Paisley thought quickly. "I'd invite Vidal, too, obviously, but she—"

"Is probably having sex right now?" Trinity replied.

"Yeah, that." Paisley laughed.

"You're at the hotel?"

"Yup."

"The place where they serve dirty peanuts?" Trinity asked.

Paisley laughed and said, "Yes, but we don't have to eat them."

"I might like dirty peanuts," Trinity said.

"Well, if that's your thing, get a strong drink so that the alcohol can kill whatever might be on those peanuts."

Trinity laughed and said, "I can be there in about fifteen minutes."

"Okay. I'll see you then."

Paisley heard the call end. She dropped the phone to the bed and thought about what she'd just done. She'd just invited a client out for a drink. That was fine. That was normal. More than that, this was a unique situation because Trinity wasn't just a client. They had a history. It wasn't a *great* history, but they were getting to know each other, discovering how different they both were now than they were as teenagers.

Paisley stood, deciding she needed to get out of her wrinkled clothes, but first, she opened her laptop to check for a response to the email she sent the client Gavin had recommended. She had one, and he'd sent a document for her to review, so Paisley read through that as well and had just finished typing her response when there was a knock on her door. Paisley slammed her laptop shut then.

"Shit," she said to herself.

She stood quickly and wiped at her wrinkled clothes. There could only be one person knocking on her door. She rushed to it and pulled it open. Trinity stood there with a lifted eyebrow and two glasses in one hand and a bottle in the other.

"I waited for ten minutes before I asked them what room you were in."

"I am so sorry," Paisley said. "I got caught up."

"*You* invited me, Paisley."

"I know. I'm sorry. Come in."

She moved aside to allow Trinity to enter her hotel room. It had been cleaned by housekeeping, but Paisley had been sitting on the bed, so that was mussed, and she'd just dropped her stuff all over the place. Her suitcase was open on the luggage rack by the dresser and had a pair of her underwear peering out. She moved to it and stuffed them inside, closing the bag and moving her other two out of the way. There was a small – very small, actually – round table by the window, so Paisley picked up the stuff she had on top of it and dropped it to the floor.

"You brought your own alcohol?" she asked Trinity, pointing to the bottle and glasses.

"No, I got this downstairs and had them put it on your room," the woman said, placing the bottle of clear alcohol onto the table along with the glasses. "I hope you like vodka."

"I do," Paisley said. "I was going to get wine, though."

"Well, you weren't there, and I ate a peanut, so I wanted the hard stuff."

Paisley smiled at her and said, "Did you, really?"

"No, I had the pretzels, and I made him pour me a fresh bowl. I would have brought you some, but I was mad at you for standing me up."

"Work is kind of twenty-four-seven for me," Paisley replied. "Sometimes, I forget to be a normal person. I have my friends when I'm home, but when I'm traveling for work, I usually just work."

"Then, why invite me for a drink?" Trinity asked.

Paisley sat in one of the two chairs. Trinity sat across from her and began opening the bottle.

"I knew I wouldn't be able to sleep for a while, and I thought you make a good drinking buddy, so…"

Trinity smiled and poured vodka into two glasses.

"Why did you say yes?" Paisley asked her back.

"What else was I going to do?"

"Hangout with friends? Spend the night in with a…"

"Girlfriend?" Trinity capped the bottle. "Yeah, I no longer have one."

"That sounds recent."

"It is," Trinity said. "But it's fine. I don't think I can really do a relationship right now anyway."

"Was that what happened? You were too busy? That's one of the reasons mine have always ended, so I've given up."

Trinity took a drink and replied, "She cheated. She's in grad school and fucked one of her classmates. Not only did she not tell me about it herself, but I overheard the woman she was with talking about it with her when I went to pick Claudia up for a date after I'd just gotten over strep throat. It wasn't a long relationship or anything – a couple of months, really – but we'd been exclusive, and as I stood there, I had to hear them talk about a potential next time and what they'd do to each other then."

"Graphic?" Paisley asked, taking a sip.

"Claudia wasn't, but the other one was, and I'm not one to easily forgive cheating. Well, maybe I can forgive, but it's hard to forget."

"Sorry, Trin," Paisley said.

Trinity smiled.

"What?" Paisley asked.

"You called me Trin."

"So? That's your nickname, right?"

"Yes, but you've never called me that."

"Your name is long."

"Says the woman named Paisley."

"It's two syllables," Paisley argued, laughing.

"So is PJ." Trinity wiggled her eyebrows.

"Stop," Paisley replied, laughing harder now and tipping her glass to her lips.

"So, you're choosing work over a relationship?"

"Yeah, to my mother's great disappointment," Paisley replied. "She's got two potential mates awaiting me at the Thanksgiving dinner I'm not even sure I'm going to."

"Two?"

"One man. One woman."

Trinity chuckled, sipped her vodka, and said, "You're still in your work clothes."

"I was going to change and meet you at the bar." Paisley pulled on the shirt she still had tucked in.

"Do you want to change now? I can wait."

"It's fine. I've lived in it all day already. What's a few more hours?" she said.

Trinity's eyes flashed for a second as if a thought had just entered her mind. They flitted to the suitcase on the luggage rack. Then, she smirked.

"Um..." she said, pointing.

"What?"

"You should tuck that back in," she said.

Paisley's cheeks pinked immediately. A charging cable was hanging out of her suitcase. It was a very specific charging cable, too, that Trinity likely knew about, given her reaction to it.

"Oh, shit," Paisley said, standing and moving to the suitcase to push it back inside.

When she turned around, she caught Trinity still with that smirk on her face.

"I guess if you're not one for relationships, you've got to take care of yourself, right?" Trinity said.

"I'm just away for weeks at a time, and I–"

"You don't have to defend having a vibrator to me, Paisley."

Paisley sat back down and tried to get her blushing under control. This was the most unprofessional she'd ever been with a client in her life.

"So… You take care of yourself instead of… looking for someone for a night or two?" Trinity asked.

"Depends," Paisley said. "Why?"

"Just curious." Trinity cleared her throat. "It can be good, I think, just…"

"Yeah," Paisley said, looking into Trinity's darkening eyes. "Sometimes."

Trinity downed her vodka and stood.

"If it can be agreed that…"

"That's all that it is," Paisley finished for her.

"Yes, and it's important. Sex, I mean."

"It's a…" Paisley stood up after finishing her drink.

"Biological," Trinity finished this time, looking Paisley up and down.

"Are we talking about what I think we're talking about right now?" Paisley asked. "Because we should *not* be talking about this."

"Then, why did you stand up?" Trinity asked.

"*You* stood up."

"So?"

"You… You had a crush on me when we were in school, Trin. I'm not her."

"What?" Trinity said, taking a step toward her.

"I'm not PJ. I'm not her anymore. If you—"

"Paisley, it's just sex," Trinity said.

"And you're my client," Paisley argued.

"You're off the clock right now."

"You know it doesn't work that way," Paisley said.

"It does if we say it does," Trinity said, reaching out and pulling at the top button of Paisley's shirt until it came unbuttoned.

Paisley gasped and closed her eyes.

"We can't do this," she said in the smallest voice in the world.

"Do you want to?" Trinity asked. "Just have sex; no strings. We can forget it tomorrow."

"Where is this coming from?" Paisley tried to stall.

"What are you talking about? We've been flirting for days," Trinity replied.

"Shit," Paisley stated.

"Shit, bad?"

"Shit, because I know you're right, and I know we need to stop this."

Trinity popped another button and said, "I've wanted to look down this shirt all day. At dinner, you leaned over the table, and I saw just a little of this pink bra."

"Trin…"

"Tell me to stop, Paisley," Trinity said, unbuttoning another button and pulling the shirt apart enough to see more of Paisley's bra.

Paisley closed her eyes, trying not to think about the fact that she'd just gotten incredibly wet and that she *had* been flirting with Trinity. She'd thought about those green eyes looking back at her own when she'd considered getting herself off that morning and had reconsidered doing that because Trinity was her client. She needed to pull herself together. She needed to remain professional.

"Just sex?" she said instead.

"Just sex," Trinity confirmed, popping the fourth button.

CHAPTER 10

Holy shit! This was happening. Trinity stared into Paisley's eyes, noting that they had darkened as she undid the next button on the woman's shirt and then the bottom one as she pulled it out of Paisley's pants. When she'd left Paisley in her car, she had nearly leaned over and kissed her goodnight as if they'd been on a date, and they *hadn't* been on a date. Paisley didn't date, and Trinity had learned recently that she, likely, wasn't cut out for it, either. So, now, she was standing in front of Paisley Hill, a woman she'd always found attractive, and she was about to have sex with her.

"This is crazy," Paisley said on a breath. "We've been drinking."

"We've had one drink," Trinity replied, moving into her body and placing her hands on Paisley's hips.

"I know, but it might be—"

"Tell me to stop, Pais. If you don't want—"

Paisley's lips moved to her own, and then they were off. Trinity kissed her back with a passion she hadn't felt in years, maybe ever. Her hands moved around Paisley's back, under her shirt, touching every bit of skin she could. She moaned. Paisley gasped and pulled back. Trinity tried to catch her breath and worried it was over before it had really started.

"If we do this, Vidal can't know," Paisley told her.

Trinity nodded and said, "Get back over here." She pulled on Paisley's now undone shirt until Paisley was back in front of her.

When Trinity had gotten home, she'd immediately gone to her bedroom to find a vibrator of her own, and just as she'd been about to turn it on and get herself off to the

70

image of Paisley leaning over the table at dinner, giving her a nice view of her cleavage, her phone had rung, and she'd dropped the vibrator when she'd seen Paisley's name. She'd been keyed up possibly since the moment she'd laid eyes on Paisley that first day.

It was Trinity who leaned back in and connected their lips for a second time. She'd imagined this so much when she'd been in school. Paisley's lips on her own had been something she'd fallen asleep to numerous times, but this... this was so much better than anything her teenage brain could have come up with. This was Paisley as an adult, Paisley who really knew how to kiss a woman, and whose hands were unbuttoning her jeans right now. Trinity had wanted to do this for a while. She thought they'd stand and kiss like this to introduce themselves to each other in this new way. But Paisley had other ideas, it seemed. Her lips moved to Trinity's neck as her hand slipped inside those jeans and instantly into Trinity's underwear.

"Fuck," Trinity said when Paisley started stroking.

"You're soaked," Paisley replied, sucking at the base of her neck.

"I need to..." she tried. "Sit."

"Lie down, you mean," Paisley said, stroking faster. "I've got you, though."

Paisley's free arm went around her back, and she held Trinity in place. Trinity's head was spinning. Maybe the alcohol *was* starting to get to her. They'd eaten dinner, but she'd hardly touched her food. She'd been too involved in the conversation and, well, staring at Paisley's boobs. Now, Paisley Hill's fingers were moving up and down her clit, and they were moving fast.

"Wait. Slow down. I don't want to... yet."

"You will again," Paisley promised.

Then, she kissed Trinity again hard, letting her tongue dip inside Trinity's mouth and flick at the back of her teeth, making Trinity elicit a soft growl. When she'd been fifteen, she'd masturbated for the first time to the image of Paisley

Hill under a shower in the girls' locker room. Trinity had been there, too, of course. She'd been showering with her. Paisley had dropped a loofa, even though they never had loofas. Trinity had knelt to pick it up for her, and Paisley's hand had been on the back of her head in seconds, moving Trinity's mouth to her sex. Trinity hadn't known at all what to do back then, but in her fantasy, she'd given Paisley one hell of an orgasm. She'd given herself one hell of an orgasm that night, too, right before her roommate walked back into the dorm room.

In the present, Trinity was on her way to what would likely be an explosive one right now, too. Paisley's fingers were working her over, while her mouth was kissing her in a way Trinity hadn't been kissed in a while; not even with Claudia, who was her girlfriend for however long. Paisley stopped then. She moved back. Trinity was breathing hard when she stared into Paisley's eyes.

"Where are you?" Paisley asked softly, her hand pulling out of Trinity's jeans.

"What?" she asked back, unable to say much else.

"You're not here."

"Yes, I am," Trinity said, holding out her hand for Paisley to take. "I'm here. I just wasn't expecting you to…" She took Paisley's hand when Paisley didn't take her own, and she moved it back to her jeans, slipping it inside and pressing Paisley's palm to her. "God, I wasn't expecting you to just do that."

"Should I really slow down?" Paisley asked.

"No, I'm already close," she replied.

Paisley moved into her then, kissing her and moving her lips back to Trinity's neck, grazing her nose over her ear.

"We have all night. You can come now," Paisley said, pressing harder against Trinity's clit.

"Oh, God," Trinity replied, lowering her mouth to Paisley's shoulder, kissing her there, and finally giving something back in this exchange.

She tugged until the shirt was low enough that she

could kiss Paisley's skin, suck on it, and moved the bra strap out of the way as well in order to bite down lightly right when she came hard against Paisley's hand, her hips bucking into Paisley hard and fast.

"That's it," Paisley said softly. "That's it. Come for me, Trinity."

Trinity bit down harder. She never thought in her wildest dreams that she'd hear Paisley Hill tell her to come for her. She did, though, and it was good. Fuck, it was amazing. Before she could come down all the way, though, Paisley pulled her hand out of her jeans. Trinity wanted to protest, but then Paisley was taking off her own shirt and trying to undo her slacks. Trinity's guess was that Paisley's right hand was a little wet at the moment, making it difficult for her to unbutton them, so Trinity reached out, undid the button, tugged at the zipper, and yanked the pants down to Paisley's ankles.

Before Paisley could say anything, Trinity pushed her back, tugging at her panties until they were down at the ankles with the pants, and Paisley was sat in the chair she had vacated moments ago. Trinity pulled Paisley's pants and underwear off her entirely and spread Paisley's legs. She pulled until Paisley's sex was at the edge and near Trinity's mouth. She licked her lips, breathed her in, and waited for Paisley to protest. When she didn't, Trinity leaned down and spread her with her thumbs, seeing Paisley Hill for the first time. She licked her lips again because Paisley was so damn wet; Trinity couldn't believe this was all for her. Moving in, her tongue lapped and pressed down hard.

"God," Paisley said.

Trinity moaned as she captured Paisley's clit with her lips, sucking hard.

"Oh, fuck," Paisley said. "Yes."

Her hand moved to the back of Trinity's head, and Trinity was pressed into her more. She had no complaints even when Paisley tugged on her hair enough to hurt, because that didn't matter. Her mouth was on Paisley. She was going to make her come. God, she was going to make her come all night long. If this was the only night they had, she'd make it count.

Paisley's grip got harder. Trinity sucked just as hard. She licked, flicked, and waited. Paisley came moments later, and Trinity went back to sucking as Paisley cried out. When Paisley's grip on her hair loosened, Trinity continued licking. When Paisley let her go completely, Trinity stopped and kissed the inside of her thighs. She looked up and watched as Paisley's head went back, her eyes closed, her mouth open, her breathing still ragged, and her chest flushed. Unfortunately, Paisley was still wearing her bra, and Trinity wanted it off. She stood. Paisley opened her eyes and looked half-still-in-an-orgasm-fog and half-worried.

Trinity held out her hands for her to take, and Paisley didn't hesitate and took them. Then, Trinity pulled her in and kissed her, knowing full well that her lips tasted like Paisley. Paisley's arms were around her neck now, pulling her in, while Trinity's were working the clasp on Paisley's bra. Unable to get it undone, she grunted. Paisley laughed and shoved her backward. Trinity ended up on the side of the bed, legs hanging over it. She watched as Paisley took care of the bra herself and let it drop to the floor. Her breasts were perfect: small, with pink nipples that looked tight and hard. Trinity wanted to suck on *them*, too.

Paisley moved to her now totally naked, and Trinity couldn't say anything about her normal ability to get bras off women; she couldn't say anything at all. Paisley lifted Trinity's shirt up and off her. Trinity's bra followed suit. Before she knew it, Paisley was on her knees on the carpet that Trinity knew now was very uncomfortable, and she was lowering Trinity's jeans, followed by her underwear. They were lousy white cotton ones, and not at all like the lingerie-type panties she'd pulled off of Paisley minutes ago.

"Sexy," Paisley said as she looked at them.

"I didn't know we'd be doing this. I wasn't exactly prepared."

Paisley tossed them onto the chair behind her and met Trinity's eyes.

"Did you think I was joking?"

"Well, yeah."

Paisley gave her a sexy smile and said, "I wasn't. They're sexy. *You* are sexy, Trinity Pascal."

She then stood back up, meaning she wasn't going to go down on Trinity, after all. Trinity tried to shove down her disappointment. She didn't have to try long, though, because Paisley was straddling her now. Trinity's arms went around her for support, and she held on as Paisley kissed her long and slow. When Trinity moved her own hand to Paisley's inner thigh, wanting to be inside her, Paisley moved Trinity's hand to her breast instead. Fine with Trinity. She held on to that breast and pulled a nipple into her mouth. Paisley's hips began to rock as Trinity sucked, and this was quite possibly the best moment of Trinity's life.

Stop it, she told herself. *Stop it. It's just sex. You're fucking. It's nothing more than that. It's not some teenage fantasy come to life, so just stop it.*

"God, your mouth," Paisley said when Trinity moved on to her other nipple.

"You want it again?" Trinity asked, biting down lightly on the nipple.

"Yes," Paisley said. "Later." She shoved at Trinity's shoulders until she was on her back. "Me first."

And Trinity almost came just from that look Paisley gave her that told her Paisley wanted this just as much as Trinity did. Trinity spread her legs, earning a smirk from Paisley, who knelt between them, and then, her tongue was swirling around Trinity's clit, and Trinity covered her face with both hands to try to keep herself from crying out already. She didn't want to come. She wanted to make this last. This might never happen again. She wanted to—

Then, she came. Since she hadn't come all the way down from her first orgasm, she was primed for this one.

"Shit. Sorry, I—"

But Paisley wasn't stopping. She sucked on Trinity's clit harder. Then, there were the fingers. God, there were fingers inside her now; at least two. Hell, Trinity was probably wet and open enough for more than that. She told herself to make it last this time, but Paisley's fingers were moving counter to the tongue on her clit, working her up faster than Trinity was sure she'd ever been worked up before, until she was coming again, and this time was even harder. Paisley didn't pull out like she had earlier, though. She stayed. She stayed and continued to massage her inside while she licked at her clit lightly, slowly bringing Trinity down until she could finally open her eyes. When she did, what Trinity saw nearly made her come a fourth time in under an hour: Paisley Hill was on her knees, licking her lips and wiping her chin because she'd just gone down on Trinity and had given her one of the best orgasms of her damn life.

"Are you okay?" Paisley asked.

"I think I need a minute," she said, chuckling.

Paisley kissed the inside of one thigh and then the other. Then, she stood and walked over to the dresser, where she had bottles of water lined up. She opened one, took a long drink, and handed it to Trinity, who sat up and took it, needing a long drink herself. Then, Paisley poured them each another glass of the vodka Trinity had brought. She took a sip of her own, took the water from Trinity when she was done, and handed Trinity her own glass. Trinity sipped the vodka slowly, wanting it and *not* wanting it at the same time.

"Want to take a shower with me?" Paisley offered.

CHAPTER 11

What *had* she done? What had *she* done? Paisley disappeared into the bathroom, needing a moment alone. She should have just said that she needed to take a quick shower to get that moment, but instead, she'd invited Trinity into the shower with her. Surely, Paisley would lose this client now. She couldn't get fired, exactly – she was her own boss – but she had just risked everything for one night of casual sex. Could it even be casual if it was with someone she'd gone to high school with and was now technically working for? Probably not. But, damn, their sex had been good. She supposed she should've known that because the moment they'd met – or reconnected, depending on how Paisley looked at it – there had been something simmering beneath the surface. The fire in Trinity's eyes that day had been so intense. Paisley hadn't known then where it was coming from. She did know now, and God, it was a good fire. The way Trinity had taken her on that chair and had brought her easily to the first orgasm only made Paisley sit there somewhat silently, hoping she could hide the fact that she'd just come at what was essentially Trinity's first touch. And she must have succeeded, too, because Trinity had continued until Paisley had come a second time. It had been a much stronger orgasm than the first one, and Paisley had needed that.

"Are you okay?" Trinity asked.

Paisley turned around to see her standing there, naked and beautiful, looking like she'd just been thoroughly fucked, but Paisley knew she hadn't done anything close to everything she wanted to do to her yet.

"Fine. Just turning on the water," she lied and bent

over slightly to reach for the faucet, turning it on to run and then lifting the silver thingy to turn the shower on.

What was that thing called? She had no time to try to remember because Trinity was behind her now, holding on to her hips from behind and pressing slightly into her.

"You are incredibly sexy," Trinity said, running a hand over Paisley's back, giving her no reason to stand back up straight, which meant her head was almost under the spray of the shower, but just off to the side enough that she could remain there indefinitely if Trinity continued to touch her like this. "I really want to be inside you, Pais." She ran her hand softly over Paisley's right butt cheek.

Paisley gasped when it went lower and between her legs.

"Can you hang on to the edge of the tub like that?" Trinity asked.

"I… I think so," Paisley replied.

"If we do this again," Trinity added, running her fingers through Paisley's wetness. "I have something at home that I would love to use on you."

Paisley nearly grunted at that implication, but she had enough dignity not to, and instead, just held on to the side of the hotel bathtub because that was what people with dignity did. When Trinity pushed inside her with two fingers, Paisley closed her eyes.

"Is that something you might like?" Trinity asked.

"Yes," she managed to blurt out as Trinity pushed in deeper.

"Good to know," Trinity said, pulling almost all the way out. "Hold on."

Paisley wasn't sure exactly what she meant at first, but when Trinity pushed back inside harder and then began thrusting her fingers in and out fast, Paisley *did* have to hold on to the side of the tub to keep herself from falling in it.

"God, this is–" Trinity didn't finish.

She just continued to thrust with one hand while her other held on to Paisley's hip, guiding her back and then away from Trinity's fingers, increasing Paisley's pleasure at least tenfold until Paisley's hips were moving on their own and Trinity's hand was around her, cupping her, stroking Paisley's clit in time with her rapid thrusts. Paisley came hard as her head hung over the bathtub... like someone who still had all of their dignity. When Trinity pulled her hands away, Paisley nearly fell, but Trinity gripped her hips and helped her stand upright again. She was kissing Paisley's shoulder, squeezing her breasts from behind, and also rubbing her own sex against Paisley's ass.

"Get in," Paisley told her.

Trinity didn't stop moving against her, so Paisley climbed into the shower and waited. When Trinity appeared in front of her, Paisley pushed her to the back wall and slipped inside her instantly.

"Fuck," Trinity said, knocking her head back against the wall.

Paisley thrust hard, wanting Trinity to know she could play this game, too. She spread Trinity's legs wider with her knee and continued to thrust until Trinity was almost there. Then, she knelt and took her.

"Yes!"

Trinity's hand was on the back of Paisley's head as it bobbed between her legs. Paisley lifted the woman's leg, encouraging her to place it on the edge of the tub to give her better access. Then, she sucked her harder, and Trinity came all too quickly. Paisley stood, and they stared at each other then. They kissed each other. At first, it was hard; all passion and fire. But then, it slowed, and they were just kissing. Hands were still moving, but not with intention, and lips sucked on lips. They slid across necks until they nibbled at the skin. The water grew cold, and they showered, but not really, and got out of the tub. Trinity passed Paisley a towel and took one for herself. Then, Trinity left the bathroom wrapped in it, giving Paisley that moment alone she'd needed before. Paisley took it. She caught her breath and wrapped her own body in the thin towel. When she finally emerged from the bathroom, Trinity was sitting on the bed, still clad in the towel.

"We should talk," Paisley said.

"I thought you'd say that," Trinity replied, looking at the window, but the curtains were drawn, so she couldn't see anything outside.

Paisley sat down next to her on the bed but left a little space between them. She sighed and placed her hands in her lap, clasping them together.

"What we just…"

"Was really fucking good," Trinity replied.

Paisley had to laugh and nodded, saying, "Yes, it was."

"And I know there's stuff to talk about because we, I don't know, know each other, but–"

"Can I just ask you something?" Paisley interrupted her.

"Yeah," Trinity said, turning her face to Paisley.

"How much of what we just did was because of boarding school?"

"My crush?" Trinity asked, nodding as if she knew the answer already. "I won't lie to you; I thought about some fantasies I'd had when you first started touching me."

Paisley nodded and swallowed, finding her throat incredibly dry. She needed something. Water? Vodka? To go back in time and not make the mistake of sleeping with a client who used to think about sleeping with Paisley in high school?

"And this was *so* much better," Trinity said, laughing more to herself than to Paisley. "That was what I was thinking about, Pais. It wasn't really about me being with you like that – it was more about how I thought about it back when we were in school, and I couldn't believe we were actually doing it *now*. Then, that all went away, and I couldn't think of anything because you… really know what you're doing."

Paisley laughed a little, too, and shrugged a shoulder.

"Is that okay?" Trinity asked her. "Is it okay that I thought about it at first?"

"Yeah, of course," Paisley said, turning to face her. "I just don't want it to be about some wish-fulfillment or something and–"

She stopped when Trinity laughed.

"A little full of yourself there, aren't you, PJ?"

"Hey," Paisley said, knocking their shoulders together.

"It's not like I've been thinking about you for all these years," Trinity said. "Honestly, I'd forgotten *all* about you."

Paisley could tell she was lying, so she smiled.

"And I've had my own share of experiences with women that didn't remind me of you at all," Trinity continued.

"Oh, yeah?" Paisley said, chuckling.

"Yes. I don't have a thing for red hair or anything," she said.

"No?"

"No. Claudia, my ex, definitely didn't have red hair."

Paisley laughed harder and said, "Of course not."

"So, I didn't think about you at all until I saw your picture in my email."

"Right," Paisley said, nodding. "Since you haven't been thinking about me at all, can you maybe tell me about the fantasies you had when you were–"

"You really *do* need me to massage that ego, don't you?" Trinity asked playfully.

"I'm curious." Paisley shrugged again.

Trinity squinted at her, smiled, and licked her lips.

"I had no idea what I was doing back then, and we were in high school, so the fantasies were location-specific."

"Location-specific? Like where, exactly?"

"Showers; my room; your room – or, at least, what I assumed your room looked like; the history classroom under the desk while there was a room full of students not paying attention to what I was doing at all; your car; the pool; the field hockey field; the–"

"Wait... A classroom with other students?" Paisley asked.

"Yeah," Trinity replied.

"Were we both under the–"

Trinity shook her head no and said, "Just me. You were sitting in your chair, rocking that plaid skirt, and I was underneath your desk."

"Oh," Paisley said, giving herself a second to picture that, and yeah, that was working for her.

"It's silly. I never would have done that, but–"

"Keep going," Paisley said softly.

Trinity looked at her, surprised, and said, "Yeah?"

Paisley's nod came half a second later.

"Okay. Well, you had this glare that you used to give people who stared at you, and I was the recipient on many occasions, and it *did* something to me. I think I got wet the first time to that glare. In my fantasy, you turned to me in class and gave it to me again. At first, I'd turn away, like always, but in my fantasy, I waited until the class was watching a movie and the teacher was at her desk." Trinity slid her hand onto Paisley's thigh.

Paisley looked down at it as it slipped under the towel.

"And I did this," Trinity continued. "You turned to me, giving me that glare again until I slipped it up a little higher. Then, you looked down and seemed to be interested in what I was doing."

"And then?" Paisley asked, swallowing still with that dry throat.

"And then, I moved under your desk, and you pushed your chair back a little, spreading your legs for me."

Paisley spread her legs now, sitting on the hotel room bed. Trinity lifted an eyebrow at her and looked down. Then, she nodded and stood. She let the towel around her fall to the floor and knelt on it. Paisley reached for the towel around her breasts, pulled it apart, and let it fall behind her on the bed.

"And after that?" she asked.

"In my fantasy, you were wearing underwear that I had to remove," Trinity replied.

"Did you tear them off or lower them down slowly?"

"Which time?" Trinity asked, smirking up at Paisley.

Paisley ran her hand through Trinity's damp hair, moving it out of the woman's face as she lowered her head, causing Paisley to lean back and spread farther for her.

"I told you to keep quiet, or they'd hear," Trinity said, pressing Paisley's stomach until Paisley fell back onto the bed. "Then, I licked you slowly, tasting you and trying to keep myself from coming just from touching you."

"Do you want to know what I did the other morning?" Paisley said.

"What?" Trinity asked, kissing the inside of Paisley's thighs.

"I got off thinking about you doing what you're about to do right now."

Trinity looked up at her at the same time Paisley put her arm behind her head in order to look at *her*.

"You did?"

Paisley nodded and said, "I did."

"Will you show me?" Trinity asked.

"You want to watch?"

"Yes," Trinity said softly and then swallowed hard.

"Later?" Paisley asked.

Trinity ran her fingers over Paisley's lower lips, smirked up at her, and nodded.

CHAPTER 12

Trinity woke up around five in the morning and realized she'd fallen asleep in Paisley's hotel room. Paisley was still asleep, lying on her side, facing away from Trinity. Neither of them was wearing clothes, and the thin blanket had been pulled up to cover them, likely, by Paisley. Trinity took a minute to gather her thoughts. They'd had sex. She'd had sex with Paisley Hill. Paisley, who was supposed to be helping Trinity's business turn a profit sometime before Trinity died. Trinity swallowed, noting her dry throat, and looked over at the table where she saw an open bottle of water. Not wanting to wake Paisley, she moved slowly until she was standing over the table and drained the bottle. She turned around, and when Paisley didn't stir, Trinity found her clothes on the floor and began dressing.

She couldn't even remember kicking off her own shoes and socks, but one sock was on the dresser and the other, on the floor by the bathroom. Trinity didn't bother with her underwear, choosing to tuck those into the back pocket of her jeans. She took one last look at Paisley and left the room, closing the heavy hotel room door as softly as she could. She'd text Paisley later and let her know why she had left. It wasn't like they had discussed sleepovers. They'd agreed it was just sex. And if it was just sex, that didn't mean there was cuddling and falling asleep next to one another, did it?

They'd talked around one in the morning about how they both wanted to do this again, so Trinity had hope that it wouldn't be the last time. She started her car unsure, though, because there was a chance Paisley would wake up and regret the whole thing. She could tell Trinity it was a mistake, never should have happened, and never should again. Trinity thought about that scenario the entire drive home. She knew she would never get back to sleep, so she kicked off her dirty clothes and hopped into the shower. After cleaning up, she changed for work and let her hair air-dry while she grabbed her laptop to get an early start on her couch. Then, her phone dinged. She reached for it and smiled when she saw Paisley's name on the screen.

PJ Hill: You left?

Trinity messaged her back and received an almost immediate reply.

PJ Hill: You could've stayed. It's just sleep, Trin.

Trinity smiled at that and replied once more.

PJ Hill: I guess we can talk rules later, if you want.

Rules? Trinity took a deep breath. If they were talking about rules, that meant Paisley wanted this to happen again. Oh, that was very good news. An hour later, Trinity left for the office and couldn't wait to see Paisley.

"Morning," Vidal said when Trinity walked into their shared office.

"Hey. You're early," Trinity said, surprised to see her.

"Yeah, well…" The woman looked disappointed.

"Ah. You didn't get laid last night, did you?" Trinity asked, setting her bag on her desk.

"No, I did not. He wanted to watch a movie and snuggle. We fell asleep after."

"Didn't you tell him you were ready?" Trinity asked.

"He's a guy, Trin; they're always ready. I thought he'd start something, and *we'd* finish it."

"That's not really fair, though, is it?" Trinity said. "He might need a signal that you're into it." She sat down in her chair and pulled out her laptop.

"How was dinner with Paisley?"

"Huh? What?" she asked upon hearing Paisley's name.

"You guys did dinner, right?"

They did *something*, Trinity thought to herself.

"Yeah, it was good. Just dinner."

"Did you guys talk software? I'm still leaning toward Paisley's recommendation."

"No, we did not talk about software. But I'll ask her when she gets here."

"She's here," Vidal said, pointing her pen in the direction of the conference room.

"She's here?"

"Got here, like, ten minutes ago. She's responding to some emails, I think."

"Oh," Trinity replied, clenching her thigh muscles because she was instantly wet. "I'll just go talk to her about that software thing now, then."

"It can wait," Vidal told her. "We're meeting in, like, ten minutes."

Trinity licked her lips and said, "Why don't you give Paisley and I, like, twenty minutes? And we'll be ready to start."

"Why are you being weird?" Vidal glared at her.

"I'm not being weird," she said, standing up.

"Yes, you are."

"No, you were right," Trinity conceded, already coming up with her next lie. "We should have talked about the software thing last night at dinner, and we didn't. So, I'll get that taken care of, and we can start mapping out the process from the time we receive the parts until it all gets sent out."

"Okay," the woman agreed. "I have a call to the Philippines to make anyway."

"Yeah, cool. Just… take your time," Trinity told her.

"Trin?"

"Yeah?"

"Your laptop," Vidal said, pointing toward Trinity's device, which was still sitting on her desk.

"Right. I'll need that, probably."

Trinity picked it up quickly, left the office, and closed the door behind her. She walked to the conference room, seeing Paisley sitting there, staring down at her computer, and looking sexy as hell with her hair pinned up and in yet another business suit. Paisley looked up just as Trinity entered the office.

"Morning," she greeted.

"Come with me," Trinity replied instead, placing her computer on the table.

"What?"

"Come on," Trinity said, nodding toward the door.

Paisley stood up, looking concerned, and followed Trinity down the hall, away from the offices, around the corner, and toward the back of the building they'd leased.

"In here."

"Trinity, what is going on?" Paisley asked.

Trinity pulled on her hand and went in with her, closing the door behind them and pulling on a string hanging from the ceiling to turn on the one lightbulb illuminating them.

"We're in a closet," Paisley noted.

"Storage," Trinity replied, locking the door. "I can't stop thinking about last night, and this morning, and–"

"We can't," Paisley argued. "We're at work."

"So? It's *my* work."

"Trinity, where is Vidal?"

"In the office, on the phone with the Philippines," she replied, leaning in and kissing Paisley's neck.

"You want to have sex with me in a closet?" Paisley asked.

"The irony isn't lost on me, but yes," Trinity replied, undoing the button of Paisley's gray slacks and unzipping them. "Just to hold me over."

"Hold you over until when?" Paisley asked.

"Until whenever we do *this* again," she said, slipping inside Paisley's underwear.

"Jesus," Paisley let out, leaning back against the shelves behind her, rustling whatever was on them in the process. "We have to be fast," she added as she reached for Trinity's jeans and undid them, sliding her own hand into Trinity's sex. "You've been thinking about this for a while; you're already wet."

"Yeah, so are you," Trinity said, stroking Paisley fast as she sucked on the woman's earlobe. "God, that's good. Don't stop; I'll come."

"We can't do this in here again," Paisley told her.

"I must... not be doing... a good enough... job... if you can still... form complete sentences," she said as Paisley slipped inside her. "God, fuck me."

"You're wearing jeans," Paisley argued, reaching her free hand to the hem and trying to push them down.

Trinity helped her until her jeans were around her ankles. Paisley turned them around, kissed Trinity hard, and pressed her against the shelves, thrusting hard inside Trinity while her thumb flicked her clit. Trinity stopped her own movements against Paisley.

"No, don't stop," Paisley spoke. "I'm close already. You're so fucking wet... Is this all for me?"

"Yes," Trinity grunted.

"God, that's good," Paisley said when Trinity picked back up again. "You left... your underwear... at the hotel."

"I put them in my pocket," Trinity replied as Paisley rocked into her hand. "Fuck."

"You must have... dropped them. They're mine... now. I'm keeping them." Paisley was breathing hard.

Trinity bit down on her bottom lip and came hard against Paisley's hand.

"Yes, like that," Paisley told her.

Trinity wasn't entirely sure if she was talking about Trinity coming or what Trinity was doing to her. Then, she realized she wasn't doing anything to Paisley anymore. Her palm was still against Paisley's center, but Paisley was doing all the work now. She rocked herself over Trinity's thigh into Trinity's hand as her head lowered to Trinity's shoulder. Then, she came. Trinity held on to her with her free hand around Paisley's back until Paisley finally lifted her head back up and tried to catch her breath.

"I can't," she said.

"Can't what?" Trinity asked, worried now.

"Do this here again," Paisley replied, slipping out of Trinity then.

"The closet?"

"At the office at all. We can't do this here again."

"Okay," Trinity said. "Sorry. I just… Vidal told me you were here, and I needed to touch you."

"No, it's okay," Paisley replied, cupping Trinity's cheek with her dry hand. "We just need rules if we're doing this."

"Like, no doing this at the office?"

"Yes," Paisley said as Trinity removed her hand from inside Paisley's pants.

She loved that Paisley grunted in protest when she did, though.

"What about tonight?" Trinity asked.

"I'm sore already, and you want to go tonight, too?" The woman laughed a little.

"You're only here for—"

"Right," Paisley interrupted. "Tonight. The hotel again?"

"Yeah," Trinity replied. "We can't stay up all night again, though. I'm so fucking exhausted."

"Me too," Paisley said.

"I'll leave after…"

"You don't have to, Trin. You can stay. Like I said, we're both adults, and it's just sleep."

"I tend to be a cuddler in bed. Big spoon, mostly, and I didn't last night that I know of, but if it's just sex, I shouldn't be spooning you all night."

"You're a big spoon?" Paisley smiled at her.

"Yeah. Why? Hard to believe?"

"No, just curious." Paisley nodded. "We should go. We have a meeting."

"And we need to…" Trinity held up her hand. "Clean up."

"Tonight? Meet me at the bar. I'll be there this time."

"Yeah, okay," Trinity said, believing her.

After they both cleaned up, they returned to the con-ference room where Vidal was waiting for them. She didn't say anything about them arriving together, and they got to work shortly after.

"What's up with you?" Vidal asked a few minutes into the meeting.

"Me?" Trinity said.

"Yeah. You look, dare I say it, happy? You never *look* happy," she replied.

Trinity blushed instantly and looked over to Paisley, who was hiding behind her computer, laughing to herself.

CHAPTER 13

Paisley heard something.

"Babe, your phone."

Someone had just called Paisley *babe*.

"Pais, phone."

There was a small shove at her shoulder. Paisley opened her eyes and saw that her screen was, indeed, lighting up. She reached for it and held it up to see who was calling her this early. Of course, it was her mother. Wait. Who had just called her *babe*? Paisley rolled over as she answered and saw Trinity Pascal lying there, with the sheet down to her hips and her breasts exposed to the cool air of the room. Paisley took a second to appreciate them before she answered.

"Mother, is there a family emergency?"

"What? No, of course not."

"Then, why on earth are you calling me at six in the morning?"

"I can never keep up with you and the time zone changes."

"You know I drove here, Mom," Paisley said, sitting up in bed.

"I'm going to get dressed," Trinity said, getting out of bed and giving Paisley an excellent view of her ass as she went in search of her clothes.

"Who was that?"

Paisley's eyes went wide. Her mother always had had bat ears.

"What was what?"

"I heard someone else there. Paisley Jane, did you have an overnight guest?"

"Mom, do not say *overnight guest*."

Trinity stopped after picking up her jeans and lifted an eyebrow at Paisley.

91

"But you have one there?"

"It is six o'clock in the morning, Mother," Paisley said.

"Listen, I wanted to let you know that Alexia Weaver asked about you."

Paisley shook her head a little and took in Trinity, who put on her jeans without underwear. Paisley wiggled her eyebrows at her, and Trinity rolled her eyes.

"Paisley?"

"Huh?"

"Are you… having sex right now?" her mom asked in a whisper.

Paisley laughed and said, "No, Mom. I'm not having sex right now."

Trinity pulled on her shirt without a bra and looked down at the sheet that was still covering Paisley's lower body. She bent over and pulled it away. Paisley had to hold in her laugh when Trinity climbed back onto the bed. She shook her head back and forth, indicating that they could *not* have sex while she was on the phone with her mother.

"Is this a one-and-done thing, or are you actually with someone, Paisley? If you're dating someone new, I need to tell Alexia and James."

"So, it *is* a setup?" Paisley voiced what she knew all along.

Trinity, who had been kneeling in front of Paisley, shifted back on her heels.

"It was an attempt to get you to start thinking about settling down; you know that," Paisley's mother replied.

Trinity stood and then sat on the chair to put on her shoes.

"Mom, I haven't figured out Thanksgiving yet. I'm sorry. Can I please just call you when I do, instead of you constantly checking in?"

"Do you need to hang up because you're *about to* have sex?"

"I'm hanging up because it's *six* in the morning. I love you. Bye."

Paisley disconnected the call and noticed the forty notifications on her phone. Her mother was on her favorites list, so phone calls from her would always go through, but text messages from her friends could get incessant since they were all in the group chat together, so those didn't notify her until after nine in the morning; preferably, once she'd had her coffee.

"Sorry, we fell asleep again," Trinity said, standing back up. "I swear, I didn't mean to."

"Trin, we've been up late so many nights now, I'm not surprised we both passed out after one round this time."

"Want to go for round two?" she asked, looking down at Paisley again.

"No, because we're going to be late if we don't start getting ready." Paisley pulled the sheet up to her neck.

Trinity held up the underwear she'd worn the previous night and said, "Want these, too?"

Paisley squinted at her and thought about saying no, but instead, she just nodded because she liked the idea of hanging on to something of Trinity's; something that she'd helped ruin last night.

"Fine, but you're buying me new underwear. I get them from Target for, like, fifteen bucks for a pack of six."

Paisley laughed as Trinity climbed back on top of her and lowered Paisley's sheet to look down at her once more. Then, she sighed, which made Paisley laugh again, leaned down, and kissed her.

"I've got to get home to take a shower," Trinity said.

"I'll see you at the office."

"I'm going to run by that coffee place. What do you want?" Trinity asked.

"Don't bring me coffee unless you're bringing everyone coffee, or Vidal will think something's up."

"She's not Nancy Drew." Trinity laughed as she grabbed her phone and wallet off the table.

"She noticed how *happy* you looked before," Paisley remarked.

"I was, like, five-minute post-orgasm," Trinity argued. "Can't blame me for that."

"Everyone, Trin," Paisley told her still.

"Fine. But if you knock them all out of my hands again, no more orgasms for you."

Paisley laughed hard and then tossed the sheet aside. She spread her legs and watched as Trinity's eyes went straight down.

"Not fair," she said.

"Whatever you're drinking is fine," Paisley replied.

Trinity stood there, looking her up and down, and said, "Okay. I'm not wearing any underwear, and I'm going to ruin my jeans, so I need to go."

Paisley smiled at her.

"Do you keep the underwear of *all* your conquests?" Trinity asked on her way out the door. "Because that would be weird, Pais."

"Just yours," Paisley said as the door opened.

"Maybe I'll just stop wearing them, then."

Paisley swallowed hard and said, "Yeah, that would... be okay. In those tight jeans, I... I mean, if you wanted–"

Trinity laughed as the door closed behind her, and Paisley flopped backward into the pillows. She let out a deep sigh and thought about their previous night. Trinity had come over. They'd met in the bar, but after five minutes, they downed their drinks and ended up back in the room, where they'd spent an hour or so all over each other before they had essentially just passed out from exhaustion.

As Paisley showered, she thought back to how she'd woken up. Trinity wasn't cuddling up to her how she'd warned Paisley she might, but she'd called her *babe*. It was probably just a slip of the tongue. Trinity was half-asleep, and it didn't mean anything.

For Paisley, though, it meant that she probably needed to at least talk to her and remind her that this was just sex for however long they both wanted it, or until Paisley went back home after the job was done. She dressed for the office and made sure to hide a little spot on her neck that Trinity had left with concealer. She'd have to talk to her about *that*, too. Then, Paisley hit the road and took the short drive to the office.

***

"Good morning," she greeted, walking into the conference room where Vidal and Trinity were already working.

"Oh, hey," Trinity said.

"Morning," Vidal said.

"I got coffee for everyone." Trinity nodded toward the cup that she'd placed in front of the seat Paisley had been occupying every day.

"Oh, thank you. That's very nice of you."

"I got one for *everyone*," Trinity repeated.

Paisley gave her a look that told her to knock it off, and Trinity laughed silently.

"We were just talking about Vidal's big night last night," she added.

"Big night?" Paisley asked, removing her suit jacket and draping it over her chair.

"*Very* big night," Vidal replied.

"She means his penis," Trinity stated.

"Oh, wow," Paisley said, not expecting that.

"It's just us, girls, in here, right?" Vidal said.

Paisley nodded at her.

"It was so good," Vidal said dreamily. "It was the best sex I've ever had. He *knows* what to do, you know?"

"Sorry, can't say that I do," Trinity replied, taking a drink of her coffee.

"You've been with women who know what they're doing," Vidal remarked. "You just told me about a woman you were with the other night."

Trinity choked on her coffee. Paisley's cheeks went pink instantly, so she opened her laptop to try to hide her face, wanting to laugh but having to hold it in.

"She was getting over her ex-girlfriend, apparently,"

Vidal explained. "Didn't you say it was amazing?"

"I think what I said was that I didn't want to talk about it," Trinity replied, coughing a little. "I don't like bragging like that. You just kept asking me about Claudia, and I was over talking about that."

"So, you've been with a woman who is amazing in bed *recently*?" Paisley asked, still trying not to laugh.

"She's all right," Trinity replied, giving her a look.

"Wait. She *is* all right? Meaning, it's happened again, or will?" Vidal asked.

"You know, I don't really know the answer to that yet," Trinity said.

"It was hot sex. Why wouldn't you see her again if you could?" Vidal pressed.

"Yeah, makes sense to me," Paisley teased.

"Please tell me about your boyfriend's penis some more," Trinity joked.

Paisley laughed this time.

"I'm just saying... I thought it would take a while for you to get back on that horse. I'm glad to see you're sewing your rebound oats."

"A lot of horse metaphors going on in there... Does that have to do with your boyfriend's penis, too?" Trinity said. "And I'm not rebounding. I'm over Claudia. I'm... having fun."

Paisley met her eyes.

"Just fun?" Vidal asked.

"Yeah, just fun," Trinity said, taking another drink of her coffee.

"Well, I'm all for that. You deserve it after that cheating cheater."

"So, can we talk about literally *anything* else?" Trinity asked.

"I have some ideas for the layout of the warehouse to maximize the space," Paisley said.

"Yes. That. That is a good topic for the workplace."

Said the woman who had me up against the shelves in

the storage closet here yesterday, Paisley thought to herself.

***

"Hey," Trinity said, walking into the conference room hours later.

"Hey," Paisley replied, looking up at her.

Trinity closed the door behind them and said, "I'm sorry about earlier. Vidal was on my case about Claudia and needing to do something new and move past her, and I got tired of listening to her, so I told her I'd slept with someone. Obviously, I left out the details, and she doesn't know it's you."

"But she knows that it's amazing, apparently. Oh, and hot."

Trinity sat down in the chair next to her and laughed a little.

"Yeah, well... It is, right?"

Paisley flushed a little and nodded in agreement.

"So, tonight?" Trinity asked. "I can swing by with dinner."

Paisley looked out the small window that opened to the hallway, where she saw Vidal and Will talking.

"I can't tonight," she said.

"No?"

"I have work for that other client I was on the phone with the other day when you got mad at me. I've put some stuff off that I need to wrap up for him."

"Okay. Sure," Trinity said. "Maybe we can talk about tomorrow night?"

"Yeah," Paisley replied.

Vidal opened the door, and she and Will walked in for their afternoon meeting.

"We'll talk more about that later," Trinity said in a deeper voice as if trying to sound more professional somehow.

"Yes, later. We must," Paisley mocked.

CHAPTER 14

Trinity tried to call Kelly to update her on the recent developments of her life, but Kelly didn't answer. She texted next, hoping Kelly would get the message soon and call her back, because Trinity *needed* to talk to someone about this. She couldn't talk to her best friend because Vidal was also her business partner. She'd done enough just by telling Vidal that she'd hooked up with someone and made it sound as if it were going to happen again. Paisley seemed unbothered by that, but she could be so hard to read at times. One moment, she's giving them advice about how to package their products to maximize space and efficiency and save on costs, and the next, she's lifting an eyebrow in Trinity's direction when Vidal wasn't looking, giving Trinity an inkling about what was going on in that brain of hers. And God, it was an amazing brain.

Trinity had known Paisley was smart when they were kids, but this was like *that* Paisley on steroids. The breadth of her knowledge spanned just about everything in business they'd need to know, and that might just be the sexiest thing about her. Trinity had always found intelligent women sexy. Intelligence, humor, and confidence were probably the top three things that got her going, and Paisley had all three of those things in spades. This woman was one of the smartest people Trinity had ever met. She was also really funny at times, and Trinity enjoyed their banter. On top of that, Paisley appeared comfortable in her own skin, in her sexuality, and in what she wanted. She was also humble and kind. Trinity never knew most of this about her back in school, for obvious reasons, but now that she did, it was hard to think of anything else.

Trinity stared at the clock on her cable box under her TV, noting that it was after nine. She should go to sleep early. She was still exhausted, despite getting to bed at a reasonable hour the night before, after all. She thought about it for a second, then stood up and went to her room to change. A few minutes later, she was out the door and in an Uber. There was a moment where she had nearly typed the address of Paisley's hotel into the app, but Paisley needed to work, and they hadn't really discussed rules around one of them just showing up, so instead, Trinity went to a bar she liked.

It wasn't a lesbian bar or even a gay bar, but it was on the outskirts of the one street that had become what the locals referred to as, "gaytown," and it often had a nice mix of people, including *her* people. Trinity ordered a beer and sat at the bar, not really sure what she was doing there. When she turned around in her stool to scope out the room, she instantly noticed someone she hadn't expected to see there. No, she noticed two people she hadn't expected to see there. One of them was Claudia. The other one was the woman Claudia had slept with. They appeared to be there as part of a larger group, and Trinity thought she recognized one of the guys as another classmate she'd met once, but she wasn't sure due to the dim lighting of the room. When the woman who had fucked her then-girlfriend noticed Trinity, she gave her a smug look, and her arm went around the back of Claudia's chair.

Trinity wanted to just leave. She didn't want Claudia anymore, not after what had happened. And when Claudia had confessed her love while trying to explain away her cheating, Trinity had worried Claudia had been way ahead of her. It was over between them now, but something about the way this woman had her arm around Claudia, as if showing Trinity that she'd won something – like a woman could be won like that – really pissed Trinity off. She smiled casually, took a sip of her beer, and turned back around in her stool, waving the bartender over and ordering a white wine as if she were expecting someone herself. Then, she dialed.

"Trinity?"

"Hey. What I'm about to say is incredibly petty, and I'm not still hung up on her or anything, but the woman she fucked is giving me a look that makes me want to just like punch–"

"What are you talking about? Why is it so loud?" Paisley asked.

"Sorry. Also, hello," Trinity said.

Paisley laughed softly and said, "Hello. Now, what's going on?"

"I'm at a bar, and the woman who slept with my now *ex*-girlfriend is here with her, and she saw me. She's giving me the look that says she got her, and *I'm* the asshole."

"Oh," Paisley said. "Okay. Are you drunk? Do you need a ride home or something?"

"No, I need this sexy as hell woman I'm sleeping with to come to the bar and just sit next to me for a few minutes. Then, we can leave like we have somewhere more important to be."

"You want me to come to the bar to pretend to be… your new girlfriend?"

"We don't have to put a label on what we fake-have," Trinity joked.

Paisley laughed a little louder and said, "Can it be for, like, ten minutes, max? I really do have work."

"Yeah, that's fine. I owe you big time for this. I would have called Vidal, but Claudia knows her and that she's totally straight."

"Text me the address. Order me something to drink, too?"

"Already did. White wine awaits you."

"Okay. I'll be there as soon as I can."

Trinity didn't want to turn back around to see if they were still there, so instead, she turned her stool just slightly toward the front door because she'd be able to see Paisley arrive and Claudia and her group leave if they decided to go before Paisley got there. Twenty minutes later, Paisley walked through the bar door, and... Fuck. She was still wearing her business suit from the day. Her hair was pinned up, and Trinity wanted to take her into the bathroom and mess all of it up. She smiled at Paisley, who smiled back, walked toward her, pushed Trinity's knees apart gently, and stood between them.

"Hey," Paisley said softly.

"Hi," Trinity replied, swallowing because she hadn't expected this.

Paisley leaned down and captured her lips in a kiss. It wasn't a deep or passionate one; that probably would've been too much if Claudia or *that woman* would have been looking in their direction.

"When we pull apart, don't look over at them; that'll give it away. Just turn your stool around to the bar, and we'll have a drink, okay?"

"But how will I get to see the shocked expression on her face, then?" Trinity asked, running her hands up and down Paisley's sides under her suit jacket.

"Whose face are you hoping to see?"

"Just the bitch who gave me that look," Trinity said.

Paisley kissed her again. It was more like a peck this time, but her arms went around Trinity's shoulders, and then they were on her back, scratching it up and down, which she now knew drove Trinity crazy. Trinity pressed her head to Paisley's neck and just sat there as Paisley scratched her back up and down over her shirt.

"Okay. If I keep doing this, you'll fall asleep." The scratches stopped, and Paisley sat down on the stool next to her, moving the wine toward herself.

Trinity marveled at the fact that already, Paisley knew that about her. Sure, she had discovered it that first night after they'd had a lot of sex, and she'd been straddling Trinity's ass while she kissed her back and scratched it a bit. Trinity had told her that back scratches like that would knock her out, so Paisley had stopped because she hadn't wanted to go to sleep yet.

"So? How did I do? Five stars?" Paisley asked, turning toward Trinity.

"At least ten," Trinity replied.

"Do you want to put your arm around the back of my chair? Really make it look real?"

"No, I want to put my hand on your thigh," Trinity replied.

"Are we going for *sleeping together* or *new relationship* here?"

"Does it matter?" Trinity asked.

Paisley sipped her wine and said, "This is awful. Is it vinegar?"

Trinity laughed as Paisley pushed the glass away.

"It's the house wine."

"It's vinegar with alcohol in it."

"It's a neighborhood bar. What were you expecting?"

Paisley reached over and took Trinity's beer, taking a drink, checking the label, and taking another drink.

"That'll do, I guess."

"You guess? You're such a snob." Trinity shook her head and laughed.

"I am not," Paisley said, laughing back at her. "Taste that." She moved the wineglass over to Trinity.

"No way. You said it tasted like vinegar."

"But I'm a snob, so I must be exaggerating, right?"

"Shut up," Trinity said. "I'll order you something else. What do you want?"

"What do snobs drink?" Paisley asked.

"I'm picturing champagne, with gold leaf floating in it and a grapefruit wedge or something on the rim because strawberries would be tacky."

Paisley laughed and said, "I'll just share your barely acceptable local beer, and we can get out of here."

"Sorry. I know you were working. Just... seeing her claim Claudia like that while I was sitting right here really irked me. Who does that?"

Paisley took another drink of Trinity's beer and said, "I thought you were over Claudia."

"I am. It's not that. It's that she looked right at me and did it."

"The audacity!"

"Who says words like *audacity*, PJ?" Trinity laughed again, stole her beer back from Paisley, and took a long drink.

"If you plan on us ever having sex again, you'll stop calling me PJ."

"Hi."

A small voice came from behind them. Trinity turned to see Claudia standing there, holding her hands together in front of her.

"Oh, hey," she said, turning her stool around a little more.

"I saw you. I was sitting over there with some friends," Claudia replied.

Trinity made a move to look over there as if she hadn't noticed. *That* woman was still sitting in the chair and was watching them closely.

"I see that."

"I'm not here *with* her. That's my whole study group."

"Claudia, you can be here with whoever you want," Trinity said.

Claudia finally looked over at Paisley and said, "Hi, I'm Claudia." She held out her hand for Paisley to shake.

"Paisley," she replied, shaking it. "Nice to meet you."

Claudia nodded and said, "So, you're doing well."

"Yeah, I am," Trinity replied without elaborating.

She wasn't here to make Claudia feel bad. She hadn't planned on talking to her at all. She'd just wanted to show the woman who had given her that smirk that Trinity was fine. More than fine, really. She was having great sex with Paisley, the sophisticated woman who used words like *audacity*.

"Good. That's good," Claudia mumbled. "I didn't hear from you after the letter. I guess I know why. I'd say this is fast, but I have no right to say that to you."

"It's not really all that fast," Paisley said.

Trinity looked over at her in surprise.

"Trinity and I go way back, actually. Boarding school. We recently reconnected."

"You went to boarding school? I didn't know that."

"There's a lot you don't know about me," Trinity said. "But yeah, I did. Paisley and I met up, and… Well, one thing led to another…"

That was true. She hadn't lied and told Claudia they were a couple; just that one thing led to another, and they'd ended up having the best sex of Trinity's life. No big deal.

"Right. Well, I should be getting back."

"It was nice to meet you," Paisley said, giving her what Trinity now knew to be her professional smile.

"You too," Claudia said. "Bye, Trin."

"Bye," Trinity said.

She didn't watch Claudia walk off. She turned back around in her stool and finished her beer.

"Come on. I'll drive you home," Paisley said, rubbing Trinity's back.

"Am *I* the asshole?"

"I don't think so. Well, not for this. You still call me PJ, so…"

"And I have you as PJ in my phone."

"You what?" Paisley asked.

Trinity laughed and said, "Hey, tomorrow night, come to my place. I'll cook us dinner. We can eat and then do whatever. Try out that thing I wanted to try on you, or not. Just whatever."

"Dinner and sex?" Paisley said.

"Yes. We've done that before."

"Not a dinner that you cooked for me," Paisley argued. "It just sounds a lot like a date, Trinity."

"It's dinner. It's not that big of a deal. I'm not proposing, Pais."

"I know. It's just that… You know I can't promise anything, right?"

"Yes, I know that. You've made that clear. I can order food in; I don't have to cook. Is that one of the rules?"

"It's not a rule, Trinity. I just don't want us to blur lines. I'm already here basically pretending to be your new girlfriend to your old girlfriend."

"We hadn't settled on *sleeping together* or *in a new relationship*," Trinity reminded her, placing a hand high on Paisley's thigh. "And I want you to come over tomorrow night; I have plans. Dinner or no dinner."

"Can I think about it?" Paisley asked, surprising her.

Trinity sat back, removing her hand, and said, "Yeah. Of course."

"Let's get out of here. I have some work waiting for me back at the hotel where the shampoo and conditioner share a bottle."

"Okay. You said that just so I'd call you a snob again and we'd change the subject, didn't you?" Trinity laughed as she waved the bartender over for her check.

"No. Shampoo and conditioner are separate things. They do *not* go in the same bottle."

Trinity couldn't help but keep laughing about the shampoo and conditioner debate all the way to her apartment, where Paisley dropped her off. They didn't kiss goodnight because that would make it seem like they'd just been on a date, but Trinity had wanted to, and that wasn't helping anyone.

CHAPTER 15

Paisley fell asleep alone, and it felt off to her. That was weird because she normally fell asleep alone, so she'd gotten used to that over the years. In fact, she enjoyed sleeping alone. It gave her the whole bed to toss and turn and wake up in the middle of the night like a normal adult. Last night, though, it was different. It wasn't like the sheets smelled like Trinity; housekeeping had replaced those. It was just... different. Yeah, that was the word. After dropping Trinity off at her apartment complex, Paisley had gotten back to the hotel, intending to finish up her work, but instead, she just stared at her laptop, accomplishing nothing.

When she'd woken this morning, she'd gone to her suitcase to pull out what she'd wear that day and ended up finding two pairs of underwear worn by Trinity. She stuffed them into the dirty clothes bag she had on the right side of her suitcase, knowing she really didn't want to wash them. Was that weird, too? Not wanting to wash them ever because then they'd always smell like this woman she slept with a few times on a work trip? Yes. That was weird, she decided. She'd have them washed and would give them back to Trinity because it was strange, keeping her underwear. Paisley shook herself out of thinking about Trinity in and out of underwear and flopped back onto the bed.

"What is wrong with me?" she asked herself.

She liked this woman. She needed not to, but she liked Trinity. Paisley liked that Trinity called her a snob last night. She liked how embarrassed Trinity got when Vidal had asked her about the woman she slept with; that leaving her underwear with Paisley was just a normal thing to do; that she'd not only started her own business, but she'd done so with her best friend, and that it worked. Their idea worked, and they'd seen major success much faster than most other companies Paisley had worked with. She liked that Trinity challenged Paisley's ideas and didn't just give in because they were sleeping together. Trinity Pascal was no yes-woman. She was strong and confident now, not at all like the shy girl she'd once been in school, from what Paisley *did* remember. Hell, could Paisley even trust her own memory of that time? She hadn't ever thought of herself as a bully, but it was clear that she'd been Trinity's, at least, in part. If she could go back in time, she would, but she couldn't, and so, she was just left with these feelings that she didn't want.

She'd pushed Trinity away last night, despite wanting to ask if she could go up with Trinity, have sex, and then come back to the hotel. She'd wanted to call the woman earlier last night and suggest Trinity come over, after all. She had managed to resist all of that, but now, she was thinking about the look on Trinity's face when Paisley told her she'd have to think about the dinner thing tonight.

It just felt like a date. Paisley would bring a bottle of good wine, not that awful stuff from the bar. Trinity would kiss her and welcome her in. They'd make small talk while she finished cooking. Maybe Paisley would help. They'd probably kiss a few times, sneak touches, make comments about how dinner could wait, and end up having sex first while it sat in the oven. They'd eat late, have sex again, and then fall asleep next to each other, and Trinity would big-spoon her until Paisley got too hot. Paisley would pull away. Trinity would find her later in the night, and they'd have sex again. Paisley would wake up in her arms, and they'd shower together before leaving for work. What was so wrong with that? That actually sounded pretty nice. It never really had before, so... Why now? What was so different about now? Paisley reached for her phone for no reason and checked her notifications.

<u>Scarlet Campbell:</u> Hey, I'm sorry about the other night.

I made it about me. Call me back, and it'll be all about you. I want to know what's going on, Pais.

Paisley smiled at her shy friend. She typed a message back to her that she'd call her later and that everything was okay. Then, she went to the group chat.

Talon Mitchell: Guys, if we're thinking about having kids one day, do we buy the house with the extra bedrooms we don't need now? It's a starter home.

Weston White: IDK. Whatever you guys think is right for you. I'd say, if you find a house you really love, and you can afford it, you buy it thinking about the future.

Aria Bancroft: Agree with Wes. Buy for the future if you love it. If it's a for-now house, get what you need today.

Scarlet Campbell: I have nothing else to add.

Eleanor Enger: Does anyone want, like, six cupcakes today? Carmen keeps making them for me, and I cannot keep eating these things all the time – I've gained three pounds since we started dating.

Aria Bancroft: Have more sex. You'll lose it.

Eleanor Enger: We have tons of sex. If we didn't, I would have gained ten already.

Weston White: You look great, El. Don't listen to Aria.

Aria Bancroft: Hey! I was just trying to help. Guys, do I bring one or two bikinis to Italy? We have a villa for a week, but it's private. Maybe no bikinis at all? We'll just skinny-dip like we do at home.

Talon Mitchell: Remind me not to just drop by your house unannounced.

Eleanor Enger: Too late for me, unfortunately. Luckily, I heard sounds and ran away.

Paisley laughed. She loved her friends so much. She missed them when she was gone, but she had a goal: grow the business; make it incredibly successful; hire people; expand from there. It was just getting harder and harder to focus just on those things now that her friends were all planning the next chapters of their lives. Weston and Annie were moving in together in January. Aria and London might be the first couple to get married. Hell, Scarlet might even come out to her parents soon and actually get a girlfriend, and Paisley would be the only one left, with one thing in her life. Did she still want that?

***

"Lunch?" Trinity asked.

"Sure," Paisley said.

"There's a decent diner, but we'd have to drive," Trinity said.

"Is Vidal coming with us?"

"Yeah, she's wrapping up a call," Trinity replied.

"Oh, okay," Paisley said, knowing that she sounded disappointed.

They couldn't exactly talk about anything with Vidal there.

"Do you not *want* her to be there?" Trinity asked.

"No, it's fine. Of course, she can be there."

"Pais…" Trinity said. "I can tell her–"

"Okay. All set." Vidal had her purse hanging over her arm. "Are we ready?"

"Yes. Let's go," Paisley said.

Lunch was fine. Well, it was a little awkward because Trinity kept looking at her like she was trying to see whatever was going on inside Paisley's head. It was unnerving, so Paisley sent her a few warning glares, but since those were turn-ons for Trinity, Paisley got back a heated stare each time. Vidal drove them back to the office when they finished, and just as she parked, her phone rang.

"I have to take this. I'll meet you two inside," she told them. "Hello," she greeted into the phone.

Trinity and Paisley got out of the car and started on their way to the office.

"Let's walk," Trinity said.

"Where?"

"Just anywhere," she replied.

"We're supposed to be working," Paisley said softly.

"And we're taking a walk after lunch to burn off the calories. That's allowed," Trinity argued.

Paisley chuckled and said, "You know, my friend Ellie is dating a baker. Carmen keeps bringing over her favorite cupcakes. It's a thing with them, but Ellie was trying to offload them because she's gained three pounds."

"I'll eat them," Trinity stated.

"They're over four hours away," Paisley chuckled.

"There's always same-day shipping. Are they good cupcakes?"

"They're great, yeah," Paisley said as they walked past the warehouse door. "And my other friend, Aria, is dating one of the other bakery owners, so she gets cupcakes, too."

"Wait. Two friends, both dating bakers?"

"Bakery owners, technically. Long story."

"Can I hear it?" Trinity asked.

Paisley looked over at her and said, "Should we really be talking about my friends?"

"Why not? We're just on a walk, Paisley. There's no set topic. Tell me about them."

"Well, we all went to college together," she began and told Trinity how they'd all met and connected instantly. "It's been an interesting year in our friendships."

"Why?" Trinity asked.

"Well, four of the six of us are now in long-term relationships that might actually go the distance, and that's all happened this year. Scarlet and I are the only single ones left, and she's out to us but no one else, including her family, so she'll probably be single until that happens, I guess."

"But you want to be single," Trinity remarked.

Paisley took a deep breath and said, "I'm trying really hard not to screw this up."

"Screw *what* up?" the woman asked.

"My work." Paisley pointed back and forth between them. "Whatever *this* is."

"I thought *this* was just sex," Trinity replied.

"Yeah, *when* has that really worked for people who actually like each other? I should have known better."

"Who said that I like you?" Trinity teased with a wink.

"Well, you *did* offer to cook me dinner."

"Yeah, to get to the sex. Everyone knows that if you cook a woman dinner, she's more likely to sleep with you. It'll probably happen before dinner, too, because she just can't wait."

Paisley laughed and said, "So, that's it? Just wanted to get me back in bed?"

"Obviously," Trinity replied sarcastically.

Paisley stopped walking and said, "I don't know if I'm ready for the whole cooking dinner thing."

Trinity stopped walking as well and said, "Okay. What *are* you ready for?"

"Can we just do drinks tonight again? But really drinks and not finish fast to rush up to my room?"

"*Only* drinks?" Trinity wanted to clarify.

"I don't know," Paisley admitted.

"It would be okay if that's all it was tonight," Trinity told her.

"That's the problem, though, isn't it? If it's *just* drinks, then it's *not* just sex."

"Pais," Trinity said, taking her hand but just letting their fingers touch at the tips a bit. "I *do* like you. I like this. It can be just sex, if that's what you want, but I'm also okay just having drinks with you tonight without expecting us to move in together."

"No? We could share my hotel room. Have you heard about the shampoo and conditioner being one bottle?"

Trinity laughed before replying, "I'll be there tonight around eight."

***

At five past eight, Paisley glanced at the automatic doors of the hotel and didn't see Trinity as they opened. Maybe she'd changed her mind. She went to text her, but when she was about to hit send, the doors opened again, and the woman walked through the doors, heading straight to Paisley.

"Sorry. I wanted to make you wait a little bit to get you back for the first time. Was that wrong of me?" Trinity asked.

Paisley laughed and leaned in, kissing her on the cheek. Cheek kisses were okay, right?

"You're insufferable."

"I'm going to start making you put a quarter in a jar for every snobbish word you use. Actually, let's adjust for inflation and say, a whole dollar."

"Insufferable is not a snobbish word. Neither is audacity."

"You sure? Let's take a poll." Trinity turned her head. "There are a whole three other people in this bar. We could ask them."

Paisley rolled her eyes and said, "No."

She leaned in a little, wanting to be closer to Trinity, and noticed something for the first time. While this wasn't an upscale hotel bar at all – far from it, actually – when Trinity turned back to her, and Paisley saw her bright green eyes, she realized it. This was her fantasy: the woman with green eyes and blonde hair in the hotel bar. Paisley was staring at the woman she'd made up in her mind.

"Paisley Jane?"

Paisley's eyes went wider than they possibly had ever gone before. Trinity looked over Paisley's shoulder. Paisley swallowed and slowly turned around.

"Mother, what on earth are you doing here?" she asked, seeing her mother standing right behind them.

CHAPTER 16

"Your father was driving me crazy, and you mentioned you were only four hours away from home, so I did the math and figured out that I could drive here myself because it's on the way to the cottage. I can take a few days there for myself and get home in time to keep planning for the holidays. You never come to Sunday dinner, Paisley Jane. You left me no choice, really." The woman looked straight into Trinity's eyes. "Well, hello there."

"Hi," Trinity said nervously.

She hadn't been expecting to see Paisley's mom tonight – or, well, ever again after high school, actually – but the woman was standing there in front of her, holding a pale blue designer bag that matched her way-too-nice-for-a-drive suit that she was wearing. Her auburn hair was not as shiny as Paisley's, and her green eyes weren't as bright, but she was a gorgeous woman, and Paisley had a lot to look forward to when she hit her mom's age.

"Mom, this is Trinity. Trinity, this is my mother. I had no idea that she was coming."

"That's my fault. I decided to come here on a whim. I was just going to go to the cottage, but decided it was worth it to take the detour."

"Are you staying here?" Paisley asked her.

"No, of course not." The woman scoffed. "I thought we could have dinner, and I could hit the road after that. The cottage is only another hour or so away from here," she explained for Trinity's sake before adding, "They're setting it up for me now, and I was hungry." Paisley's mom sat down in the chair opposite the booth Trinity and Paisley had been sharing. "So, Trinity?"

"Yes," Trinity said, wondering if she should say *ma'am* after it.

"And you are *friends* with my daughter?"

"Mom, let's get you a drink. Martini?"

"I'm driving, Paisley. I'll have wine, and I'll sip it slowly. What do they serve in this bar? I assume peanuts or something." She rolled her eyes.

Trinity had to laugh at that.

"I'll ask them for a menu." Paisley stood, walked until she was behind her mother, and mouthed, "I'm sorry," to Trinity.

"So, you two met at the hotel?" Paisley's mother asked Trinity.

"Um… no," Trinity replied.

The woman squinted at her. Trinity was determined not to give anything away until Paisley got back and took over this conversation.

"No? Where did you meet?"

"Technically, we met when we were fourteen."

The woman looked at Trinity, confused.

"We went to the same boarding school," Trinity explained.

"Oh," Paisley's mom said, seemingly excited now. "You went to Pemberton?"

"I did," she said.

"Excellent school. Were you on the field hockey team with Paisley?"

"No," Trinity replied.

"Would I know your parents? I went to Pemberton, you know? I'm on the alumni council. I'm certain we would have met."

"Unlikely," Trinity said. "My mom worked at the boys' school. My dad passed away when I was a kid."

"She worked at the boys' school?"

"Yeah, that's how I got to go to Pemberton. We wouldn't have been able to afford it otherwise."

"I see," the woman said, contemplating something.

This was where Trinity assumed she would make an offhanded comment about scholarship kids or about how Paisley was so amazing and deserved whomever she was trying to set her up with today.

"Maybe I know your mother. I worked with the boys' school a lot, too. My husband went there. What's her name?"

"Sharon Pascal," Trinity replied.

"Oh, I know Sharon." Paisley's mom leaned over the table.

"You do?"

"Yes, she helped me plan a dance once with the girls and the boys. She was delightful."

Trinity smiled and said, "She is, yeah."

"She's not still there, is she?"

"No, she actually got a job as a high school principal at a public school about three years ago."

"That's great. I really did enjoy working with her on that dance. She had some great ideas about keeping the boys who wanted to spike the punch away from the punch. One of them involved putting that Miss Driscoll by the punch bowl – she'd been in the Olympics for weightlifting, and your mom thought all the boys were afraid of her."

Trinity laughed and said, "That sounds about right."

"So, how did you two reconnect? Was it through Facebook or Snapchat?"

Trinity gave her an expression that undoubtedly showed surprise.

"I'm not *that* old," the woman argued almost playfully.

Trinity laughed just as Paisley walked back with a glass of red wine and a menu for her mother.

"It's Merlot. I'm sure it's bad. Just drink it anyway," Paisley said, placing it in front of her mom.

"I swear, I raised her with manners…" She took a sip of the wine. "Oh, that's awful! Do they not let it breathe here?"

Trinity laughed again as Paisley sat back down next to her. Automatically, Trinity's arm went over the back of the booth. She turned to Paisley and gave her a look that told her silently that things must run in the family.

"Shut up," Paisley said, laughing at her.

"No one said anything," her mom replied, pushing the wine away. "No danger of me driving drunk with *that*. So, what are you two having for dinner?"

"We weren't. We were just having a drink, Mom."

Her mom looked from Paisley to Trinity.

"I see. You were having a drink and then…" She pointed straight up. "Going upstairs."

"Mom, you're killing me here," Paisley said, looking down.

"We hadn't gotten that far yet, Mrs. Hill. We were just having a drink. We both had a long day."

"What is it you do, Trinity?"

"Oh, let me tell her." Paisley patted Trinity's leg. "She owns a company that invented this really cool thing and got backing from Kickstarter. Now, she's got investors offering her more money to expand, and she's totally kicking ass."

Trinity smiled and watched as Paisley enthusiastically continued to brag about her to her mother.

"That's pretty amazing," Mrs. Hill said.

"Right now, they're in this really cool space in the warehouse district that they're renovating, and they'll be hiring like crazy soon."

"Really?" her mom said.

"It just kind of took off," Trinity replied this time. "Vidal, my best friend and business partner, is really the brains behind the operation."

"That's not true," Paisley argued as Trinity winked at her. "Vidal's great. I really like her, but Trinity's idea is what got them here, and they've got raving fans online already."

"You sound very proud, dear," Mrs. Hill said.

"I am," Paisley replied. Then, she turned to Trinity. "Is that weird? Me being proud of you?"

"No," Trinity replied, chuckling, and pushing a piece of rogue hair back behind Paisley's ear.

She realized what she'd done only too late, turned, and caught the elder Hill lifting a curious eyebrow at her.

"So, you two work together and are also doing more than working together?"

"Isn't it getting late?" Paisley replied quickly. "I'd hate for you to be on the road after eleven, Mom. You should–"

"You're an adult, Paisley – I know what happens between two people who like each other when they're adults. I should assume you two like each other, have plans for the rest of the night, and I'm getting in the way."

"We really didn't–" Trinity tried to interrupt.

"We're on a drinks date, Mom," Paisley stated.

"You don't use the *date* word often," Mrs. Hill noted.

Trinity hadn't expected that word, either.

"We're… It's complicated, okay? We didn't really know each other in school, so we're getting to know each other now. And yes, we were having drinks and doing that when you walked up."

"On a date?" Mrs. Hill asked.

"A date, huh?" Trinity said.

"Oh, don't *you* start," Paisley told her, pinching Trinity on the thigh through her jeans.

"Hey! That hurt," she said, laughing.

"Trinity, has Paisley invited you to Thanksgiving yet?"

"Mom!"

"No, she hasn't," Trinity replied, leaning forward and nodding.

"Well, I keep asking her to confirm if she's coming alone or bringing a plus-one."

"You don't say?" Trinity said, getting a thigh squeeze under the table for her trouble.

"I haven't even confirmed if *I'm* going yet," Paisley remarked.

"Would you like to join us?" Mrs. Hill asked. "Of course, if you have plans with your mother, we'd be happy to have her as well."

"Oh, my God," Paisley muttered, covering her face with her palm in embarrassment.

"I usually have Thanksgiving with her, yes, but this

year, she splurged on a four-day cruise that weekend," Trinity told Mrs. Hill.

"Well, that's unfortunate. I would have loved to have seen her," the woman replied.

"You would have?" Paisley asked.

Trinity slid her hand down from the back of the booth to Paisley's tense back and ran her hand under her shirt, pressing a palm gently into Paisley's lower back.

"You should really join us. That is, if my daughter actually comes," Paisley's mom told her. Then, she added, "You know what? Even if she doesn't, *you* should come – we can talk about her behind her back."

"You're talking about me with me sitting right here, so that wouldn't make much of a difference, would it?" Paisley said.

Trinity laughed and said, "Let me talk it over with PJ here, and I'll make sure she gets back to you."

Mrs. Hill laughed and said, "I haven't heard anyone call her PJ in years."

"Mom, if you're hungry, order and take the food to-go," Paisley replied.

***

"Well, *I* had fun. I don't know about you," Trinity said.

"Shut up, and come here," Paisley replied while laughing and pulled Trinity into her. "I thought she'd never leave."

"She ordered appetizers *and* an entrée. That woman is my hero," Trinity said as Paisley unbuttoned her jeans.

"Do you want to have sex tonight?"

"What? Yes."

"Then, you should stop talking about my mother."

Trinity laughed again as Paisley pulled her own shirt off. When she removed her bra, Trinity's eyes looked down at the breasts she hadn't been able to see the previous night.

"Damn," she said softly.

CHAPTER 17

Paisley dipped her tongue into Trinity's belly button.

"This is a really good way to wake up," Trinity said with a groggy voice.

"Yeah? Should I continue?" Paisley asked, repeating the movement.

"Definitely. But I think what you're looking for is a bit lower."

Paisley chuckled and said, "Oh, I know. I don't think I've *missed* yet, have I?"

"Nope. No missing. Definitely no missing," Trinity said.

They'd had another night of ridiculously amazing sex, even after her mother had interrupted their drinks date. *Paisley* had called it that; she still couldn't believe it. She rarely used the word *date* unless she was telling someone she wasn't interested in one. Now, she was between Trinity's legs, licking her, and preparing to make her come after she'd used that word last night.

"God," Trinity said. "*Best* way to wake up."

Paisley smirked, but she doubted Trinity could see it, given that the woman's eyes were closed, and her head was already tipped back. Paisley had woken with too many thoughts in her brain, and they were all mixed up, so she'd decided to wake Trinity up like this to help focus on something else. But, as much as she was enjoying this, it wasn't helping. Paisley's mind was racing now that she was fully awake and listening to Trinity's sounds as her orgasm built.

They'd had a late dinner with her mother last night, who had asked Trinity a lot of questions, leaving Paisley out of most of them, which only meant one thing – her mother liked Trinity. Her mother liked Trinity for *her*. She had invited Trinity to Thanksgiving dinner with the family. Hell, she'd even invited Trinity's mom. *Paisley* hadn't even met Trinity's mom. And she shouldn't meet her mom – they were just having sex. Right? No... They'd had a date last night. Paisley shook her head rapidly, mainly to get her thoughts in order but also because she knew Trinity liked that when Paisley's lips were wrapped around her clit.

"I'm close," Trinity said.

But Paisley felt so far away. They'd had a dinner date with her mother last night, and it had gone *well*. Not just because her mother had liked Trinity, but because Paisley did, too. Paisley liked the hand that had appeared on her back. She'd liked putting her hands on Trinity, essentially claiming Trinity in front of her mom and the few people in the bar. When her mom had gone to the bathroom in the lobby, she'd even leaned over and just kissed Trinity. It wasn't a preamble to anything, and it wasn't on the cheek, either. It was just a kiss, and when Trinity had deepened it, Paisley had not only allowed it, but she had also encouraged it, enjoyed it, and wanted more kisses just like that. Her mom had cleared her throat when she returned to the table, and Paisley's cheeks had flushed – not just out of embarrassment, but from the heat of Trinity's touch.

"Yes!"

Trinity held her head in place as she rocked her hips against Paisley's mouth. Paisley tried her best to focus on what was happening because she loved this; she loved making Trinity come this way. Trinity was so responsive. She had no problems expressing herself, what she wanted, what she liked and how much she liked it, and that was almost enough to make Paisley come herself. She couldn't stop thinking about the fact that they'd had a date last night, though. Moreover, she couldn't stop thinking about the fact that she liked the idea. What did that mean? Did she want to date Trinity? Go out for dinner and a movie and go back to someone's place to either have sex or just fall asleep like normal people do? Was Paisley normal now?

"Pais?" Trinity said softly.

And it was then that Paisley snapped out of it and realized she was on her back now, with Trinity on top of her, kissing her. Paisley, likely, hadn't been kissing her back.

"Hey," Paisley said, trying to smile her way out of what was coming next.

"You're not here right now," Trinity replied, nudging her nose to Paisley's.

"I am," Paisley said, running her hands through Trinity's hair.

"No, you're not. Or, you weren't just a second ago. What's going on?"

She rolled over beside Paisley onto her side, facing her.

"You were doing something," Paisley said, rolling to face her.

"And I'll pick it right back up if you want me to, but tell me what's going on first."

It wasn't supposed to be like this. They were supposed to sleep together, work together, and then Paisley would leave for home. And maybe, if they were both still single later, and she were in the area, she and Trinity could hook up again. That was the extent of it. At least, it was supposed to be the extent of it.

"Pais," Trinity said softly again.

She cupped Paisley's cheek, and Paisley leaned into it automatically.

"Why am I PJ in your phone?" she asked eventually.

"What?" Trinity said, smiling back at her.

"Why?"

"Is *that* what's bothering you?" Trinity asked.

"I'm not PJ anymore, Trin."

"You are, though," Trinity replied, moving closer to Paisley when Paisley shifted back a little. "We can't just pretend we aren't who we were in high school – it's always going to be part of us. I'm still shy at times. My acne reappears at will. I have no business being on a field or court of any kind." She pressed a kiss to Paisley's nose. "And I still think about you all the time."

"Still? You said you hadn't thought about me in years," Paisley teased.

"Oh, *big* lie," Trinity said, laughing. "But, babe, you're still a little bit of PJ, too. You're confident and comfortable in your own skin. You own a room when you walk into it or make a presentation. I would know; I've had to force my eyes off you in the office so that Vidal doesn't get any ideas about us. I bet if you picked up a field hockey stick, you'd still score goals. You're still kind of a snob, too."

"I am not," Paisley said, laughing.

Trinity wrapped an arm around her waist and said, "Yeah, you are. Now, I happen to like it and think it's cute."

"Cute?"

"That face you made when you didn't like that wine was really cute," Trinity replied. "We're also different now; both of us. We've changed, but – I don't know – it feels like maybe we've changed in all the right ways to–" Trinity paused for a second. "Do this."

"And what is *this*?" Paisley asked her.

"Oh, no. You can't ask me that. You're setting all the rules here, Pais."

"I thought you wanted the rules, too," Paisley said. "They work for both of us, right? You just got out of a relationship with Claudia and didn't want anything serious."

"True, and I love having sex with you," Trinity said, winking at her. "But last night, you said we were having a drinks *date*. Obviously, we got interrupted, but before your mom showed up, it was like an actual date, with all the possibilities that are attached to that, and I had my hands kind of all over you. You were touching me, too, even with your mom around. Do you still want to just have sex?"

"No," Paisley said immediately, surprising herself.

Trinity laughed and rolled onto her back.

"Wow! Your expression right now."

"What?" Paisley asked.

"Your mouth just said that, but your brain hadn't caught up yet, had it?"

Paisley moved on top of Trinity, straddling her hips, and smiling down at her.

"I will admit, I hadn't planned on saying that."

Trinity slowly stopped laughing, held on to Paisley's hips, and asked, "Is that what you want?"

"I don't know," Paisley replied. "I didn't plan this."

"I didn't, either," Trinity stated. "You think I planned on running into PJ Hill and sleeping with her?"

"Trin?"

"Yes?"

"I'm not PJ anymore. I'm not the person who did those things to you or who didn't stand up for you. I'm sorry I ever was that person, and I wish I could take it back."

Trinity ran a hand up her abdomen and placed it between Paisley's breasts, over her heart.

"Then, let me get to know all of who you are now," Trinity replied softly. "Don't hold back because we're only sleeping together. Let's actually try it."

"A date?"

"A second date, technically."

"So, my mom was on our first date, then?"

"Good point," Trinity said, dropping her hand.

"And about that Thanksgiving thing…"

"No way. We'll go there next. First, tell me what I want to know, Paisley." She gave Paisley's hips a light shake.

"We can go on a date," Paisley replied. "But, Trin, where is it even going to go? You live here… I live somewhere else, but I'm never really there anyway. We're both so busy… This is why I don't date – it's just too hard."

"Well, when you put all that pressure on it – yeah. If you just go on a date and see if there's something more there than chemistry in the bedroom, though, it gets easier to think about it."

"I wouldn't know," Paisley replied.

"Just don't make it all about days, weeks, and months for now," Trinity told her. "Make it about a day at a time. Maybe we'll end up hating each other, and it'll be a moot point."

"I doubt it," Paisley replied.

"Obviously, you're obsessed with *me*, but that doesn't mean I–"

Paisley tickled her, causing Trinity to break out in laughter.

"Stop!" she managed through her laughter.

"You've thought about me for years," Paisley noted.

"Yeah, about my head between your legs," Trinity replied, still laughing. "And yours between mine. I never…" Laughter overtook her for a moment. "Thought of actually dating you. Stop it. I can't–"

Paisley stopped tickling her and smiled down at Trinity's flushed skin and beautiful green eyes still filled with laughter.

"But you're thinking about dating me now?"

"Yes," Trinity replied.

"Change my name in your phone," Paisley said.

"Fine, but I'm changing it to Paisley Jane."

"Paisley Jane is what my mother calls me," Paisley argued, leaning down to hover over the woman and settling her hips between Trinity's legs.

"Never mind, then. Paisley it is," Trinity said, brushing Paisley's hair away from her face. "And I don't have to go to Thanksgiving. I was mainly teasing you because it was fun. Although now, I kind of want to go."

"God, why?"

"Because if I don't go, there will be two people there whose sole purpose is to flirt with you, get to know you, and see if there's something there."

"Jealous now that we're dating?" Paisley said, smirking down at her.

"Oh, we're not dating. We're going on one date," Trinity teased. "And we'll take it from there." She rubbed Paisley's back up and down with both hands. "And yeah, a little."

"It's a family meal, Trin. It's the holidays. Bringing someone home to that–"

"What if it's actually a good thing?" the woman interrupted. "Get out of your head for a minute, Pais. What if me showing up there as a date – or even if you wanted to call us *girlfriends* just for the sake of the holiday – gets your mom off your back? It doesn't have to mean we actually *are* girlfriends. Your mom would have to disinvite the two people she's already told you're available, or she'll at least have to update them on your relationship status, and you'd have a family holiday free of pressure to meet someone new."

"That just means the pressure will shift on when one of us is proposing, who will have the kids, when are we moving in together–"

"Okay. Calm down. I get that you like me a little bit, but I'm nowhere *near* ready to move in with you," Trinity teased.

Paisley smiled down at her. Then, she kissed her and rocked her hips into Trinity.

"That's nice, though. I'll take more of that."

"Say, 'Please,'" Paisley teased back as she rocked again.

"I'll do you one better." Trinity paused to kiss Paisley. "I'll change your name in my phone to Paisley Hill."

Paisley smiled and nodded in thanks.

"And I'll put a bunch of hearts around it," Trinity added.

Paisley slipped out of bed quickly.

"Hey!" Trinity laughed.

"Just meet me in the shower."

Paisley laughed, too, and it was nice. Waking up like this, holding Trinity, talking to her about this stuff was really, really nice.

CHAPTER 18

"Okay. I need help," Paisley stated.

"Like, psychological?" Aria asked.

"No, asshole," Paisley replied and shifted the phone as she stared down at the bed and the clothes she'd laid out on top of it.

"Well, I hope it's not physical because you're far away, so I can't save you, and if you're interested in anything else physical, my girlfriend might take issue with that."

"Aria, focus. I called you for a reason," Paisley said, sitting in the desk chair.

Aria laughed and said, "What's going on?"

"Are you alone or with London right now?"

"She's at the bakery. I'm at home. Why?"

"Because sometimes, it's hard talking to you because she's always around."

"Damn, Pais. Tell me how you really feel."

"I don't mean it like that. I love London. Happy for you both. Blah. Blah. Blah."

"Straight from the heart there, friend."

"You're all with people now," Paisley said. "All of you. Well, not Scar, but she's Scarlet, so…"

"She's still on the whole coming out thing again," Aria finished for her, likely nodding on the other end of the line.

"I know," Paisley sighed. "I can't even talk to *her* about what's going on right now because she just turns the conversation to that."

"What's wrong, Pais?"

"I love you guys, and I love your girlfriends, but I miss just hanging out with you – just the six of us. I miss having at least a few single friends that didn't have a girlfriend sitting next to them, interrupting our conversations."

"Or your friends talking about their new relationships all the time?"

"That too." Paisley sighed. "I get it; I do. I love how happy you are. I just still need my friends, you know?"

"I know," Aria replied. "And if I've been too busy with Lo recently, I'm sorry. Sometimes, it's hard with you, Paisley. You're kind of in and out of our lives at times. You're traveling so much that it's hard for us to get together, just the six of us, on the days that you're here, but maybe we can figure it out and make it a priority."

"Maybe, but that's not really why I called," Paisley admitted.

"Okay. Tell me what's going on in your world, then."

"I might be dating someone."

There was silence. Then, it sounded like Aria shifted.

"I'm sorry. What?"

"I know." Paisley leaned back in the hotel chair and heard it creak. "I called *you* for a reason."

"Me, specifically?"

"Yes, you met London back in school."

"Y-e-a-h," Aria dragged out the word as in question.

"My client is a company with two owners. Vidal is the one that I talked to and signed with, and I hadn't met her partner until I got here. The partner's name is Trinity Pascal. I went to boarding school with her."

"And you're dating Trinity?"

"We're going out on a date tonight."

"Okay. So, a first date with someone you went to school with?" Aria asked.

"Yes, but there's more to it than that," Paisley replied. "I wasn't nice to her in school… You and London fell in love at first number two pencil or whatever – I can't listen to that story again, by the way."

Aria laughed and said, "Noted."

"I didn't know this, but I was kind of a bully to her. I

have no real excuse. I don't think I was the worst bully in the world, but I was mean, and I let my friends be mean to her, too."

"Paisley Hill was a bully? Never would have known."

"I was different in high school," Paisley told her.

"I guess so," Aria said.

"Anyway, when I ran into her here, it didn't go well at first. But there was like this… heat between us. She remembered me; I didn't remember her."

"Oh, that's not good…"

"But we were flirting, and then she told me who she was, and I apologized, and we were having drinks." Paisley paused. "Then, we were having *sex*."

"Hold on. What?"

"Yeah…"

"You slept with her?!"

"I've slept with her multiple times now. We've sort of put the past behind us, I guess. We've had a lot of sex, and it is…" Paisley smiled at the memories.

"You're sleeping with her, but your first date is tonight?"

"It was supposed to be just sex."

"Oh, Pais… That never works; you know that."

"Hello, you had Pia as a friend with benefits for years."

"Pia always wanted more, and I always pushed her away and felt terrible about that. I should have ended it long before I did because of that, but I was selfish. Now, we're just friends, and it's working so far."

"Well, still," Paisley argued.

"And now, it's not just sex with you two?" Aria asked.

"I like her," Paisley admitted. "I didn't want to. I'm here to work, and she's a client, but–"

"The sex was amazing," Aria said, laughing at her.

"Best sex of my damn life. God, what she does to my body…"

"So, it's more than just that, though?"

"Yes. She's smart and self-deprecating about it, which

is adorable to me. She's also sexy as hell, calls me on my shit, she held her own with my mother, Aria, and–"

"Wait. Your mother?"

"She showed up last night," Paisley said. "Trinity and I were at the hotel bar, and my mom just shows up." Paisley told her the full story. "And now, she may or may not be joining my family for Thanksgiving dinner, to where my mother has also invited two people who think they're being set up with me."

"Your mom is hilarious," Aria replied, laughing. "So, you'll have an actual date there, and then two people who want to date you at the Thanksgiving gathering? Is she giving you a rose to hand out at the end?"

"I said the same thing," Paisley replied, laughing, too.

"Well, it *could* make an interesting reality show," Aria laughed some more.

"That I would *watch*, but I don't want to participate in."

"Pais, what's going on here? You like her, and you're freaking out? You've dated before; you're a big girl. I know you have this whole 'no serious relationship' thing because of work – which is dumb, but your choice – but I'm not sure what the deal is here."

"You went on a first date with London after years of whatever. I wasn't in love with Trinity as a kid, but… I don't know. I guess I'm just looking for some advice."

"On what to wear? What to do?"

"I guess."

"Well, I don't know that I have any of that for you because I've never met Trinity, but it was different for London and me – we had a friendship back then. We also went on dates prior to seeing each other naked."

"So, you're no help, then?" Paisley concluded.

Aria laughed at that and replied, "Pais, be yourself. Wear something comfortable. Actually, let me rephrase that: wear something comfortable to the rest of humanity; not a business suit."

Paisley chuckled a little and said, "I have jeans and sweaters lying on my bed right now."

"Good. Go with that. And don't sleep with her tonight."

"What? Why?"

"Because you've already done that. Make it clear that tonight is the first date."

"Can we sleep over?"

"Up to you; I'm not your mom, Pais. I just recommend not having sex since you've been doing that already."

"Yeah, right," Paisley agreed, nodding for no one. "You're right."

"You're thinking about having sex with her, aren't you?" Aria chuckled.

"Yes," Paisley said with a loud grunt. "It's really good, Aria."

Aria laughed and said, "But if you think this is more than just that, you need to explore the other stuff, too."

"I know…"

"So, pick out something to wear, let your hair down tonight, and no clips all up in there. Don't wear makeup, either."

"Not even mascara and some lipstick?" Paisley asked.

"Nope. Just show up looking casual and comfortable."

"Literally none of what you just told me is casual or comfortable to me," Paisley remarked.

"Maybe it's time for a change, then, Pais," Aria replied. "Your life is more important than your work. Your life isn't *about* your work. You're more than that."

Paisley sighed and thanked her friend. When they hung up, she felt a little better but also wasn't sure she was ready to change *that* much about her life just yet. So, she stared at her clothing options, made her choice, got dressed, brushed her hair, trying to make it look less frizzy without adding a bunch of products, which she normally did for work, and resisted the urge to apply some light makeup. On the bed, she'd placed the vibrator earlier that they'd yet to use and which she had planned on putting into her bag to bring with her, but given the conversation with Aria, she decided to leave it behind. Shoving it into her suitcase and closing it, Paisley sat down once more, took a deep breath, and then stood again right after.

"Okay. I'm ready."

Minutes later, she was standing at Trinity's front door, staring at the number under the peephole and thinking about turning around.

"You know I can see you, right?" Trinity spoke from behind the door.

"You know it's weird to wait for people at the door and watch them through the peephole, right?" Paisley asked through the door.

"Are you going to knock, Paisley?"

"I was planning on it, yes. Now, I'm reconsidering."

Trinity pulled open the door and met Paisley's eyes with intensity in her own.

"Take the risk, Pais."

"*You're* the one taking the risk on me. I'm not good at this," Paisley argued.

"You've been great so far," Trinity replied. "You look amazing, by the way. I love when your hair is down like that."

Points for Aria, Paisley thought to herself.

"You look great, too," she said, looking at the jeans with holes in the knees and the green V-neck T-shirt Trinity was wearing. "Brings out your eyes."

"Yeah, well, I have to compete with those," Trinity said, pointing at Paisley's eyes. "Come in, Pais."

Paisley entered the apartment, and Trinity closed the door behind her. When Trinity walked back around her, facing Paisley, she leaned in and kissed her hello.

"I missed you," she said softly against Paisley's lips. "That doesn't have to mean anything; it's just a statement of fact. And I'm glad you're here." Trinity kissed her softly again. "Also, a fact." She kissed her a third time, and Paisley deepened it, not wanting Trinity to let go just yet. "And I really like just kissing you."

"I like it, too," Paisley replied.

Trinity kissed her one more time and pulled back to look at Paisley again.

"You really know how to rock casual."

"You rock casual every day. The way you wear a T-shirt…"

"Oh, yeah? Business-suit-wearing Paisley loves a good T-shirt, huh?"

"On you? Absolutely," Paisley replied, tugging on the hem of Trinity's shirt. "Your breasts look so fucking good in just a T-shirt."

"But you like them *out* of it better, don't you?" Trinity asked, reaching for that hem.

Paisley placed her hands on top of them and said, "Yes, I do, but… tonight, I don't want to… do that?"

"See my boobs?"

"Have sex," Paisley said.

Trinity let go of her own shirt, and Paisley watched her eyes as they glimmered a little with what looked like recognition.

"Okay. I'm cooking us dinner, then."

"I'll help," Paisley replied.

CHAPTER 19

"Just how long has it been since you've been on a real date?" Trinity asked.

"I don't know. A while," Paisley said, looking around Trinity's apartment.

"You're so talkative tonight. That'll make us not having sex tonight much easier," she said sarcastically. "Maybe we'll just play charades or something."

Paisley turned around to face Trinity, who was in the kitchen, chopping vegetables.

"Sorry, I'm being weird."

"Yeah, you are. Did you forget how to talk to me since I saw you last?"

"No," Paisley said, walking into the kitchen and stealing a piece of a carrot. "Your place is nice."

"It's okay; not exactly nice. What's your place like? Mansion? Castle? Is there a moat?"

"Yes," Paisley said, eating the carrot. "The drawbridge is a little tricky. I have to use WD-40 on the lever at least once a month to get it to open."

Trinity laughed silently as she tossed chopped onions into a pan, earning a nice sizzle.

"Can I come over?" Trinity asked. "Will you open your drawbridge for me, Paisley?" She winked at her.

"Not tonight," Paisley said, laughing a little.

"And is that because you don't sleep with people on the first date?"

"It's because I was talking to my friend Aria before I came over here, and she suggested that because you and I have already been having sex, and now we're taking things to the next level, we shouldn't be having sex tonight."

"Next level? Isn't it usually the other way around? Dating and then sex?"

"Who cares?" Paisley said, "We're here, right?"

"Are you not going to stay over?" Trinity asked. "I mean, if we're not having sex."

"I think I can keep my hands off you for the night if we just sleep next to one another, but I can go back to the hotel if you want."

"I want you to stay here," Trinity replied. "But are you sure?" she asked, chopping pancetta. "Can you really keep your hands off me all night?"

"No one said we couldn't make out a lot and maybe have a little under-the-shirt action," Paisley replied, leaning against the counter.

Trinity leaned over and kissed her.

"So, I can stay?" Paisley asked.

"Yes, but only because of the under-the-shirt action," she joked.

"I brought a bag. It's in my car."

"You brought a bag? Weren't *you* presumptuous?"

"No, I left it in the car. Had you said no, you never would have known about it," Paisley countered. "I can go get it now."

"I can get it for you later," Trinity replied. "I kind of like you standing right there while I cook." She leaned over and kissed Paisley again.

Then, Trinity moved to the sink to wash her hands. After drying them on a towel, she moved in front of Paisley and placed her hands on the counter behind her on either side.

"I'm going to kiss you for a while now. Then, you're going to go sit down and find a movie for us to watch while we eat on the couch, and I'll finish up in here."

"Warning me that you're about to kiss me?" Paisley lifted an eyebrow.

Trinity shook her head and said, "*Preparing* you. I'm about to use tongue and make you go weak in the knees."

Paisley smiled into the kiss. When her arms wrapped around Trinity's neck and pulled her in, Trinity's were around Paisley's back under her sweater. They kissed like that until Trinity smelled slightly burning onions. She pulled back, kissed Paisley on the nose, and moved to the pan.

"Go. Sit. Find," she said.

"You're bossy when you cook," Paisley replied.

"Says the field hockey player who wasn't the captain but still bossed everyone around."

"I *was* the captain senior year," Paisley remarked.

"But the bossing began long before then."

"How do *you* know that? You weren't on the team."

"I had nothing better to do than watch you practice," Trinity said, moving the pancetta into the pan with the onions.

"You watched us?" Paisley moved into the living room.

"No, I watched *you*," Trinity replied.

"How often?"

"I had no activities other than the ones that were required, so... often."

"And?"

"And what?"

"Did you like what you saw?"

"I masturbated to you, Paisley. Repeatedly. What do you think?"

Paisley laughed and said, "I masturbated to you, too."

Trinity turned around with wide eyes and said, "You what?"

"Not in school."

"Oh. Recently?"

"Kind of. It's hard to explain," Paisley said, sitting on the couch, which faced away from the kitchen, but she turned to the side to meet Trinity's eyes. "It's actually really weird."

"Getting off to me is weird?" Trinity asked.

"No, I just..." Paisley took a deep breath. "So, I've had this fantasy, and I use it to get myself there in a pinch."

"Go on."

"I'm usually in a hotel bar. Like, a really nice one, not like the one we were in the other night."

"Come back in ten years; maybe it'll be renovated."

"Shut up," Paisley said, laughing. "You're never going to let that go, are you?"

"Unlikely."

"Anyway, I'm sitting next to a beautiful woman, and she tells me she wants to go up to my room."

"I thought you said this is about me," Trinity noted.

"It *is* about you. I said, 'beautiful woman,' Trin."

"I know. That's why I asked."

"Trinity, you're gorgeous," Paisley told her. "I've spent several nights now looking at and touching your body. Trust me; you're perfect. Now, *shut up*."

Trinity swallowed. Paisley thought she was gorgeous.

"Anyway, she's wearing a skirt, and I slip my hand under it, and I get her off in the bar with everyone around. Then, we go up to my room and continue. I usually come before that part, though."

"You get her off in the bar?"

"Yes."

"And that's a turn-on for you?" Trinity asked.

"Apparently," Paisley replied.

"You've never done it?"

"Not like that, no."

"Do you want to?"

"I don't know," Paisley said.

"With me?"

"So, here's the thing about that. The woman I always picture has long blonde hair." Paisley pointed to Trinity. "And bright green eyes."

"That's not me; that's a lot of women in the world." Trinity pushed the onions and pancetta around in the pan.

"No, it's you. I don't know how I knew it, but last night, when we were just talking in the bar, it dawned on me. It's been you, and I just didn't know it."

"Pais, you didn't even remember I existed."

"Maybe not, but my subconscious did."

Trinity rolled her eyes.

"Trinity, I get off about thirty seconds into that fantasy, and I get off about thirty seconds after you touch me. Sometimes, it's faster."

Trinity dropped the spatula into the pan with a clang and said, "Sorry, just slipped there."

***

"So, there's my mom and my dad. Then, there will be my grandfather on my dad's side, most likely. I'm not sure; he might do Thanksgiving with my uncle in Pennsylvania instead. He's not much of a planner. Then, there's the Lofton family. Mr. and Mrs., and their son, James. Alexia Weaver will be there. James and Alexia are fine, but–"

"Your mom wants one of them to marry you one day?" Trinity interrupted as she put her plate down on the coffee table.

"Well, she *did* invite you, so not sure she's too picky."

"I'm choosing to take that as a compliment," Trinity said. "How was dinner?"

"*You* are a great cook," Paisley said, setting her plate down next to Trinity's.

Trinity's arm went around the back of the sofa. A second later, Paisley moved into her side and rested her head on Trinity's shoulder.

"Will that win me parent points?" Trinity asked.

"Probably."

"Do I care about parent points, or are you going to remind me that this is one date?"

Paisley wrapped an arm around her waist firmly and replied, "You care about parent points."

Trinity smiled and kissed the top of Paisley's head.

"Especially because you cooked with pancetta and not bacon," Paisley added.

Trinity laughed softly and said, "I was cooking for a

snob. We're having bacon for breakfast, by the way."

"You're cooking me breakfast, too?"

"Yes, with eggs and strong coffee."

"That would be a great breakfast after a night of hot sex," Paisley said.

Trinity had an image of herself, strapped-on, with Paisley on the bed in front of her, and shook herself out of it. They weren't having sex tonight. This was their first official date, and it was going really, really well.

"I'll keep that in mind for date number two," Trinity said.

"Trin?"

"Yeah?"

"We wrap up at work soon. Then, I go home."

"I know," Trinity said.

"I know you said not to think about all of that yet, but it's happening. It's soon."

"I know," she repeated.

"So, what happens then? It's just something I think we should start talking about."

"We will. Later," Trinity replied. "Let's just finish the movie and go to sleep. I can big-spoon you tonight because this is an actual date."

"What if *I* want to be the big spoon?"

"Then, we can alternate. I'll take tonight and the next, like, year or so. You can have, like, a day or so then, and we'll go back."

Paisley laughed, lifted her head, and smiled at her.

"Make out with me during the movie?" she asked.

"Oh, that's a great idea," Trinity said.

"Good. I'm going in for that under-the-shirt action, too."

"Promise?" Trinity joked.

Paisley's hand slipped under her T-shirt and cupped her breast.

CHAPTER 20

"What are you talking about?"

"Just what I said," Trinity replied.

"I'm confused. You're at the beginning of it all, Trin. This is the exciting time."

"Babe, I just had an idea – I never expected it to get this far," Trinity replied.

Trinity had been calling her *babe* more and more. Paisley had been called that before, of course. She'd been called *babe, baby, honey, sweetheart,* and her least favorite, *dearest* by any number of her partners, sexual and otherwise, but it was different with Trinity. Paisley liked it this time. She smiled as they walked around the building while on their lunch break.

"But your idea was so good, a whole company got created from it."

"And that's cool, but Vidal was the one who wanted to do all of this; I just had an idea."

"What would you be doing if you weren't doing this?" Paisley asked.

"No idea," the woman replied with a shrug. "When this happened, I was in grad school."

"And what were you going to grad school for?"

"Finance," Trinity said.

"Finance? Really?"

"Surprised?" Trinity asked, looking over at her with a playful smile.

"Not really. From what I've seen, you're great with numbers."

"Well, I was going for my MBA, technically."

"Jesus, Trin. You never told me that."

"I went to Dartmouth for my undergrad and got into Harvard Business School after that."

Paisley shook her head and said, "Of course, you did."

"What's that mean?"

"Just that you're smart. You like to pretend you're not, and you let Vidal make a lot of the decisions for the company, but you're smart."

"I didn't graduate. I dropped out when this thing took off," Trinity explained. "So, not smart enough to stay in school."

"But you didn't need it. People go to business school to get into business. You found a way to do that on your own."

"Tell that to my disappointed mother who was bragging to all of her friends that I'd made it," Trinity said. "And I really want to hold your hand right now."

"We're walking around the office," Paisley noted.

"Yes, but you're almost done here, and we're not just sleeping together anymore. Vidal is my best friend; I want to tell her."

"That we're not just sleeping together anymore?" Paisley said.

"That we're dating," Trinity replied. "Smart-ass."

"Let's just wrap everything up first, okay?"

"Then, I can tell her?"

"Fine with me. But is she going to ask for her money back because I was sleeping with her business partner?"

"I will defend your honor if it comes to that," Trinity replied, taking Paisley's hand.

"Trin…" Paisley said softly, pulling away.

"Today is the last day. It's wrapped enough, babe."

Paisley looked around them for a second, and seeing no one she recognized, gave Trinity her hand to hold.

"When we get to the door, you drop it until I'm officially off the clock, as you like to call it. Then, you can tell her."

"Deal," Trinity said.

***

Usually, the weeks Paisley spent on-site with clients slowly rolled by like tumbleweeds in only a mild breeze. She'd be bored and ready for them to end almost right away. Her work was fun enough for Paisley, but she did it alone, always alone, and the evenings in the hotels were the worst. She could get through the days just fine, but when she got back to the hotel and checked the messages from her friends asking about drinks at the bar or going to see a movie, it hurt knowing that she was missing all of that. This trip was different. Paisley wasn't sure she'd been bored once since arriving, and that was all due to Trinity Pascal, the woman she was now *dating*. Paisley was dating someone, and that was a good thing.

"To Paisley Hill! Thank you for helping us get to the next level," Vidal toasted.

Trinity cleared her throat, only to earn Paisley's glare.

"You've helped us so much; you have no idea. We're light-years ahead of where I thought we'd be. I met with our investors this morning, and they're thrilled at our progress and the cost savings. Thank you." Vidal held up her champagne flute.

"Yes, agreed," Will said.

"Can't wait to put all of this into action," Chad said, holding up his own glass.

"Trinity?" Vidal nudged.

"Yeah?" she asked.

"Anything to add?"

"Oh," she said, looking at Paisley. "Just... I'm really happy... with the progress."

Paisley smiled at her. They all clanged their glasses and took sips of their celebratory champagne. That was it; Paisley was done. She'd move on to the next client after this. She was set to check out of the hotel tomorrow and head home. She'd given in to her mother and had postponed any more travel until after the holiday because it was just easier to let her mom have this one. It was even easier because Trinity was scheduled to be there for Thanksgiving.

***

"So?" Trinity asked later when Paisley was packing up in the conference room.

"Oh, my God. I'm not even out of the building yet," Paisley said, laughing.

"I was going to tell her with you here," Trinity said.

"Oh. Really? I thought I'd go back to the hotel, and you two could talk."

"I thought we could go to the hotel together after and get your stuff."

"My stuff?"

"It's your last night, Paisley. Check out and stay with me tonight. In fact, if you want, you can just stay with me until Thanksgiving. We can leave together."

"That's, like, seven days."

"Yes, and *I* was the one who was good with numbers," Trinity teased. "So?"

"That's a lot of days."

"For my commitment-phobe of a girl–" Trinity stopped. "I just meant that we could have more time to-gether. You can work from my place – or even work here if you want; I'm about to tell Vidal we're together anyway."

Paisley watched the woman cringe at her own words.

"Not *together*," she added, correcting herself quickly. "Sorry. I just mean that we're dating."

"Hey," Paisley spoke softly. "You keep saying things and then taking them back – it's okay to say them. And I don't have a phobia of commitment. I'm perfectly capable of committing to someone, *babe*." She winked at Trinity. "I just haven't in a while, so I worry that I'll mess it up because the last person I want to hurt is you, Trin."

Trinity smiled and took Paisley's hand, entwining their fingers.

"Do you want to stay with me?"

"Yes, tonight. Then, I have to go. It's not about you, though. I have work; I have a house I have to check on; I have friends I haven't seen in weeks that I miss. If I stay here, and we leave together, we'd have to drive four hours separately so you could drive back later."

"There are trains," Trinity remarked. "But I guess I get your point."

"So… Let's just enjoy tonight, say see you later tomorrow, talk while we're apart, and I'll see you for one of the most awkward holidays ever in the history of the world. It'll help us figure out if this can work with the distance, anyway."

"Nice spin," Trinity said, chuckling.

"Not a spin." Paisley moved into Trinity and wrapped her arms around the woman's neck. "I really mean it – I want to see how it'll work. We'll be long-distance for however long."

"And what is going on *here?*" Vidal asked, standing in the doorway.

"We're dating," Trinity stated bluntly. "So, there's that. And no, you can't have your money back."

***

Later that evening, Paisley checked out of the hotel. Trinity helped her with her stuff, making comments about how much stuff Paisley had brought the entire time they were lugging it up to her apartment. Just to shut her up, when they closed the door, Paisley kissed her. Trinity kissed her back and walked her to the bedroom, keeping their lips connected as she did. When they arrived, clothes went to the floor. Paisley was pushed backward onto the bed, lying under Trinity now, who stared at her before she kissed Paisley more slowly. They took their time with each other, and Paisley lost track of how long they kissed and grazed before Trinity finally pressed into her with two fingers and brought her to orgasm once. She moved down Paisley's body and did it again with her mouth, and Paisley was really going to miss this, even if it was just for a week.

Paisley took her time as well, making sure to touch Trinity everywhere she could before she finally touched her with intent, and Trinity came beneath her. Then, they lay there silently for a while. Paisley ran her hands through Trinity's hair, and Trinity stroked Paisley's stomach. They talked about Vidal taking the news well, how Paisley wanted to think more about hiring help, how they could make their schedules work after Thanksgiving, and for the first time, Paisley wanted to put in the effort. She wanted to spend the last part of her nights on the phone with Trinity, talk to her in the morning before she started her day, arrange weekend trips, and make plans for who would go where this time. It was scary as hell because she hadn't allowed herself to feel this way about anyone before, and now, here was Trinity, a girl she'd once made fun of in high school, who was now lying on her chest, making soft sounds as her hand drifted lower and into Paisley's dark-red curls.

"I'm going to miss you," Trinity said.

"I'll miss you too," Paisley replied, meaning every word.

"Are you going to tell your friends about me?"

"Aria already knows about you. I'll tell the rest when I see them."

"Yeah?"

"Yes, Trin. You're not a secret. I just don't get to talk to them as often as I'd like; not in person, anyway."

"Will I get to meet these amazing friends?"

"Maybe," Paisley said.

"Maybe?" Trinity sat up and straddled her in one quick movement.

"Yeah, we'll see," Paisley teased, gripping her hips. "Why? Do you want to?"

"Yes, obviously. They got you to stop your bullying ways. Plus, they probably have a ton of embarrassing stories about you."

"Not that many," Paisley said.

"Oh, come on," Trinity argued.

"From college, probably," Paisley entertained the possibility. "But I started the business, and I've been traveling ever since, so I'm not around all that often for them to have embarrassing stories saved up to tell."

"That makes you a little sad, doesn't it?" Trinity guessed.

"It's starting to, yes."

"Are you really going to start hiring so you can travel less?"

"I think so," Paisley confirmed, running her hands up Trinity's sides.

"And that's because you miss your friends?"

"Are you fishing for something there, Miss Pascal?"

"Yes. It should all be about me, obviously," Trinity replied with a wink.

Paisley laughed and said, "It would potentially give us a little more time together once I have people trained up and ready to go, yes."

Trinity smiled and said, "I like that."

"What?"

"Well, it'll take you time to hire and then train people. I like that you're thinking that far ahead when it comes to us having time together."

"Me too," Paisley replied, smiling up at her. "Kiss me?"

Trinity's smile widened as she lowered herself down onto Paisley and kissed her in that perfect, slow way she had that told Paisley it wasn't going to turn into anything more. It was just about them expressing this to each other; that they were thinking about their future together no matter how complicated it might appear to figure out right now.

CHAPTER 21

Paisley walked into the restaurant with a wide smile on her face. All of her friends were here, and none of their girl-friends were. This would be the first time just the six of them got to hang out without significant others since at least February, when Weston started dating Annie.

"Pais," Aria greeted, standing up from the table and closing the distance between them to embrace Paisley. "I told everyone no girlfriends," she whispered.

"Thank you," Paisley said.

"Hey, welcome home," Weston said, hugging her after Aria.

"Are we doing the hugging thing now?" Paisley asked as Ellie hugged her next.

"Yes, we are," Eleanor said.

As ridiculous as this felt because they were in the mid-dle of a restaurant and her friends were acting as if she'd been gone for a year, Paisley rarely hugged people outside of her parents, and she hadn't realized that she'd needed this from her friends until now.

"Hi, Ellie," Paisley replied.

"Welcome back. How long are you here for this time?" Talon asked, hugging her next.

"At least until after Thanksgiving."

"Really?" Scarlet asked, smiling at her as she pulled Paisley in for a quick hug. "You're hardly ever here for that long. There's usually at least a two-day trip somewhere mixed in there."

"Well, it was just easier with the holiday, and I have enough work to do at home."

Hugs finished, Paisley sat down next to Scarlet at the end of the table. The waiter approached, took their drink order, and Weston and Talon ordered them a few appetizers for the whole table. When Paisley ordered a white wine, she thought of Trinity calling her a snob. The wine wasn't cheap, but it also wasn't the most expensive one on the menu. She smiled to herself, hearing Trinity's voice in her head.

"How have you been?" Scarlet asked.

"Good. You?"

"Yeah. Really good, actually," she replied.

Paisley hadn't heard Scarlet say she was *really* good in years, maybe ever.

"*Really* good?"

"Yes, but I'd like to hear more about *you* first. Then, I can fill you in."

"There's something to fill me in on?"

Scarlet smiled coyly as she nodded. Well, *that* was new.

"So, Pais, tell everyone your news," Aria nudged her.

"The job went well."

"Not *that* news," Aria replied, tossing a roll from the breadbasket at her.

Paisley caught it, but just barely, and laughed.

"Come on. You were late, and we've all been waiting," Talon said.

"Yeah, and Aria wouldn't tell us anything," Weston replied.

"I'm a good friend." Aria shrugged.

"I'm trying not to be offended that Aria knows and I don't," Ellie remarked.

"Okay. Everyone, just calm down," Paisley said. "It's not really a big deal, okay?"

"You hired someone else?" Talon tried to guess.

"You got an office space and won't be working out of your house anymore?" Weston guessed.

"Oh, your mom is marrying you off to a prince of some country none of us know exists," Ellie chimed in.

"Or princess," Scarlet added.

"Right; or princess," Ellie said.

"I'm dating someone," Paisley finally spoke out.

The noise of the restaurant continued around them, but had they been alone, the room would have gone silent.

"You're dating someone?" Weston asked. "As in, *really* dating?"

"Not just a one-night stand?" Talon asked.

"Yes," she replied with a nod as she placed the roll down onto her plate.

"When? How?" Ellie asked. "Where?"

"Also, who? That's pretty important," Scarlet said.

"Her name is Trinity."

"That's a pretty name," Ellie said with a smile.

"It is," Paisley replied, smiling herself now. "She was technically my client."

"Oh, shit," Talon said. "Really?"

"Two business partners, and she was one of them, yeah, but we actually met back in school."

"College? Would we know her?" Weston asked.

"No, boarding school. We didn't hang out back then or anything."

"Paisley was a bully," Aria said.

Paisley glared at her.

"What? It's true," Aria contested that glare. "Paisley Jane Hill of the Mayflower Hills was a big old high school bully."

"We weren't on the May–"

"*You* were a bully?" Eleanor asked, cutting her off.

"I didn't know that I was," Paisley said in defense. "I was going through stuff, like everyone else. I guess I made fun of Trinity, and glared a lot at her, but it turned out that was a good thing because she likes when I glare."

"She likes when you glare at her?" Talon asked.

"She did back then, too," Paisley said proudly. "She had a little crush on me."

"While you were making fun of her?" Ellie said.

"I guess she's a masochist," Talon stated.

"Anyway, we're dating now. So, there's the story."

"No, there's way more to it than that," Ellie argued. "You can't just tell us that and not keep going."

Their drinks arrived, and they ordered their entrées, giving Paisley a reprieve while she figured out exactly how to tell the rest of the story, which now had so many layers to it, she had to get more practiced at telling it if they kept dating. She'd have to practice before Thanksgiving, too, in order to introduce Trinity to the people at the party. No, she didn't need to do that. She could just tell them Trinity was her date and leave it at that. They didn't need to know anything more. When the waiter left, Paisley continued. She told them about Trinity overhearing her call, the coffee spill, the flirting over mustard, which got her made fun of a bit, and then their first night together when it was just sex.

"Best sex of your life?" Scarlet asked softly when the waiter dropped off their appetizers.

"Yes," Paisley said softly right back.

"What's that like?"

"You'll find out one day," Paisley replied softly.

Scarlet flushed and looked away.

"You're letting your new girlfriend near your parents?" Talon asked.

"Technically, we're not together," Paisley replied. "We're still just dating."

"Did you text her the moment you pulled your car into the garage to let her know you were home?" Weston asked.

"Yeah. Why?"

"Are you calling her right when you get home while you're still changing clothes because you can't wait until after?" Talon asked.

"I don't know. Probably."

"And will you message her good morning tomorrow?" Ellie asked.

"I guess."

"Girlfriend," they all said at the same time.

Well, all of them save Scarlet, who was reaching for another roll.

"You guys are hilarious. We both have to agree that that's what we want first," Paisley said.

"And do *you* want that?" Aria asked.

"It's only been a few weeks. It's not like what you and London had when you met at school. I hardly knew Trinity. I didn't even recognize her when we first met this time. You and London were BFFs and got to know each other. I'm just now getting to do that with her."

"Is she seeing anyone else?" Weston asked.

"No."

"Does she want to?" Weston asked some more.

"I don't think so," Paisley replied.

"But you haven't asked?" Talon said.

"Not specifically, no."

"You might want to," Ellie said. "Not to put pressure on it or anything, but you should know if she's going to while you guys are just dating."

"And you'll be long-distance," Aria added. "So, good to just clear the air."

"Can we talk about something else now, please?"

"Paisley has a girlfriend," Talon teased.

Weston chuckled and said, "You're blushing, Pais. I don't think I've seen that happen in a long time."

"It looks good on you," Ellie said, smiling back at Paisley.

"So, London and I will be gone for three weeks."

"Aria, that's not until after the holidays. Why do you keep saying that?" Talon asked.

"Because my girlfriend has a new obsession with plants and keeps reminding me that we need to find someone to watch them *and* the house while we're gone. None of you have volunteered yet."

"Carmen and I can do it, but we *will* be having sex in the hot tub," Eleanor replied. "I still need to get you back for walking in on you and London."

"You showed up uninvited," Aria said, laughing.

Paisley sighed as the subject was changed to Aria and

London's upcoming trip to Europe, followed by Weston's book having an official publication date, a cable network being interested in the series, and Annie's first book being with the editor. Eleanor talked about her brother Emmett and how he loved working at the bakery with Carmen, Mariah, and London and was going to enroll in culinary school when he could afford it. He wanted to learn all about food, but he would likely have a pastry focus one day. Talon and Emerson were still looking for a house, so Talon asked them a bunch of questions about house-hunting. Paisley answered a few. Weston and Aria both chipped in, too.

When it was time for Scarlet to update the group on what had been going on with her, she passed the baton back to Aria to talk more about Italy and the upcoming trip where London would meet Kate and Pia, who both had had relationships with Aria in the past and were now a couple themselves. Paisley was a little worried about her shy friend, but she wouldn't say anything with the whole group around. When the dinner was over, they all said their goodbyes-for-now. Paisley knew most of them wanted to get home to their girlfriends, and Scarlet skedaddled pretty much right after the check had been paid.

Paisley drove home and laughed when she parked the car because her first instinct had been to pull out her phone and text Trinity that dinner had been great and that she was in for the night. She resisted until she was inside her bedroom, at least. Then, she just called her.

"Hey. How was dinner?"

Paisley smiled at the sound of Trinity's voice and said, "It was great. I really missed them."

"Yeah? Good, babe."

"What are you up to now?" Paisley asked.

"Nothing. Just watching TV, hoping this woman I'm dating calls me to say goodnight."

"Yeah? What's she like?"

"I mean, she's all right. A snob sometimes, but I think it's cute."

"I thought of you tonight," Paisley admitted.

"I'd hope so," Trinity replied.

"I meant when I was ordering wine," Paisley chuckled as she kicked off her shoes in her walk-in closet.

"Did you order the most expensive stuff and *still* send it back?"

"No," Paisley said, laughing now as she emerged from the closet and sat on her bed. "Hey, can you come here early?"

"What do you mean?" Trinity asked.

"Instead of driving to my parents' house on Thanksgiving, come here the day before. We can drive there together."

"I'm working Wednesday, but I can drive up when I'm done; try to leave a little early. It's a short week with the holiday, and you gave us a lot of work to do, Miss Hill."

Paisley stood back up and unbuttoned her jeans.

"What was that?" Trinity asked.

"What was what?"

"Did you just unbutton your jeans?"

"No way you heard that through the phone."

"I know that sound, Paisley. That's a sexy sound that my brain has cataloged now."

Paisley unzipped them.

"*And* the zipper. What are you doing, Pais?"

"Babe, I'm changing into pajamas. I just got home from dinner, remember?"

"Now, I'm thinking dirty thoughts," Trinity stated.

"Come here Wednesday night, and we can have dirty thoughts together."

"I'll be there," Trinity replied. "But can we also have dirty thoughts *now*?"

Paisley laughed softly and lay down on her bed.

"I really miss you," she said on a sigh.

CHAPTER 22

It was the night before Thanksgiving, and Trinity was getting annoyed. She'd checked the time for the drive when she'd left the office, and it had been four hours then. It had *actually* been closer to five and a half, and she was supposed to be lying next to Paisley in bed after having great sex by now. Trinity kept telling herself it was okay. She had more than just one night. They'd agreed that she'd stay for a few days, which she considered to be Paisley taking a pretty big step. It was a lot to ask of someone who didn't date because work took priority. It was already a lot that Trinity was going to Thanksgiving dinner tomorrow with Paisley's family, of course, but that had been Paisley's mom. While she knew Paisley would tell her not to go if she didn't want her there, Trinity also didn't want to make too much out of this. Paisley's mom had not one but two potential suitors there for Paisley, and Trinity being there was helpful for Paisley because it meant she was off-limits to said suitors. It didn't have to mean more than that.

After Paisley left, Vidal and Trinity talked at length about what would happen next for them, and Trinity realized she had no answers. She'd been the one to tell Paisley that they'd take it day by day, that they'd figure it out in time, and it would all be okay, but now, she had five and a half hours of thinking behind her, and all the scenarios were rolling through her head. They were still only dating, but Trinity wasn't someone who dated around. Paisley was, even if she didn't call it dating. The woman at least had sex, and Trinity was ready to tell Paisley that she wanted to be exclusive in that regard, even if they weren't an official couple. Trinity wanted that, though. She wanted Paisley Hill to be her girlfriend, and even that sounded strange to her: Paisley Hill could eventually be her girlfriend. Trinity shook her head and made the last turn her phone told her to take in order to finally arrive at Paisley's house.

Before the car was in park mode in the driveway, she saw the front door open. The house wasn't as large as Trinity had thought it would be, considering Paisley's family money, but she knew Paisley now – she should have understood that the woman would have a modest home, not a mansion like her parents probably had.

"I'm so glad you're here," Paisley said, walking briskly as Trinity got out of the car, and wrapping her in a hug. "I'm sorry traffic sucked."

"Worth it for *this* welcome," Trinity replied, meaning it. "I missed you."

Paisley pulled out of the hug and smiled at her.

"I missed you, too."

Trinity then looked down to notice that Paisley wasn't wearing any shoes.

"Why are you barefoot?"

"I saw you pull in and didn't want to wait to put on shoes."

"So cute," Trinity said, smiling at her.

She leaned in and kissed Paisley sweetly, missing those lips.

"I have dinner in the oven for you since I'm sure you're starving, and I can draw you a bath after if you want so that you can unwind from the drive. I was thinking–"

Trinity cut her off with another kiss, but this one wasn't sweet. She cupped Paisley's cheeks and pulled the woman into her body. Paisley's arms went around Trinity's waist and pulled right back until they were standing in Paisley's driveway, kissing slowly, enjoying each other for the first time in a week.

"Trin?"

"Yeah?" Trinity asked as she moved her lips to Paisley's jawline.

"Babe, I'm freezing," Paisley said.

"Oh, shit," Trinity replied, remembering just now that it was winter. "I'll grab my stuff. Get inside."

"Should have put on shoes," Paisley muttered as she turned and ran into the house.

"And a coat," Trinity added. "I'm telling your mother on you tomorrow!" she yelled as Paisley rushed inside.

"I'll tell her that you defiled me in the hotel!"

"She already knows that!" Trinity yelled back.

Paisley laughed and turned in the doorway with her arms crossed over her chest.

Trinity walked around to the trunk and grabbed her bags. She'd brought one small roller and her backpack with her computer in it in case she was able to get a little work done. Locking the car as she passed it, Trinity made her way up the sidewalk, which had been shoveled, despite there only being a couple of inches of snow on the ground.

"You walked outside in this," Trinity scolded as she handed Paisley her roller bag to wheel inside the house.

"I was excited," Paisley replied.

"Are you still?" Trinity asked, closing the door behind her.

Paisley chuckled and said, "Yes. Why?"

"Because," Trinity said, moving behind her, wrapping her arms around Paisley's waist, and pressing her front into Paisley's back. "I'm not starving, so dinner can wait."

Her hands moved under Paisley's T-shirt, and she lifted it off her and tossed it to the floor in the foyer, because Paisley's house *did* have a foyer.

"You just got here," Paisley noted as Trinity cupped her breasts over her bra.

"So? It's been a week."

"What happens when it's longer between visits?" Paisley asked.

Trinity smiled as she kissed Paisley's neck. She liked that she was asking that question.

"We have sex in the driveway."

Paisley laughed but unbuttoned her jeans. When she

unzipped them, Trinity slipped a hand inside and cupped her.

"I promise, we can eat dinner and take a bath, but I need you."

Paisley leaned back against her then. Trinity stroked her softly at first until Paisley gasped, and Trinity dipped lower, finding the wetness she wanted and coating Paisley's clit, circling it with her fingers. Her other hand worked under the cup of the bra and massaged Paisley's breast.

"I want to turn around. I want to see you," Paisley told her.

"Babe, stay," Trinity replied, pressing into her back more. "I want you like this. Just like this."

She stroked her harder, and Paisley's hips bucked into her hand.

"We can go up–" Paisley stopped.

Her arm went around to the back of Trinity's head and encouraged Trinity to kiss her neck again.

"We will. We have all night; we will," Trinity said.

"I have things... set... up."

Trinity stroked faster, applying even more pressure now, and asked, "Things?"

"The bed…"

"What's on the bed, baby?"

"Not us," Paisley replied, bucking again. "There!"

Trinity rubbed her and said, "What did you set up?"

"Harness," Paisley moaned. "Vibrator."

"I brought my own," Trinity told her, sucking on her neck, knowing she was leaving a mark, and hoping Paisley was going to be wearing a turtleneck tomorrow.

"For me," Paisley said. "For you. Fuck!"

Paisley came against her hand, and Trinity held her in place, letting Paisley use her palm to continue her orgasm until she finally slowed her rocking and went slack in Trinity's arms.

"For me, to wear for you," Paisley said finally.

"Yeah?"

Paisley nodded and said, "I bought a new toy for it."

"Oh, I like that," Trinity replied, still stroking Paisley but slower now. "Do you want to go upstairs now?"

"I don't know if I can walk right now," Paisley said.

Trinity laughed and said, "I'll catch you if you fall."

Paisley made no move to head up the stairs that were off to the right. She stood there, letting Trinity hold her, stroke her, and Trinity thought she could do this all night. Hell, she could probably stay here forever if it meant holding Paisley like this, touching her like this.

"You'll have to stop doing that if you want me to move," Paisley told her.

"Why would I want you to move?" Trinity whispered in her ear.

"Because you're going to want what's upstairs," Paisley replied.

"Yeah?"

"It's a double-sided dildo."

Trinity swallowed. She removed her hand from Paisley's jeans, which allowed Paisley to turn around and face her.

"I've never used one of those before."

"No?" Paisley asked, wrapping her arms around Trinity's neck.

"Have you?"

Paisley shook her head and said, "I went to the sex shop yesterday. I was just going to get a regular one, which I did, but then I saw the one I bought, and thought about trying it with you."

"With me?" Trinity asked.

Paisley nodded and kissed her softly.

"Upstairs?" she asked.

Trinity nodded this time. She wouldn't get a tour of Paisley's house for the next several hours, and that was completely fine with her. When they made it up to Paisley's bedroom, there were flameless white candles around the room, the lights were dim, and the bed had been turned down.

There was a harness lying on it with a double-sided dildo to its right, a regular dildo below it, and a vibrator to the left.

"It has two vibrators in it already. That one is just the one—"

"It's the one you had with you before," Trinity spoke.

"Yes," Paisley said, standing in front of Trinity as she undid Trinity's pants. "Which do you want to try first?"

"The one we'll try together for the first time," Trinity said, stepping out of her jeans.

Paisley removed Trinity's shirt, and they each took off their own bras and underwear. When Trinity was also shoeless and sockless, she climbed onto the bed with the most amazingly soft sheets she'd ever been on and waited. She watched as Paisley grabbed the toy they'd be using. Then, she reached between her own legs to do a check. Touching Paisley downstairs had been the right move. She was soaked and ready for what they were about to do. Paisley hovered over her, kissing her slowly as she rocked her hips down into Trinity's. Trinity held on to her, loving how they seemed to melt together in all the right ways. When Paisley moved to take a nipple into her mouth, Trinity could only think about the fact that she was ready to come; foreplay could happen later.

"Babe, please," Trinity said, pushing Paisley's hair away from her face.

"Already?" Paisley asked, looking up at her.

"Already? I drove for five hours."

Paisley laughed silently as she reached for the dildo. First, Trinity spread her legs. Paisley gave her a sexy smirk as she slid the toy up and down, coating it. Then, she pushed it slowly inside. Trinity closed her eyes and let her head roll back into the pillow. She wasn't normally the one to have something this large inside her, so it took a moment for her to adjust, but she loved how full she felt. When she opened her eyes, it was just in time to watch Paisley slip over the toy.

"Oh, fuck," Trinity said mainly to herself.

Then, the vibrators were turned on, and Paisley was over her, kissing her, rocking into her, and Trinity was holding on to her back, her ass, Paisley's neck.

"God!"

"Yes, so good," Paisley said. "God, so good."

"Harder, baby," Trinity encouraged, pressing Paisley's ass down.

"I'll come," Paisley said.

She thrust then. It was no longer a rock; it was a thrust. God, it was so fucking good. Paisley was thrusting into her, and her back was all sweaty now. They were breathing hard. Trinity lay there, her body moving up and down with the silk sheets, because she had nothing of substance to hold on to, and her orgasm built from the middle of her body and tore out of her, reaching the tips of her toes within seconds as she screamed Paisley's name into the bedroom.

"Yes! Yes! Yes!"

That wasn't Trinity. Trinity was barely able to open her eyes, but what she saw was Paisley coming above her at the same time she was, and that only made it all better. Trinity pressed her hips up, allowing Paisley to take anything she wanted from her right now.

"Trin!"

"Yes, baby. Come for me."

Paisley did. She came once, turned off the vibrators for them, and crashed down into Trinity, who held her and whispered to Paisley about how amazing that was in her ear. Minutes later, when she assumed Paisley would get up and remove the dildo from between them, Paisley reached down there instead, and Trinity felt the vibrators working inside and against her again.

"I like this thing," Paisley said.

And she didn't rock at all this time; she thrust. Trinity held on to her, and when Paisley stilled as her second orgasm took over, Trinity watched her and knew she was in love.

CHAPTER 23

"Okay. So, just pick some safe small talk topics," Paisley suggested. "The weather is good, but not global warming. No politics. Maybe talk about sports. My dad loves sports. Well, he loves golf, anyway. Is Tiger Woods still golfing? Has he retired? Do you retire from golf? It's usually a bunch of old guys he's watching on TV, so I don't know. You could try talking charities with my mom; she works with a bunch of them. Oh, for my grandfather – he's like a typical old rich white guy who donates to Republicans, so maybe just avoid him altogether. If he's without a drink, grab him a bourbon. At any point before, during, or after the meal, just get him a bourbon. The staff will actually make it. You can just deliver it to him. He'll give you at least a two-minute speech about why bourbon is the best alcohol in the world. You don't ask questions; you just smile and nod while he talks. Then, you're dismissed. It's weird, but if you go with it, you'll get a better result. The Loftons are good people. Their son James is a music producer in New York. He might have some interesting things to say. Alexia Weaver, apparently, just got her Ph. D, but I don't know what in, so maybe ask her–"

"Paisley," Trinity said, placing her hand on Paisley's thigh.

"Yeah?"

"Babe, it's okay. I can handle it."

"They're a lot," Paisley said, turning to her. "And my mom told me the other day that she also invited a few other families."

"A few?"

"There will be about thirty people here, including us," Paisley replied.

"Thirty?"

"Well, twenty-eight to worry about, because you're

160

you, and I like you already," she said, smiling awkwardly. "Hey, do you just want to go? We can go. I can text my mom and tell her I'm not feeling well, or that you came down with something, so I'm taking care of you."

"Will she even fall for that?" Trinity asked.

"No," Paisley admitted. "But she'll be too busy, and it's a long drive for her to get to my place, so she'll read me the riot act tomorrow."

"Do you *want* to go?" Trinity asked.

"I'm not one for this much time with these people. I love my parents. They've been very supportive, considering I went a whole different way with my business than they expected. On top of that, how lucky am I? My mom made sure to include a man and a woman in her setup scheme. I mean, misguided? Yes. But she doesn't ignore that part of me, and neither does my dad. My grandfather doesn't really acknowledge it, but he also doesn't seem to care much, either, so I'm lucky, yeah."

"Pais, do you want *me* here?"

"What?" Paisley asked.

"Your mom invited me," Trinity noted. "You've never actually said *you* definitely want me here. And I know we're already sitting in this crazy long driveway right now, about to go in, but if you don't want me here, we can do what you suggested and go back to your place."

"I don't even want *me* here," Paisley replied.

"That's not really what I asked, though."

"Paisley Jane Hill, *what* are you doing out here?"

Paisley sighed and turned to look out the window, where she saw her mother walking down the driveway toward the car. She'd yelled loud enough for Paisley to hear her through the closed windows.

"Moment of truth," Trinity said softly.

Paisley turned away from her mom toward Trinity again and saw a look of disappointment on her face. Paisley had put that there, but she had no idea how to remove it. Trinity had been right: Paisley's mother had invited her.

Paisley, herself, never would have. They were still so new, and Paisley hadn't ever brought someone home for the holidays. During college, she'd dated the guy her parents thought was suitable for her. She'd given them that. He'd gone home with her a few times, but neither of them was committed to their relationship.

Once that was over, she decided not to bring anyone home unless things were serious, very serious. They either lived together or were at least talking about that as their next step. She'd been sleeping with Trinity for a few weeks. That was all, really. They'd been dating officially for maybe a week and a half, and they hadn't even talked exclusivity. She didn't think Trinity was dating anyone else, and Paisley could barely date *one* person, so that wasn't something she planned on doing, either, but they'd had sex last night instead of talking about this stuff. They'd had a lot of really powerful sex last night.

That was how Paisley would describe it. It was amazing, yes. It was also sexy and hot. It was soft, slow, and then demanding and fast. It was hard and against things, but it was also powerful because they'd stared at each other throughout. They'd made a point of connecting their eyes at every possible occasion. They stroked backs, legs, cheeks, necks, and hair, as well as the parts that would make them scream. They took pleasure in holding one another and exchanging kisses that went nowhere, and it was the most powerful thing Paisley had ever experienced.

That had her nervous, but not because of Trinity. Paisley was nervous because she wasn't sure she could take that look of disappointment off of Trinity's face. At least, not right now as her mother stood outside the driver's side door, with her arms crossed over her chest. If she answered Trinity's question honestly, she'd tell her that she didn't want her here. She'd rather Trinity be at Paisley's house or even her own. Paisley wished she could do this dinner alone and go meet Trinity and tell her about her wacky family after instead. So, she didn't answer at all.

"Hi, Mom," Paisley said, opening the door.

"We're having drinks, and you're in your car," her mom remarked.

"We were just talking, Mom," Paisley said. "I had to give Trinity the rundown on who's going to be here. You invited some people last minute."

"No, they *accepted* last minute, which means they had other plans first that fell through. They get the cheaper champagne," the woman joked, pulling Paisley in for a hug. "Hello, honey."

"Hi, Mom," she said, hugging her back.

"Hi, Mrs. Hill," Trinity said as she arrived to join them.

"Trinity. Hello, dear. How are you?" she said, moving away from Paisley and hugging Trinity now.

Paisley smiled away her nerves because her mom really *did* seem to like Trinity. Was that even a good thing? What would happen if it didn't work out between them? She'd be lectured by her mom as if it were her fault. Well, it probably *would* be her fault.

"I'm so glad you could join us," Paisley's mom told Trinity.

"Thank you for having me. I wasn't sure what to bring, and Paisley told me nothing, but my mom wouldn't let me get away with that." Trinity opened the back driver's side door and pulled out a beautiful bouquet of autumn flowers they'd bought on their way over. "I hope these are okay. I was told not to bring wine or any food."

"Yes, we're picky about our wines here, and we have more than enough food. We'll take what's left over to the soup kitchen after dinner. We do that every year because I always order too much, and it would just go to waste."

Trinity smiled as Paisley's mom took the bouquet from her.

"Thank you, dear," the woman said.

Trinity nodded and took Paisley's hand. Paisley's mom looked down between them and lifted an inquisitive eyebrow.

"Mom," Paisley warned.

"I was just thinking about how to introduce Trinity here," her mom said. "Girlfriend? I forgot to talk to Alexia and James. Well, truthfully, I remembered, but I wasn't sure Paisley would bring you, so I told them you'd been dating someone."

"We *are* dating, yes," Paisley said.

"Good." Her mom smiled. "Let's get inside; it's freezing out here."

They walked up the driveway hand in hand at first, but Trinity let go of Paisley's when they arrived at the front door. Paisley thought it was just because they were walking inside, but even after their coats had been taken and hung up in the coat closet, Trinity didn't take her hand back. She stood there awkwardly with her hands clasped in front of her. Paisley took her in then. Trinity was out of place. That was how Paisley would describe it. She looked beautiful. Her long blonde hair framed her face in subtle waves. Paisley hadn't ever seen her dressed this formally, and Trinity Pascal could wear a damn dress. This one was a burnt orange with some subtle red and browns, making it perfect for the occasion. Paisley had told her she could wear her usual jeans and a T-shirt, but Trinity had chosen to get dressed up.

"Are you okay?" Paisley asked, placing a hand on the small of Trinity's back.

"Yeah, I'm good," Trinity told her.

"Let's introduce you," Paisley's mom said, taking Trinity by the hand and pulling her into the party.

Paisley stayed behind for a moment, took a deep breath, and followed. Trinity was introduced as Paisley's date. She shook hands with everyone and even had a few hugs thrown in there by the more excited in the bunch of party guests. Paisley did the small talk and kept an eye on Trinity. In the moments where it looked like she could use a hand, Paisley walked over and made sure Trinity knew she was there.

"So, you run your own company?" Alexia asked.

"With my best friend, yes. You have a doctorate, right?" Trinity said.

"In public policy, yes. I'm also on my city council and will make a run for mayor next cycle," Alexia replied.

"That's cool," Trinity said.

"I'm hoping to be the first lesbian mayor and then the first lesbian governor of my state," the woman added.

"We need that," Trinity replied. "That's awesome. Personally, I'd like to feel like I live in this time period, and not like a hundred years ago."

Alexia laughed and said, "Yes, exactly. We had this amazing period where we were looking forward, and then we regressed as a nation. It's so disappointing."

"It's horrible," Paisley said, chiming in.

Alexia smiled at her and said, "Paisley, how have you been?"

"Good," Paisley said. "Sounds like you're doing well."

"I was when I heard *you* were still single and finally thinking about settling down from your mother, but now, I see that's no longer the case." She winked at Trinity. "So, now, I'm good, but not great."

"Hey," Trinity joked.

"Your girlfriend's a catch, Trinity, but it seems you are as well," Alexia replied.

"Hey," Paisley said, placing her hand on Trinity's lower back again.

"We're not technically girlfriends. We're just dating right now; seeing how things go. Paisley is..." Trinity looked at her. "Pacing herself?"

Paisley gave her a forced smile but nodded.

"Well, lock her down already, Paisley. She's a keeper. Now, if you'll excuse me, I see your grandfather is without a bourbon, so I'm going to get the points this time. I'm hoping I can get him to contribute to a democratic campaign for the first time in his life."

"I wouldn't hold your breath," Paisley said.

"We're ready, everyone," Paisley's mother announced.

"Dinner's ready," Paisley clarified with Trinity.

"I'm starving. Those appetizers were nuts," Trinity replied. "I couldn't even tell what they were, and I didn't want to ask because I'd look like a poor person. Please tell me dinner is something I'll be able to recognize."

"It's turkey," Paisley said, stating the obvious. "With three sauce options."

"Just point me to the one that most closely resembles gravy," she said.

"That would be the gravy," Paisley replied, taking Trinity's hand as they walked into the formal dining room.

"I'm going to wash up. Is that okay?" Trinity said, dropping Paisley's hand.

"Yeah, sure," Paisley replied.

Trinity kissed her on the cheek and headed toward the guest bathroom. Paisley watched her go.

"Paisley Jane?"

"She's just washing up, Mom."

"No, honey. I wasn't going to–" Her mom sighed. "That girl cares for you. You care for her. Don't be stupid, you hear me?"

"What? Mom, I–"

"Don't argue with your mother," her mom cut her off. "She's sweet, smart, and endearing. She's also beautiful and funny. She's the kind of woman you bring home to Mom and Dad, and she's here when I can tell she doesn't exactly feel welcome. Considering *I'm* the one who invited her, I think that's something *you* need to be addressing."

Paisley nodded as her mom walked off to join the rest of the party.

CHAPTER 24

"I brought you a bourbon," Trinity said, handing the old man a glass.

"Do you know that my grandfather drank a glass of bourbon on the Titanic as it went down?"

"I did not know that, no," Trinity replied, wondering if the man even knew who she was or why she was handing him a drink. "He was really on the Titanic?"

"Oh, of course. He'd been in London on business and met with the Prime Minister."

"Wow! Really?" she asked.

"He would only travel back on the most glamorous ship in the world, so he went to Southampton and had one of the best-state rooms."

"He went down with the ship?" Trinity asked, sitting next to him in the armchair on the other side of the small end table.

"He did. He wasn't about to scramble for a lifeboat. He made sure his wife, my father, and my aunt were on one, waited until they were a safe distance away, and went back inside to pour himself a drink."

"Did they make it?"

"Of course, they did. Minor frostbite on my dad's hand wouldn't keep him from taking over the family business one day, either."

"Of course not," she replied.

He took a drink and leaned over the table.

"Who are you again?"

"Trinity Pascal," she said. "I'm friends with your granddaughter."

"Paisley Jane?"

"Yes," she replied.

The man had to be in his late eighties or early nineties, but he looked good for his age. Maybe it was all that bourbon he drank.

"She's doing well?" he asked.

Trinity smiled and said, "You should be very proud of her. She's amazing."

He gave her an inquisitive look and said, "Friends?"

"We're dating, actually," Trinity replied.

"I see," he said, nodding and taking another drink. "Have I told you about how my father fought in the war?"

"No," Trinity said, smiling at him. "I'd love to hear it, though."

He nodded and started telling her old war stories. Trinity sipped on the best wine she'd ever had in her life and now understood a little of what Paisley and her mother had been going on about. As Trinity listened, she wondered if anyone just listened to the man, or if they handed him a fresh drink, earned a few points for that, and walked away. When he finished with one story, he had another one all lined up and ready to go. Trinity asked him questions, learning things about the family and about history at the same time. He laughed a few times, and Trinity laughed a few times. When she looked up, she saw Paisley's father watching them; he nodded with a smile that told Trinity he was grateful. She nodded back and asked another question. When his glass was almost empty, Trinity rose to get him a new one, but Paisley was right there, holding it out for him.

"Here you go, Grandpa," she said.

"Ah, thank you, Paisley Jane." He took it from her. "I was ready for another one."

"How *are* you?" Paisley asked him.

"Stuffed and tired," he said. "I'll finish this and head up to bed. It's getting too late for this old man."

"You're not old; you've still got moxie," Paisley replied, standing next to Trinity's chair.

"I do; you're right," he said, laughing. "I like your girl here. She's funny."

"She is, huh?" Paisley asked, placing an arm over Trinity's shoulders.

"She's smart, too," he said.

"That, she is," Paisley agreed.

"We were just talking history," Trinity replied.

Paisley's grandfather downed the bourbon in one gulp, which he probably should *not* be doing at his age.

"I need to hit the head," he said, standing up slowly. "And I'll take my leave."

"Do you need help up the stairs?" Paisley asked.

"I do not," he said with pride. "I've got that moxie, remember?" He looked down at Trinity. "You come by anytime, dear. I'd be happy to chat with you again."

"Thank you. I'd love that," Trinity replied, meaning it.

Paisley sat in his chair after he walked toward the stairs.

"It *is* getting late," she said.

"Are you ready to go?" Trinity asked.

"We've done dinner, dessert, after-dinner drinks, and small talk. I think we can say goodbye now."

"Okay. I'm good if you are," the woman told her.

"Hey," Paisley said.

Trinity looked at her then.

"Thank you."

"For what?" Trinity asked.

"Spending so much time with him. He's normally on his own at these things."

"I like him," Trinity said with a smile. "And I got to learn a little more about your family history, which was great."

"Yeah, he embellishes a lot, so take everything with a grain of salt. Maybe a boulder of salt, depending on what stories he told you."

"The Titanic?"

"True, but his grandfather didn't drink as it went down – he clung to the side like everyone else." Paisley shrugged a shoulder. "There were sergeants in wars, not captains or majors, either. There *was* a governor and a couple of senators, but if he told you my great-uncle was almost President – he lost in the primary, by a lot."

"Ah," Trinity said, nodding. "Oh, well. Doesn't make the stories any less interesting."

"Let me get our coats, and we can head home," Paisley said.

As she walked away, Trinity thought about that word. They weren't going home; they were going to Paisley's house. Paisley, who wasn't her girlfriend – she'd made a point to mention that earlier. Yet, Paisley had been by her side most of the day, finding excuses to touch Trinity, claiming her as her own. Trinity needed to get herself in check because she couldn't be falling in love with someone who wasn't ready for that yet. She'd risk everything and would just get her heart hurt in the process.

***

The drive home was relatively quiet. They listened to Christmas music on the radio, and Trinity watched the houses they passed as their lights flickered red, green, and yellow once they were out of the fancy neighborhood Paisley's parents lived in, where the lights were all an elegant white.

"Trin?" Paisley whispered.

"Huh?" Trinity said.

"Babe, we're here," Paisley said.

Trinity had fallen asleep in the car. She lifted her forehead off the window and turned to Paisley, who was smiling warmly at her.

"Sorry. I guess I was tired," Trinity replied.

"It's okay. It's late; let's get you to bed," Paisley said.

Once in the house, Paisley put the whole pumpkin pie her mother had insisted they take in the kitchen to deal with tomorrow, and they walked upstairs to her room. They changed for bed in silence and slipped under the blanket shortly after. Trinity was in love with Paisley, but she was also in love with these incredibly soft sheets.

"Hey, what do you want to do tomorrow? We haven't talked about that yet," Paisley said.

"If you're thinking of waking me up at five in the morning to make me go shopping, think again," Trinity replied.

Paisley laughed and said, "I was thinking about taking you out for breakfast or brunch."

"Sounds good. Maybe around eleven or even one or two so that it's not at all before noon."

Paisley laughed again and said, "Get some sleep." She leaned over to kiss Trinity quickly on the lips. "Night."

"Good night," Trinity replied.

But it wasn't. Trinity couldn't sleep. She tossed and turned a few times. When Paisley stirred, Trinity didn't want to wake her up, too, so she grabbed her phone and went downstairs. Grabbing a glass of water, she sat on the sofa in the living room and called Kelly.

"Hey, it's late," Kelly said.

"And you're wide awake," Trinity replied.

"I have kids under three."

"Is it okay?"

"Yeah, it's fine. What's up?"

"I think I might be in trouble." Trinity sighed.

"What kind of trouble?"

"I'm falling in love with her," she admitted.

"Why do you sound like that is a bad thing?" Kelly asked.

"She's not even close to there yet," Trinity replied.

"So? That's okay. People get there in their own time."

"We're only dating, but it's like… I think even after a few weeks, she's who I might want."

"Forever?" Kelly asked, sounding surprised.

"I don't know. Maybe. Is that crazy?"

"I've just never heard you talk that way before."

"I've never *felt* that way before," Trinity said.

"And you're worried she's not there *yet*, or that she won't ever be?"

"I don't know. Both, maybe."

"She invited you to her house for a major holiday. That's a big deal, Trin."

"Her *mom* invited me, remember?"

"She still could've told you not to go. I actually expected she would. Like you said, you're not *together*, as you put it, and she's new to this whole thing."

"Maybe, but having me there today meant Alexia Weaver and James Lofton didn't try to hit on her."

"Who?" Kelly asked.

"Her mom had been trying to set her up before she knew about us; they were both there. Alexia is probably going to be a lesbian icon or something one day, and James produces music and lives in an artist loft in the city. He works with some really well-known artists, too."

"So?"

"So, they're much more accomplished than me," Trinity explained.

"Who was she there with today?" Kelly asked.

"Me, but—"

"No. She was there with *you*. She could've easily told you not to come. She could've gotten to know those two and gone out with both of them, but she took *you* instead, Trin. How was she with you?"

"Fine. I mean, she made a comment to her mom that I was just her date, not her girlfriend, but she was great."

"Did she touch you?"

"Yeah, of course."

"Telling people you were there with her?"

"Yes," Trinity replied.

"Then, you're fine. Just give her time, okay? You said this was new for her."

"It is."

"So, that's all it is, okay?" Kelly told her.

"Yeah, I guess," she replied.

"And, Trinity?"

"Yeah?"

"Don't ever let me hear you denigrate yourself or your accomplishments again or compare yourself to others like that. You are remarkable. You went to Dartmouth and Harvard, Trinity. You left because you got successful long before your classmates will. You didn't drop out – you didn't need it. You and Vidal are building something. You're just as successful and important as the future lesbian icon."

Trinity nodded to herself and said, "I guess."

"What do you mean, you guess?"

"I don't like it anymore," Trinity replied. "Vidal loves it. All I did was just have an idea. I liked building it, working with everyone to make it real, but the day-to-day of it all isn't what I ever really wanted."

"Okay. What are you going to do about it?"

"Nothing. It's my idea and my company."

"If you don't like it anymore, you should talk to Vidal."

"It's fine. We're in that weird growth phase. I'll be fine once we've got things really moving. I'm just a little bored right now."

"Because you're not being challenged," Kelly replied. "You loved being challenged – probably one of the reasons you're falling in love with PJ Hill."

"God, she's great for me," Trinity said. "I just want her to see that I'm great for her, too."

"I'm sure she does," Kelly replied. "Now, you should get some sleep, and I have to go."

"Yeah," Trinity replied. "Thanks, Kell."

"It's all going to be okay."

Trinity wasn't so sure, but she hung up the phone and took a long drink of her water before she went back up to bed.

CHAPTER 25

Paisley woke up and rolled over, expecting to find Trinity lying next to her. When she didn't, she checked to see if the light in the bathroom was on under the door. It wasn't, so she put on her robe and walked downstairs.

"Her mom invited me, remember?"

Paisley stopped before she got to the kitchen. Trinity was talking to someone.

"Maybe, but having me there today meant Alexia Weaver and James Lofton didn't try to hit on her." There was a slight pause. "Her mom had been trying to set her up before she knew about us; they were both there. Alexia is probably going to be a lesbian icon or something one day, and James produces music and lives in an artist loft in the city. He works with some really well-known artists, too."

Paisley leaned in, pressing her shoulder to the wall.

"So, they're much more accomplished than me." Trinity paused again. "Me, but–"

Paisley knew this was wrong. She should *not* be listening in on Trinity's conversation like this, but she stood there, not announcing herself, all the same.

"Fine. I mean, she made a comment to her mom that I was just her date, not her girlfriend, but she was great."

Paisley closed her eyes, hearing that.

"Yeah, of course." A pause. "Yes." And another. "It is." And another before Trinity said, "Yeah, I guess."

Paisley wiped her hand over her face. She'd hurt Trinity. That was, apparently, something she was very good at. She'd done it when they were teenagers, and she was doing it now, when all Paisley wanted to do was hold her.

"Yeah?" Trinity said. Then, there was another long pause. "I guess." Another pause. "I don't like it anymore," Trinity said.

Shit. What does Trinity not like anymore?

"Vidal loves it. All I did was just have an idea. I liked building it, working with everyone to make it real, but the day-to-day of it all isn't what I ever really wanted."

Paisley sighed when it was clear it was work and not her that Trinity didn't like.

"Nothing. It's my idea and my company," Trinity said and paused. "It's fine. We're in that weird growth phase. I'll be fine once we've got things really moving. I'm just a little bored right now." There was yet another pause. "She's great for me. I just want her to see that I'm great for her, too."

Paisley looked up at the ceiling and let out a deep breath.

"Yeah," Trinity replied. "Thanks, Kell."

She'd done this to her. Her indecision, her inability to be a normal person and go for something she really wanted because it might interfere with her job, was causing Trinity pain, and it wasn't fair. No, it wasn't just that; it was also stupid.

When Paisley heard Trinity get up, she made her way quickly back up the stairs, took off the robe, and slipped into bed. When Trinity made her way into the room, Paisley didn't feign sleep or even pretend like she just woke up. She was sitting up, and she gave Trinity a small smile.

"Couldn't sleep?" she asked.

"Sorry, no. I was trying not to wake you, though."

"I woke up on my own and noticed you weren't here."

Trinity got under the blanket and said, "Need me to big-spoon you?"

"I'd love that, actually," Paisley said, lowering herself down into the bed.

***

<u>Aria Bancroft:</u> I got your message. What's up?
<u>Paisley Hill:</u> SOS. I need help.
<u>Scarlet Campbell:</u> What's wrong?

Weston White: You okay?

Talon Mitchell: You can't just say SOS like that unless you're in real trouble, Pais.

Eleanor Enger: Shut up, Talon. What do you need, Pais?

Paisley Hill: Is the bakery open today?

Aria and Eleanor both started typing.

Aria Bancroft: Yeah. Why?

Eleanor Enger: They're getting the Black Friday crowd. Why?

Paisley Hill: What are you all doing today?

Scarlet Campbell: Nothing.

Aria Bancroft: Waiting for my girlfriend to get home.

Eleanor Enger: What Aria said.

Talon Mitchell: Nothing. We did the family thing yesterday.

Weston White: Annie and I are at the cabin. Why?

Paisley Hill: Can any of you maybe get to the bakery around one? I want Trinity to meet you guys.

Talon Mitchell: Holy shit. Really?

Eleanor Enger: I can be there. Carmen and Emmett are there already anyway.

Weston White: Can I bring Annie?

Paisley Hill: Sure.

Scarlet Campbell: I can be there.

The messages went on until all of her friends said they'd drop what they were doing in order to meet Trinity. Paisley really loved her friends. She missed not having time with them, but she could work on changing that later. First, she had to let Trinity know that she was really in this.

"Hey," Trinity said, walking into the kitchen. "Want to maybe cut into that pumpkin pie? I'm actually finally hungry after that massive dinner."

"How would you like to have a fresh-baked good of your choosing instead?" Paisley asked, wrapping her arms around Trinity's waist.

Paisley was seated on a stool at her kitchen island.

Trinity had just come out of the shower. She wore her usual jeans-and-T-shirt look with still-damp hair, and she looked perfect. She placed her arms on Paisley's shoulders as she approached her.

"That's a weird question."

"Want to go to the bakery?" Paisley clarified.

"*The* bakery?"

"Yes, *the* bakery. They're open today. Capitalizing on all those Black Friday shoppers, I guess."

"Okay. You want a scone or something?" Trinity asked.

"No, I want you to meet my friends," Paisley replied.

Trinity looked down at her, a little confused, and said, "Meet your friends?"

"They're going to be there, yes."

"And you just found out and want to meet up with them?"

"No, Trin. I *asked* them to meet us there." Paisley smiled up at her.

"You did?"

Paisley leaned forward then, placing her lips against Trinity's collarbone, and said, "I did. I want them to meet you. God, you smell good."

"I smell showered; there's a difference."

"No, you smell like you," Paisley replied, kissing the spot, and looking up at her. "So, do you want to go?"

"I guess, yeah."

"Don't sound so excited about it," Paisley said, moving her lips up to Trinity's neck.

"I just wasn't expecting it."

"Is that bad?" Paisley asked, nibbling on her earlobe now.

"No, it's good. I want to meet them."

"Okay. Well, let's go."

"I have to dry my hair first," Trinity replied.

"I like it like this," Paisley said, running a hand through it. "But if you must."

Trinity pulled her in for a kiss and said, "What time again?"

"One," Paisley said. "And it's only noon…"

"After," Trinity replied, kissing her again.

"After?" Paisley said, almost disappointed. "But I was just kissing your neck, and you smell so good."

"I don't want to look like a total slob when I meet your friends, Pais."

"What does us having sex have to do with you looking like a slob?" Paisley asked.

But Trinity was already heading out of the kitchen.

"They'll know!"

"They already know we have sex, babe. I've told them about it," Paisley said, following her.

"They'll know we *just* had sex!" Trinity yelled as she ran up the stairs.

"Not if we don't have it," Paisley argued, walking up behind her.

"Exactly."

"I don't understand. Are you *for* or *against* sex now?" Paisley asked, laughing.

Trinity popped her head out of the bedroom and said, "Always for it."

"Great. Take off your–"

"After," Trinity interrupted.

Paisley laughed and joined her in the bedroom to get ready.

"So, what should I wear?"

"What you have on now," Paisley replied.

"No, I need to dress up a little. I have another dress I brought in case you didn't like the one I brought yesterday. I didn't hang it up, so it's probably wrinkled, but I can iron it and–"

"Trinity?" Paisley wrapped her arms around Trinity's waist from behind as she searched through her bag that was on the chair by the bed.

"Yeah? I have pants I could–"

"I am crazy about you," Paisley stated.

Trinity stopped moving.

"And I would really like to introduce you to my friends today as my girlfriend."

Trinity stood up fully. Paisley placed her head on Trinity's shoulder then, kissing her through her T-shirt, heart pounding in her chest as she waited for her answer.

"You do?"

Paisley nodded with her lips pressed to Trinity's T-shirt.

"But yesterday, you said we were just dating."

"We were *just* dating. We hadn't talked about this yet."

"And you want this? Exclusivity? You and me?"

"I do," Paisley said, moving her lips to Trinity's neck. "I'm scared, and I'm not good at this – I don't know how to make things work when we're both so busy – but I want it."

"It's only a four-hour drive," Trinity replied, leaning back against Paisley finally.

"Four hours is a lot when we're both exhausted from work. And I travel, so it won't always be four hours. I'm in San Francisco one week, El Paso the next, Miami after that. It's all over the place, and it means I can't just get in the car and drive to you whenever I want."

"But you do want to?" Trinity asked, placing her arms over Paisley's.

"I want to try," Paisley said.

"As my girlfriend?"

"Yes," she chuckled against Trinity's skin. "You're just the best big spoon in the world."

"That's all you want me for?"

"No, I tried to get you to sleep with me a minute ago, but you turned me down," Paisley joked.

Trinity turned around in her arms, cupped Paisley's cheeks, and kissed her with abandon. Paisley took two steps backward, trying to keep herself from falling over, but she had nothing to worry about because Trinity had her. She held on to her as she deepened the kiss, and before Paisley knew it, she was on the bed on her back, with Trinity spreading her legs with her knees and kissing her neck. When Trinity's hand moved into Paisley's sweats, Paisley bucked up into her. When she came, it was with a yell first, and then a sigh because she loved how Trinity touched her. It was like nothing else, and she had no idea how they'd make this work, but it would be worth it for moments like this; for moments like the one downstairs when she'd been able to just breathe Trinity in and feel like she was home.

CHAPTER 26

"Yeah, they totally just had sex," a woman said when Trinity and Paisley walked through the doors of the bakery. "I can see the mark right there, Pais."

"Talon, you better shut your damn mouth," Paisley said as she slapped the woman's hand away and laughed.

"You really went *all*-in, didn't you? That thing is dark," the woman Trinity now knew to be Talon said, pointing to Paisley's neck.

"I wanted her to have something to remember me by when we're apart," Trinity replied.

Paisley rolled her eyes at the comment, but she took Trinity's hand and walked them farther into the bakery.

"Really? You're participating in this?" Paisley asked her.

"It's the truth," Trinity said.

"That mark is also very fresh," another woman said. "Couldn't wait?"

Paisley laughed and said, "Okay. Here it goes. You ready?" She turned to Trinity, who nodded. "That is Talon. That one is Talon's more well-behaved girlfriend, Emerson. We like her. Jury's still out on Talon, though." She pointed from one woman to another. "This is Eleanor."

"Ellie," Eleanor corrected.

"And Eleanor's girlfriend, Carmen, is where?" Paisley asked.

"In the back, doing bakery-type things. They just had a massive morning rush. Thankfully, it's over now, just in time for us to have the place pretty much to ourselves."

"Okay. So, that's Aria." Paisley pointed. "And London is *her* girlfriend."

"Hi," London said, wiping off a table but pausing to greet Trinity. "I'll be done in a second."

"Weston and her girlfriend, Annie," Paisley continued,

pointing to a couple who was sitting at one of the tables.

"Hi," a woman who was sitting at a table by herself said, waving.

"Oh, that's Janet. Her girlfriend is Mariah, who is…"

"Also in the back," Janet said.

"And this is Scarlet," Paisley finished, pointing to a woman who was standing off to the side, alone. "Did I miss anyone?" she asked, looking around.

"I think you got all of us. Want to introduce us to whom you're holding hands with now?" Aria said.

"Everyone, this is my girlfriend, Trinity."

Trinity flushed for some reason and allowed herself a small smile at the sound of those words coming out of Paisley's mouth.

"Wait a minute… Girlfriend? Paisley Hill has a girl-friend?" Eleanor said.

"She does," Paisley said. "This is her." She pointed to Trinity. "Now, none of you embarrass me because I've told her you're good people."

"We're all right," Talon said, reaching out for Trinity's hand. "Welcome to the family."

Trinity shook it and said, "Thanks?" She turned to Paisley, silently checking with her eyes on the use of that term and hoping it was okay.

Paisley just smiled back at her.

"Nice to meet you," London said. "Can I get you a coffee? Something to eat? All new girlfriends in the *family* get their first cupcake on the house."

"I get *all* my cupcakes on the house," Aria said.

"Is that an innuendo?" Trinity asked.

"Yes," Aria stated.

"No," London said at the same time.

"They have this pumpkin cream cheese cupcake. In-terested?" Paisley asked her.

"Sounds good," Trinity replied.

"Sit. I'll order for us," Paisley said, kissing her quickly before walking off to the counter.

Trinity looked around the bakery with mismatched, brightly colored tables and a large group of women staring back at her.

"You're wishing we all wore name tags right now, aren't you?" Talon asked.

Trinity laughed and said, "Or, that Paisley would have had notecards or something and quizzed me."

"Hey, did I miss her?" a woman with short red hair said, coming out from the back of the bakery.

"No, babe. She's here," Eleanor replied.

So, that would make this woman Eleanor's girlfriend, Carmen.

"Hi," Trinity said.

"Paisley's *girlfriend*," Eleanor introduced her with an added emphasis.

"Yes, surprising to us all," Trinity replied.

"I heard that," Paisley said from the counter.

Trinity smiled wider and said, "So, this is your bakery?"

"Mine, London's, and Mariah's. She's in the back, but she should be out soon. She's showing Emmett how to do something," Carmen said.

"Emmett?"

"Ellie's little brother. He works here," the woman explained.

"This *really* is a family affair," Trinity commented.

"He started not that long ago, and he's doing great so far. He is, right?" Eleanor checked.

"He's doing great. And he seems to really like it, which is a perfect combination."

"Babe, grab us a table?" Paisley said from behind her.

"*Babe*," Talon and Aria said at the same time in a high-pitched, mocking tone.

"Shut up," Paisley said loudly.

Trinity took the closest table for their own and sat down.

"So, you and Pais, huh?"

Who was this again? It was a W name.

"Yes," Trinity replied. "Is it really *that* strange for her to have a girlfriend? I know she doesn't usually date, but…"

"She used to, but when things took off at work, she stopped. It's good to see that she is again, though. Paisley's great. She deserves the best," the woman with the W name said.

"So, you own your own business, too?" her girlfriend asked.

Anne… Annie… Anna? God, there were too many of them to remember. She should have studied for this exam.

"I do," Trinity replied. "My best friend and I run a company, yes."

"That's great."

"I know Paisley told me, but there are so many of you. What is it that you two do?"

"Writers," the W name said.

Weston! It hit her then. Weston was the writer, and her girlfriend's name was Annie.

"Weston's book is going to be released early next year. Mine's still being worked on by the editors, but it should go out later next year," Annie said.

"That's amazing. Power couple," Trinity replied.

"Like you and Pais," Talon commented, sitting across from Trinity.

That name, she remembered.

"Oh, I don't know about that," Trinity said. "Pais is the super successful woman in a business suit."

"Your company is pretty successful," Talon argued. "From what Paisley tells us."

"She tells you things about me?"

"You *are* her girlfriend," Eleanor said, pulling a table over with Carmen to join them.

"Talon, you're in my seat," Paisley said, placing a cupcake on a plate with a fork in front of Trinity, followed by a coffee. "Move it."

"Sit next to her," Talon replied.

"Here," Talon's girlfriend said, pulling an extra chair

over next to Trinity and then adding one next to Talon.

Talon turned and smiled when Emerson put her arm around Talon's chair.

"Are we ready for the interrogation now?" Eleanor asked, sitting down on Trinity's other side.

"*I* didn't get interrogated," Carmen said, sitting down opposite her girlfriend.

"We already *knew* you," Aria noted, pulling up yet another table.

"As our friend, but not as my girlfriend. Should I be jealous Trinity is getting the full interrogation treatment, but Carm didn't?" Eleanor asked.

"I think you used the wrong word there. Shouldn't be jealous of this," Trinity replied, heart racing in her chest.

Then, Paisley sat down next to her with her own coffee, wrapped an arm around her chair, leaned in, and kissed her on the cheek.

"They're harmless. Only I have to like you. I don't care what they think."

"Liar," Trinity said, chuckling.

"So, how's the cupcake?" London asked, sitting by Aria.

"I haven't tried it yet. Where's yours?" Trinity asked Paisley.

"Oh, you're sharing." Paisley reached over and stole the fork off the plate with her free hand.

Trinity smiled as Paisley took the first bite.

"So, tell us all about you," Eleanor said.

"What did I miss?" someone else said, coming from the kitchen.

Great. Another one. How in the hell was she supposed to remember all of these women?

"That's Mariah. She's a co-owner of the bakery. We all met her when London and Aria reconnected. That's how Ellie met Carmen," Paisley said.

"Thank you."

"And her girlfriend is Janet," Paisley added, pointing

to the woman who stood when Mariah walked over to her.

They kissed, and it wasn't a chaste one. Janet went all-in there.

"They're new," Paisley explained.

"*We're* new," Trinity said, turning her face to her.

"You know? You're right," Paisley said, leaning over and kissing her.

This one also wasn't chaste; Paisley was really kissing her. Trinity kissed her back, and when Paisley's tongue slipped into her mouth, Trinity heard the fork clang on the plate. Paisley's hand was cupping her cheek a second later. The kiss slowed naturally until they finally broke apart.

"Better?" Paisley asked.

Trinity could only nod. Then, she turned and noticed every woman in the bakery was staring at them.

"Damn!"

Trinity turned to see a boy, who didn't look like he was out of his teen years yet, standing just inside the door to the kitchen.

"Emmett, get it together," Eleanor said, laughing at him.

"Yeah. Sorry. I'll just…" he said in a hurry and disappeared into the kitchen again.

"I don't think I've ever seen you kiss anyone like that," Talon said. "And that includes senior year of college."

"What happened senior year?" Trinity asked.

"Nothing happened then," Paisley replied. "Eat your cupcake."

"Innuendo?" Talon asked.

"Yes," Trinity replied.

"No," Paisley said at the same time.

A few minutes later, Trinity had the details on Paisley's senior year, where she'd decided to kiss a whole lot of people on first dates to see if there was any chemistry there. Her theory had been that if it wasn't at least a good first kiss, it wasn't worth pursuing. That sounded so much like Paisley that Trinity had to laugh.

An hour later, the bakery got busy again. London, Carmen, and Mariah went to work. Janet left to go home and get ready for a party she and Mariah were going to later that night to meet someone named Aubrey. Weston and Annie left to drive back to the cabin where they'd been spending their weekend prior to Paisley asking them to come to the bakery. Talon and Emerson were off to do some more online house-hunting. Eleanor stayed to help Carmen on the espresso machine when the line started to get long. Aria went back into the kitchen to help with any manual labor. That left Scarlet, who hadn't said much of anything since they'd arrived. She was definitely the shyest one in the group. The three of them talked for a bit, but mainly about Trinity before the bakery got so busy, they needed to vacate the table for paying customers. They said their goodbyes to the ones who remained and left, walking Scarlet to her car.

"She seems happy," Paisley said when they walked away.

"That's good, right?" Trinity asked.

"Yeah, but she's shyer than usual."

"*That's* shyer than usual? I think she said ten words."

"Our group has gotten much bigger this year. When it's just the six of us, she's fine. She's good with London, Annie, and Emerson now, and she'll get comfortable with you and Carmen soon enough. Mariah is sort of in the group, but also not. It's a lot for Scar."

"Can I help get her comfortable with me faster? I don't want her to feel like she can't talk to you if I'm around."

"You're sweet," Paisley said, taking her hand. "And no, Scarlet just needs time. She likes you, though."

"How do you know?"

"Oh, just that whole ten-years-of-friendship thing."

Trinity laughed and said, "Okay. Got it."

"She's happy right now, but she didn't tell me what's going on, which isn't like her, so I'll have to call her later to talk to her."

"Need me to give you space?"

"No, not right now anyway. You're only here for a couple more days; I want you all over me," Paisley replied, resting her head on Trinity's shoulder.

"That can be arranged."

CHAPTER 27

"Where did you go?" Paisley asked.

"I'm in here," Trinity said loudly.

Paisley walked down the rest of the stairs and into the living room through the kitchen, seeing Trinity sitting on the couch with her laptop.

"I came out of the bathroom, and you were nowhere to be found. Last I saw you, you were naked." Paisley sat down next to her.

"Yeah, sorry. I know we were going to… Vidal just texted that we have a slight hiccup with our game plan for one of our parts."

"You can work in my office if you need to," Paisley said, running a hand through Trinity's hair.

"No, it's okay. I just need to email a supplier and explain that we need this part, or we can't produce. I think he's trying to get more money out of us."

"Vidal can't handle it?"

"She can. I felt bad about leaving her there while I'm here with you this weekend, so I told her I would."

"Doesn't she have a new boyfriend?"

"They're just dating. She told me before I came here that the sex is amazing but he's only okay, so I think she might just enjoy herself for however long, and that'll be the end of that."

"Bummer," Paisley said.

Trinity looked at her with a smile and said, "Say *bummer* again."

"Why?"

"Because it's *so* not something you'd say."

"I'm not *that* much of a snob," Paisley argued.

"Still."

"Fine." She sighed. "Bummer."

Trinity laughed, and Paisley kissed her quickly.

"Happy?"

"Yes," Trinity said quickly. "And yes," she added that with intention in her eyes that Paisley could easily read.

Paisley smiled back at her and asked, "Should I leave you alone?"

"No, I like having you here," Trinity told her. "I just hate this stuff." She turned back to her computer.

"What stuff?"

"This." Trinity pointed at the email she'd been typing.

Paisley thought back to the other night when she'd overheard Trinity talking about not liking her job.

"Emails? I don't know anyone that loves *that* part of the job," she said, trying to make light.

"Not the emails; the day-to-day stuff."

"What do you mean?" Paisley asked her.

"I remember being in business school, thinking how lucky I was that I got in and trying to avoid worrying about massive student loans. I was at one of the top business schools in the world, and I liked *some* of it. But what I liked was the idea part of it; thinking of something, creating it when it didn't exist before, figuring out how to build a business around it, problem-solving, and seeing it all come together. Now, I'm just replying to emails, coordinating with suppliers, and hiring people."

Paisley rested her head on Trinity's shoulder and said, "Look at it this way: you're doing all of that because your business is growing, Trin. That's a good thing, baby."

"I know. I just thought it would be more exciting for me. The most exciting thing that's happened recently was you."

"Um… Should I take offense to that?" Paisley lifted her head.

"I didn't mean personally – I meant professionally." Trinity kissed Paisley's forehead. "You showing up and us brainstorming in that conference room, looking at tools, and coming up with ideas was fun. I liked it. I mean, I also liked staring at your ass when you were presenting something, and looking down your shirts when you had a button open, or staring at your lips once I knew what they could do."

"You objectified me," Paisley said, nodding.

"Absolutely," Trinity replied, winking at her.

"What's that say about me that it worked?" Paisley asked.

"That you like what *my* lips can do, too," Trinity suggested.

"I like more than just your lips," Paisley told her.

"That makes for a healthy relationship, I think," Trinity replied.

Paisley checked Trinity's tired eyes to see if there was more to the tired than the fact that they hadn't gotten much sleep this weekend.

"Babe, do you really not like it?"

"I like working with Vidal; she's my best friend. But... I don't know. I just wanted to make a thing... The thing is made now."

"You should tell her," Paisley said, cupping the back of Trinity's neck and massaging it.

"I can't. I got her into this."

"She's a grown woman; she got herself into it. Is there something else you could be doing there? Maybe you could be in charge of coming up with new products for the company? You could sit in that conference room, add a dry-erase board, and spend all day doing what you love."

Trinity closed her laptop and said, "What I loved was doing that with *you*."

"I loved working with you, too," Paisley said. "I can come to the office sometimes when I'm not traveling; be your muse."

Trinity smiled at her and said, "I'd love that." She sighed right after.

"Trin, you really don't like what you're doing, do you?"

"Not as much as I thought I would. After you left, it was just different. I've never worked with a consultant before. I mean, we have investors, and they get a say, but they're not consultants. Now, I feel like it's back to just business: forecasts, goals, plans, people to hire, places to be."

"That *is* business, babe."

"I know. But in business school, I thought about dropping out *before* I had the idea. I wasn't a huge fan of most of my classes, and the work wasn't inspiring. You know how in undergrad business classes, you usually have a group project to build a business?"

"Yeah."

"I loved that. We worked together, created a fake company, presented that to the class, got a grade, and moved on. I didn't have to send supplier emails."

"You also didn't make any real money," Paisley reminded.

"I know. I just mean that I liked doing that."

Paisley rubbed Trinity's neck again and said, "I think you should talk to Vidal. Maybe you guys can come up with something that is more suited for what you like."

"Maybe," Trinity said. "Let me send this email, and we can go back upstairs if you want."

Paisley watched Trinity send the email. The woman looked unhappy, which made Paisley wish she could fix this for her. When Trinity finished, instead of going back upstairs to have sex, Paisley suggested Trinity take a nice hot bubble bath while she talked to Scarlet, who had texted earlier. It would give Trinity time to think and relax, and Paisley could find out what was going on with one of her best friends.

"Hey," Scarlet said.

"Hey. Sorry, I was with Trin. What's up?"

"You just said you wanted to talk when we were at the bakery."

"I do," Paisley confirmed. "What's going on with you? You seemed different."

"I... came out to my siblings."

"What?" Paisley said, cupping her hand over her mouth. "Really? Scar, that's great. How did they take it?"

"They were good about it, and they promised not to say anything to my parents until I'm ready to tell them myself."

"Scar, that's such good news. I'm so proud of you."

"Thanks. I just didn't want to tell you with Trinity there because it was your day to show off your new girlfriend to everyone."

"Scarlet, you still could have told me."

"I know. But before, you made a good point when you said I was talking about myself and my own issues when you'd called me to talk about your stuff; and there's the fact that girlfriends are everywhere these days, and it's hard for just the six of us to get together."

"This is big, Scar. You have my permission to interrupt me when I'm talking about myself to tell me you came out to your family," Paisley told her.

"Not all of it," Scarlet replied.

"Still. They were really good about it?"

"Yeah, they just want me to be happy."

"I must have perceived some relief at the bakery, then," Paisley concluded.

"Well, there's more," Scarlet said.

"More?" Paisley asked.

"Kind of the reason I wanted to at least tell *them* about me being gay."

"Scarlet Sophia, you tell me right now."

"I'm dating someone," she replied.

Paisley cupped her hand over her mouth again in disbelief.

"Her name is Dakota. You've been a little out of the loop lately. Did you happen to check the group texts about me needing help picking out date clothes?"

"Honestly, no. I've had my phone on do not disturb a lot lately."

"I can tell you all about her later, but she's great. We've gone on a couple of dates, and I really, really like her Pais."

"Scar, that's so great."

"Yeah. She knows I'm not out, but she's supportive of me being wherever I am in my journey. I just felt like I wanted my brother and sister to know because I can maybe see them meeting her one day."

"Yeah?"

"Maybe. I don't know. It's early, but I like her a lot."

"Does that mean we'll get to meet her?" Paisley asked.

"Oh, I don't know," Scarlet said quickly.

"Why that response?" Paisley laughed. "You met Trinity, and we just became a couple."

"You're better at handling Talon's antics than I am; and when Eleanor and Talon get together, Ellie feeds off of her. She met Ellie and Carmen last night, but that was because Ellie called to see if I wanted to go to dinner, and Dakota was already here. Maybe *you* can meet her by yourself. I can't do the whole group thing with her yet, though."

"That actually sounds like a smart move, waiting to meet all of us at once," Paisley said, laughing.

"I don't want to mess this up," Scarlet said.

"You won't."

"I've never…"

"I know," Paisley said.

"She knows, too."

"And?"

"She understands."

"That's good. She sounds like a good person, Scar."

"She is," Scarlet replied, and Paisley could hear the happiness in her tone.

"I'm happy for you."

"How's Trinity?"

"She's good. Well, she's got a work thing going on right now, so I put her in the bubble bath to try to relax, but it's good."

"You have a girlfriend," Scarlet said.

"And I'm terrified," Paisley admitted.

"Why?"

"She's four hours away when I'm actually home, and I'm hardly ever home. It's been a few days, and I'm used to her being here already. Like, I'm already expecting her to be in bed when I come out of the bathroom, or in the kitchen, making us coffee like she did this morning."

"That's tough," Scarlet said.

"The tough part hasn't even started yet," Paisley replied.

CHAPTER 28

Trinity didn't want to leave tomorrow. As she sat in the bathtub, she thought about work and how she liked it enough. She could deal with the part of it she wasn't a fan of, but it was the fact that she'd be leaving Paisley that had her wishing she could stay here forever. *If fifteen-year-old Trinity could see her now,* she thought to herself. She was lying in PJ Hill's bathtub, in a bath drawn by her girlfriend, who was freaking *PJ Hill.* Trinity laughed to herself, thinking back to her rough high school days and how much had changed between then and now. Fifteen-year-old Trinity hadn't even had the guts to talk to PJ Hill, let alone argue with her over spilled coffee. Trinity was the poor kid at a rich school, and PJ was at the top of the food chain, so to speak.

She'd wondered a little since meeting Paisley again. What would have happened back then had she actually spoken to Paisley in any way other than just as a classmate when required? Would PJ, the bully, have told her to go away? Would Paisley, the girl who was struggling with her sexuality in the same way Trinity was, have given her the time of day? Maybe they would have been secret friends or something. Maybe more. Maybe not. Part of the reason they worked now was because they were both so different from how they used to be. Trinity was confident and comfortable now. Paisley had obviously won the friend lottery, and they'd helped her get off that high horse once she got to college.

"How's your bath?" Paisley asked, walking into the bathroom.

"Missing something," Trinity replied.

"What's that? You have my best salts and bubbles in there."

"You," Trinity said, holding out her hand for Paisley to take.

"It's *your* bath," Paisley replied.

"And I'd like you in it. Sit in front of me?"

"Is the water cold yet?"

"No, it's perfect," Trinity replied.

Paisley seemed to consider for a moment, but she stripped, and Trinity watched, enjoying every moment of it until Paisley was leaning back into her, between Trinity's legs, and all seemed right with the world.

"I don't want to go home tomorrow," she said after a few minutes of silence.

"I know," Paisley replied. "I leave tomorrow, too, though, so *I* won't even be here," she added.

"Can you postpone?" Trinity asked.

"It's just two days in Chicago, and then I'm back."

Trinity kissed Paisley's shoulder and said, "Can I come back then?"

"Yes, but how will you get away from work?"

"I can work in the morning and drive in the afternoon to miss traffic if you don't mind me working at night a little."

"If you're working at night, babe, how will we have any time together? And you'd have to leave crazy early in the morning or miss work in the morning, too."

Trinity sighed and said, "Yeah, I know. I can drive that morning, get to work by noon, and work through the evening to make it up to Vidal."

"We could wait for the weekend," Paisley said. "I have another client meeting, but we're doing it remotely to get a feel for each other before I fly out. It's most of the day on Thursday, but I'll just be working on their business plan on Friday. You can come then."

"I have a supplier meeting on Friday. They're actually coming to the office. We're doing dinner with them after to try to lock in the best prices we can."

"Saturday morning?" Paisley asked.

"Can you come to me?" Trinity suggested instead.

"I fly out of here Sunday afternoon," Paisley said. "But yeah, I can figure it out. I'll leave super early so that we can have the day together, and stay over. I'll leave early the next morning."

"No, that's too much for you," Trinity said. "I'll come here again."

"I can do it," Paisley replied.

"No, I'd rather just come here," Trinity told her.

"Are you sure?" Paisley asked.

"Yeah, it's no big deal."

"It'll turn into one, though," Paisley said softly.

"No, it won't. I don't mind driving."

"The weather's getting worse. It's going to take five hours instead of four, just like it did the other day," Paisley replied.

"Hey, I'll be here this weekend. That's what we're focusing on."

"I like you here," Paisley said, tightening Trinity's arms around her middle with her own.

"I like me here, too," Trinity replied.

"Why do you have to live so far away?"

"Why do *you* have to live so far away?" Trinity argued playfully, smiling into the kiss she gave Paisley's shoulder.

"This is why I haven't done this, you know?"

"Done what?"

"Relationships," Paisley said.

"Pais…"

"No, it's okay. I just think it's clicking that you're leaving tomorrow, and we have to start the real work to make this happen. I don't want to get to the point where you're resenting me because it's easier for you to drive here than it is for me to get there, and you're tired of doing it, we're fighting about it, and you decide not to come one weekend. Because that's how it goes; that's the beginning of the end, Trin."

"Hey, I won't get tired," Trinity tried to tell her.

"You will," Paisley said. "I will, too. I'll be exhausted from a trip and just want to sleep for two days, but I'll miss you, so I'll drive to see you, ending up sleeping the weekend away, and that'll start a fight, too."

"Why are you going there right now?" Trinity asked, loosening her arms around Paisley's waist.

"Because it's the reality," Paisley replied.

"Why are you trying to predict how this will go? I'm not whomever you dated before, Paisley. I won't just give up."

"I'm not saying *you'll* give up," Paisley remarked. "I'm just saying it's hard, and that's why I've avoided this for a long time now. You can find someone back home who's a hell of a lot easier to date than me."

"You know I don't want anyone else," Trinity replied, getting frustrated now.

Paisley shifted until she was facing Trinity in the bathtub and said, "I don't, either. But seeing each other once a week won't always be possible. I was with you and Vidal for a few weeks; I've been with clients for up to two months before, staying wherever and living out of a hotel room and on appetizers until I finally got home."

"I can fly to you on the weekends," Trinity said. "I have points from flying around the world when we first started the business, looking at facilities and stuff."

Paisley smiled, but it didn't reach her eyes.

"I don't want to ruin the rest of our time with this right now," Paisley said.

"*You're* the one that brought it up," Trinity replied.

"I know. I'm sorry. This is new for me, too, Trin. With my previous relationships – the few there were, at least – I didn't care this much."

Trinity at least liked the sound of that.

"You didn't?"

"No," Paisley said, placing her hands on Trinity's knees.

"Then, we'll figure it out."

"It's one thing to say that, babe, but it's harder to really do it, so I think I'm stuck on that part."

"We'll map it out," Trinity said.

"Map what out?"

"Our trips to see one another. You'll pull out your travel schedule, I'll grab my calendar, and we'll map out the next few months."

"Months?" Paisley asked, eyes widening.

"Paisley, you *are* driving me crazy. One minute, you tell me you don't want anyone else and say we're girlfriends. The next, your eyes get big at the thought of me planning the next few months of our relationship."

"No, it's not that. I just don't know where I'll be yet."

"When will you know?"

"I have some stuff booked for January and February, but not everything. I have meetings with prospective clients to get the rest of the months booked out."

"Can you maybe do some of the work remotely instead of traveling? Like, Zoom meetings instead of in person? You could work from my office, or I could work from here."

"Rarely," Paisley said. "I do that; I have some remote stuff that's small, but the big jobs require me to be there, babe."

"And you can't take more small jobs?"

"I can. It's just a step backward for me. I'm finally getting the big clients and referrals I've been working toward this whole time, so—"

"I'm offering to drive here pretty much every week. Can you give me something, Pais?"

Paisley's glare nearly gave Trinity shivers. It wasn't the kind of glare that turned Trinity on. It was the kind she hadn't seen from Paisley before, one that told her Paisley was angry.

"You're asking me to change a whole lot about my life right now. I'm doing the best I can, Trin. I didn't exactly plan on going to a job and finding a girlfriend. I can try to take some remote stuff between bigger jobs, but I've worked my whole life to get here – I don't want to just stop growing."

"What about hiring so you don't have to do it all yourself?"

"I'm going to figure that out this week. It takes time to train them and money to hire them."

"Paisley, you have money," Trinity noted.

Paisley stood up abruptly. Water went everywhere. She stepped out of the tub, and Trinity knew she'd gone too far.

"I think you're trying to start a fight right now, for whatever reason," Paisley told her. "And I'm trying not to argue with you, but you're starting to piss me off, so I need to get out of the tub and put some clothes on."

"Pais, don't. I'm sorry," Trinity replied, standing up.

"No, just–" Paisley wrapped herself in a towel, with bubbles smelling of vanilla still around her calves and ankles. "I need a minute."

"I didn't mean–"

"You did," Paisley stated. "I get that you're upset because I've been playing catch up to you this whole time. I hesitated when I should have just called you my girlfriend and shouted from my parents' house that we were together, but I fucked that up. I thought I'd made up for it, Trin. I introduced you to my best friends as my girlfriend. *They're* my *chosen* family; they matter to me. And you met them even though this is still so new and scary. I'm trying here. I– "

"I know." Trinity stepped out of the tub as well. "I'm sorry, babe. Can we just get back in the tub? I'll stop. We can talk about dinner with Talon and Emerson tonight instead."

"I don't know if I want to go anymore," Paisley said.

"At all? Or do you just want to go without *me*?"

"You knew this going in, Trin. You knew what my job was. You've benefitted from it at work. I'm good at what I do."

"I know you are," Trinity said.

"And it gets tedious at times, but I love what I do," Paisley added. "I love helping companies improve, grow, and see the results from my work in the same way you loved making something and seeing it become a reality."

"I know," Trinity said softer.

"I said I would try to take some smaller jobs; I said that. That's me trying."

"I know," Trinity repeated even softer.

"I don't have money, Trinity – I don't take money from them. You know how important that is to me. I have my house; I have my business. Everything is in one of those two things."

"I get it," Trinity said.

Paisley shook her head and said, "I want this to work, Trin, but…"

"But what?" Trinity asked, swallowing hard.

"Maybe it's too much, too soon. We met less than a month ago. You can't say we met in high school because we didn't know each other back then. We slept together and *then* started dating. Now, you're meeting my family, and we're together, and it's a lot. We're putting all this pressure on the next few months. It's–"

"A lot," Trinity finished for her.

"Yeah," Paisley uttered.

"So, what do you want to do?" she asked.

CHAPTER 29

"So, what do you want to do?" Trinity asked.

"I don't know," Paisley said.

"Pais, we're standing in your bathroom naked right now. What do you want?"

"I want to postpone this conversation."

"What?"

"I want to go to dinner with my friends and pretend like we don't have this whole thing hanging over our heads right now," she said.

"We can't pretend. You're the one that keeps bringing things like this up. I've been trying to stay in the moment."

"Can you put a towel on or get dressed? I can't talk to you in here like this," Paisley told her, leaving the bathroom and heading to her dresser, where she pulled out a sweater.

"I don't want to go to dinner, Paisley," Trinity stated.

"Fine. I'll cancel," she replied, throwing the sweater back into the drawer.

"No, that's not..."

"Trin, you said we could do this," Paisley said, staring down into her top drawer.

"We *can.*"

"But you want me to change–"

"Nothing," Trinity interrupted. Suddenly, her arms were around Paisley's middle from behind. "Nothing. We're fine. It's fine. Let's just go to dinner."

"You said–"

"No, let's go. It'll be good." She kissed Paisley's neck, holding on to Paisley tightly.

"You're only saying this because you're worried," Paisley responded.

It took a moment, but Trinity finally said, "Yes, I am."

"I'll look at my schedule and see what I can move around," Paisley said.

"Okay."

"And you'll come here this weekend."

"Yeah," Trinity said.

"Okay," Paisley agreed.

She didn't feel at all like they were done with the conversation. They were putting it off, and they both knew it. Paisley wasn't sure she could actually move anything on her schedule. She'd made plans, signed agreements, booked travel, and in some cases, accepted payment already. She wasn't sure how to do this, which was why she hadn't. It wasn't that she didn't want to find ways to make this work with Trinity, but she had worked so hard to get here with her business; and the thought of taking smaller clients or jobs that didn't require her to be gone as long, seemed like she'd be going backward. Even though it would give her more time with her girlfriend, which Paisley wanted, it was a lot to ask this early in their relationship.

So, instead of having the conversation they both knew they needed to have, they got dressed in silence and drove to the restaurant to meet Talon and Emerson for a double date. It had been Talon's idea, and Paisley probably should have said no in order to have their last night together alone, but she liked the idea of Trinity becoming more of her everyday life, and that included spending what time she could with her friends.

"You leave tomorrow?" Emerson asked, taking a bite of her asparagus.

"Yeah, afternoon," Trinity replied, sipping her wine. "This is good."

"Told you," Paisley said, smirking at her plate.

"She's a wine snob," Trinity said.

"Oh, *we* know," Talon replied. "Have you had a beer with her yet? She checks the label and kind of–"

"Does the nod thing?" Trinity said.

"Yeah. Tilts her head back and forth–"

"Like she's considering giving it a score out of ten," Trinity finished for Talon again.

"I don't do that," Paisley argued.

"Yes, you do. It's very cute," Trinity told her, smiling over at her.

"I think it's less cute, but you *do* do it." Talon winked at her.

"Do you score them in your head?" Trinity asked her. "Like, this ale is a two because it tastes like... battery acid with a side of alcohol."

Paisley laughed silently and said, "No."

"She does," Talon said. "She just doesn't want to admit it."

"A-n-y-w-a-y..." Paisley dragged the word. "Emerson, how's work going?"

Emerson wrapped an arm around the back of Talon's chair and said, "Fine."

"Is it weird, working together and living together?" Trinity asked her. "Like, do you ever get sick of each other?"

"Nope," Talon said immediately. "I mean, maybe we will one day. We've only been together for nine months, so it could happen, but I can't see it becoming a thing."

"I hope not," Emerson added. "It's nice now that everyone knows we're together. We don't have to sneak around. We drive in together, go home together, talk about our days, and we know all the same people. We're in most of the same meetings, too, so when I tell her that someone was an asshole, she knows what I'm talking about. She knows if I had a bad day because she probably witnessed it, and I know the same for her."

"You want to hear something even worse than us living and working together?" Talon asked.

"Worse?" Trinity asked.

"We share an office now," Talon replied. "I had my own, and she used to share with another director. She moved into mine last week. It's sickening how much we like each other, isn't it?"

"You moved into Talon's office?" Paisley asked.

"My officemate was hardly ever around when I first

got the job. Then, he moved to a different team, so I got a new one. He is literally *always* there, and he's super loud. He has a ball he bounces against the wall by my head." She looked over at Talon. "And here, my amazing girlfriend had her own office with space to spare."

"She took it," Talon said, finishing her chicken.

"You offered," Emerson said.

"Yes, because I like you. And you're quiet. Sometimes, I forget she's even there. She just sits and works at her computer, and I'll look up, and it's like my girlfriend is just there."

"That sounds really nice," Trinity replied.

Paisley looked over at her and heard the sadness in her voice. She swallowed and took another drink of her wine because she didn't know what to say.

"It is," Emerson replied. "I thought it might be weird, but it's been fine so far. Talon mainly writes on the dry-erase wall and stares at it for a while. Really, they shouldn't be paying me to do my job anymore – I just stare at her all day."

"You do not," Talon said, laughing.

"Sometimes, I do. You remember that day I spilled my coffee?"

"Yeah."

"You were wearing those–"

"No way," Talon said, laughing.

"Way," Emerson replied. "Sexy."

"Babe!" Talon laughed again.

Paisley pushed her plate away. Trinity turned to look at her, and she placed a hand on Paisley's thigh. Paisley took it and entwined their fingers. How had Trinity become so important to her so quickly? Listening to how happy Talon and Emerson were because they got to spend so much time together at home *and* at work made Paisley jealous. She was actually jealous of the fact that they saw each other every single day for hours at a time, and she was about to say goodbye to her girlfriend for a week. It was only a week. She'd done a month and a half away from the last person she had dated before she'd given it up. They'd talked on the phone, video chatted, had phone sex, and the six weeks didn't bother her at all. Now, Paisley couldn't think about falling asleep alone tomorrow night. She couldn't think about kissing Trinity goodbye tomorrow or watching her pull out of the driveway. She didn't want calls, video chats, and phone sex. She wanted Trinity in person all the time. How had things changed so fast? It had been weeks, not months or years, and she was already trying to figure out how to cut back on travel in order to have what she wanted.

"Pais?"

"Huh?" Paisley said, looking up at Talon.

"Where are you going next?"

"Oh, Chicago," she replied.

"What are you bringing us back?" Talon asked.

"Nothing," Paisley replied.

She said the same thing whenever any of her friends asked what she'd bring them from wherever she'd be traveling to next. It had become one of their many inside jokes.

"Bitch," Talon said.

Paisley squeezed Trinity's hand tighter.

"Do you guys want dessert?" Emerson asked.

"They don't have churros here, babe," Talon said.

"Churros?" Trinity asked.

"She's obsessed with churros," Paisley explained.

"I'm not obsessed. They're just my favorite dessert, and the food truck is just down the street tonight."

"And you looked it up, didn't you?" Talon asked, laughing. "She stalks this churro food truck on Twitter."

"They're two blocks away," Emerson replied. "I'm buying."

"Not a big fan of cinnamon, but I'll go with you," Trinity offered.

"You don't like cinnamon?" Paisley asked.

"*In* stuff, it's okay. I just don't like it covering stuff."

"So, no French toast for breakfast? Got it," Paisley said.

"Light on the cinnamon, and I'll eat it."

"Breakfast tomorrow, then?"

"Send-off breakfast," Talon commented. "Complete with sex before and after, probably."

Paisley cringed at the *send-off* part.

"Dessert?" she asked, wanting to change the subject.

***

They spent the next hour walking to the food truck, ordering churros for Emerson, Talon, and Paisley, and getting Trinity a cup of ice cream sans churro. They ate it on a bench nearby, and Paisley was content to let Talon and Emerson carry the conversation. Trinity didn't say much, either, so she must have been okay with that, too. Dessert finished, they walked back to their cars. Emerson and Talon walked ahead of them hand in hand, talking and laughing mainly about houses. After the first block, Trinity reached over and took Paisley's hand. Paisley leaned into her, wanting to be as close as she could get to Trinity because as silly as it seemed when they'd be seeing each other next week, it felt like a year from now, and she needed this closeness.

"You smell like you," she said, breathing in Trinity's shirt.

"I'll leave this for you," Trinity replied, seemingly understanding exactly what Paisley needed. "I mean, you already have my dirty underwear, so what's a shirt?"

Paisley laughed and said, "I still haven't washed them."

"Dirty girl," Trinity teased, letting go of Paisley's hand to instead wrap her arm around Paisley's shoulders.

"I'm going to be that girl, okay?"

"What girl?" Trinity asked.

"I'm going to put my hand in the back pocket of your jeans while we walk," Paisley said.

Trinity laughed softly. Paisley slipped her hand into the pocket and squeezed Trinity's ass.

"Save that for home, Paisley Jane," Trinity said.

Paisley leaned her head on Trinity's shoulder, not caring that it was awkward as they walked. When they got to Emerson's car, they all exchanged hugs and said their good-byes-for-now. Then, they walked around a corner to Paisley's car and drove home. Paisley turned on the lights in the hallway, and Trinity stood against the wall as if waiting for instructions.

"Pumpkin pie in the kitchen?" Paisley offered.

"After churros and ice cream?" Trinity asked her.

"Movie?"

"Pais, take me upstairs," Trinity said softly.

Paisley nodded, took Trinity's hand, and they went up to her bedroom.

CHAPTER 30

"I'll see you in a week," Trinity said, cupping Paisley's cheek.

"Yeah, it'll fly by," Paisley replied.

Trinity gave her a soft but unsure smile. It was only a week; she'd been telling herself that for about the past twenty-four hours. A week would be easy. Three weeks or six weeks because Paisley was on the other side of the country, working with a client, would be harder. Yes, it was true that technology meant they'd be able to see each other on video and talk all the time, but it wasn't the same. She couldn't touch Paisley, smell her, taste her lips and her skin on video chat. She couldn't wake up next to her and roll over to hold her close instead of getting out of bed to go to work.

"I'll call you when I get home," Trinity said.

"Okay."

"And if I get stuck in traffic, I'll text you."

"I'd rather you be safe," Paisley replied, hands on Trinity's stomach under her shirt.

This was the part where they were stalling. They both knew it, but neither had said it out loud. Trinity was supposed to be on the road by now, but they'd sat on the sofa snuggled up for twenty extra minutes, and now, she was running behind.

"Okay," Trinity said.

Paisley leaned in and kissed her softly. Trinity kissed her back, deepening it, memorizing this moment because she was still worried. They'd made a very tentative schedule for December. With the holidays, Paisley didn't have as many clients to meet with in person toward the end of the month, but it was Christmas, so Trinity had her mom to think about, and Paisley had her own family to consider. So, they'd left that week alone and decided to spend New Year's

Eve and Day together instead. Now, Trinity was thinking about their midnight kiss as Paisley pulled her closer right there on her driveway, kissing her deeper.

She knew Paisley wanted this, but she always went straight to the fact that it hadn't worked for her in the past, so it likely wouldn't now. Trinity worried that the woman might deliver upon a self-fulfilled prophecy and end things with Trinity before they had a chance to see what could be between them. She didn't say that, though, because now wasn't the time. They were saying a temporary goodbye, and Paisley's lips were on hers. Trinity only wanted to focus on that.

"You should really get going. The weather is supposed to get bad," Paisley said, taking a quick step back and wrapping her arms around the sweater she had on.

Trinity had told her to put on a jacket, but Paisley hadn't listened. She was probably freezing, and Trinity wanted to take her inside, make them something hot to drink, and sit right back down on that couch, holding Paisley until she warmed up.

"Yeah," Trinity said instead. "I'll call you."

"Okay," Paisley replied.

After repeating that for a third time in a few minutes, Trinity finally got into her car, turned it on, and gave Paisley one last longing look before she backed out of the driveway and onto the road. It only took a few minutes before Trinity began to cry, which made no sense. She would see Paisley in a few days, and they hadn't been together long enough to feel this way, but Trinity knew – she knew this was love. And maybe Paisley wasn't there yet; maybe she needed time. But Trinity didn't.

Paisley hadn't been kind to her in high school, but Trinity knew now that she'd seen something in Paisley even back then. Yes, there had been attraction and confusion because Trinity was a teenager realizing she was gay, but it had been more than that. She just hadn't known it then. The reason she'd gone to those field hockey practices and games, and the reason she'd gone to the slopes in the winter and failed to ski was that Paisley had been there. Trinity had loved her smile, her laugh, how she always seemed so confident, how her hair fell over her shoulders, and how it made her look sweeter when she wore it in a French braid. She'd been in love with Paisley back in school, too. It was a different kind of love, a naïve one and one that wasn't easy to understand because Paisley had picked on her some days and left her alone completely other days, but it was there and had been the whole time.

"Hey, sweetie," Kelly said.

"Hey," she said, wiping tears from her cheeks.

"Oh, no. What happened?"

"Nothing. Sorry, I'm just kind of a mess for no reason."

"I doubt it's for no reason," Kelly replied.

"Can you talk?"

"Yeah, the kids are occupied."

"I'm sorry I keep dumping this on you. I can talk to Vidal about it when I get back, but she's with this guy she's dating today."

"It's okay; you're not bothering me. Trin, what's going on? Did you guys breakup?"

"No," she said, sniffling and trying to get herself together. "I just left."

"You miss her already?"

"Yeah. Stupid, huh?"

"Not stupid. You love her."

"It's been a few weeks."

"Doesn't change how you feel," Kelly reasoned. "So, not worth bringing up."

"I guess. But she's not there yet; or if she is, she's not saying it."

"Did you tell *her*?"

"No. I know her. She's so worried this won't work, she's not ready to go there."

"Did you guys talk about what happens next, at least?"

"Yeah, sort of. I'm coming back here this weekend."

"That's good, then; it's only a week apart."

"For now, anyway. But I screwed up yesterday. I got upset when she started talking about how hard it would be, and I started a fight."

"Trin…"

"I know. She called me on it, and we talked some. Not as much as we should have probably, but I didn't want to drag us back into that place where Paisley is talking about how she'll be somewhere for six to eight weeks, and it will be hard for me to get away from work to visit."

"I get it," Kelly replied. "But you're going back this weekend. That's what matters."

"Why does it feel like I can't breathe?"

"Really, or you just mean–"

"I mean, like I can't breathe without her."

"Oh, honey," Kelly said. "You're in love for the first time, aren't you?"

"I think I was in love with her in school."

"Probably. But this is different because neither of you is trying to be cool in a competitive high school full of rich, entitled brats with self-esteem issues. Now, it's real. It can actually turn into something."

"I was so angry when I first saw her again," Trinity said, thinking back to overhearing Paisley on the phone. "She seemed like the same entitled rich kid I'd been in school with."

"But she's not, and *that's* the scary part." Kelly paused. "You can see a future with her, but at the same time, you can't because of the distance and work. Right?"

"Yes," Trinity admitted. "And I feel like I have to move slower when I don't want to. I want it all."

"I think you have to risk scaring her if you feel this way, Trin."

"No way."

"Trinity, you're crying right now, and you'll see her in less than a week."

"She doesn't need to know that," Trinity argued. "Look, had we been talking about any of my ex-girlfriends, I might have done what you're–"

"Had we been talking about any of your ex-girlfriends, we wouldn't be having this conversation in the first place," Kelly interrupted.

Trinity knew her friend was right. She stared ahead at the rust, orange-colored sedan in front of her, needing to focus on anything else.

"It shouldn't be this hard, this soon. That's what she'll say. I know her," Trinity said.

"Well, she's an idiot," Kelly replied, chuckling. "I think it *should* be this hard. The harder it is upfront, the better you will be long-term. If it's easy, you take it for granted. You aren't challenged to get through something together to see how you can do that when things get tough later, and they *will* get tough later. The more you talk about this stuff now, the better you'll be then. You could be fighting about putting the cap on the toothpaste or squeezing it from the bottom one minute, and the next, one of you is bringing something up from a long time ago that still bothers you, and you're in a full-blown argument. The time you spend now figuring out how to deal with the time apart is time well spent, in my opinion."

"I want the good stuff, too, Kell," Trinity said.

"Have you not had that? If you haven't had any good so far, I'd wonder why you even want to be with her."

"No, that's not what I meant. I–"

"You call *me* to talk about this stuff because we're friends, yes, but you also call me because I'm getting a Ph. D in psychology, Trinity. Let's not kid ourselves here. Vidal has a business degree and is probably a good friend to you, but you call me because you know I'll give you my thoughts not just as your friend from high school but as someone who counsels couples."

Trinity sighed.

"Yeah, that's what I thought. You have the good stuff,

or you wouldn't be crying. You want more of the good stuff? You work on it. You talk to her, tell her how you feel, no matter what that is. If she's the one for you, she'll at least listen, even if she can't tell you she's exactly where you are yet. I've talked to probably a hundred couples so far in my career. I've heard at least fifty of them talk about how they met, where one of them was ahead of the other. Sometimes, it worked just fine. Other times, it caused a fight. A few times, they told me they broke up over it only to come back together later. Put in the work now, Trinity. It's worth it if *she's* worth it."

Trinity nodded slowly, even though Kelly couldn't see it.

"You're right," she said mostly to herself.

"So, what are you going to do?" Kelly asked.

"Talk to her," Trinity said. "Tell her that I'm nervous about not having things planned out more for the future because I want a future with her. I don't know that I'm ready to tell her that I'm in love with her yet. I know it's there, but saying it out loud is a whole other thing."

"That's okay, though," Kelly said.

"I don't want to talk to her about this stuff over the phone, though," Trinity added.

"You might have to if your schedules prevent–"

"I'll see her this weekend, at least. I'll tell her then."

"I'm here for you, you know? I know I'm busy – it's going to take me another thirty years to get this damn doctorate off my back – but I'm here."

"I know," Trinity replied, grateful for her friend. "Do you want to talk about *you* now? Selfishly, I could use a break from talking about my crap. And I know you have crap, too."

"So much crap," Kelly said.

Trinity laughed.

"Sometimes, actual crap. Ever seen a kid still in diapers but old enough to get around take the poop out of his diaper and spread it all over their crib and the wall behind it?"

"What? No," Trinity said, laughing.

"Well, that happened the other day, and despite having cleaned the kid, the crib, and the wall more times than I can count, I still smell poop whenever I walk into the room. I'm considering just selling the damn house and starting over in a new one."

Trinity laughed again and said, "But you have another kid who will hit that stage soon."

"Yeah, maybe we'll wait until they're both over that phase and then move," Kelly replied.

Trinity listened to Kelly talk about her dissertation, her husband, who was a great guy that Trinity had only met a couple of times but really liked, and the kids. They made plans *to make plans* to meet up after the New Year, which gave Trinity something else to look forward to, and they hung up when Trinity had about two hours left to go in her drive. She stopped to fill up her gas tank with about an hour left so that she wouldn't leave it on empty, and got back in the car just in time to see a call come in on the screen.

"Hi," she said with a smile.

"I know I said I wanted you to be safe, but it's been four and a half hours, so I wanted to check on you," Paisley said into the phone.

"I'm at the gas station, about to get back on the highway. Weather has been fine so far, but there was an accident about an hour ago that I got caught in."

"Okay. I can let you go. I just… I got worried, and I'm at the airport, so it's loud here."

"I *like* that you got worried," Trinity replied, pulling out of the gas station.

"I have a feeling it'll be a regular occurrence on these drives, especially in winter," Paisley said.

"How am I going to handle you flying all over the place?" Trinity asked, getting onto the highway entrance ramp.

"Planes are fine. Cars – not so much."

"I don't know about that. I have no idea who's flying

that plane; if they've had any drinks; if the plane itself is maintained well; if–"

"So, you'll be tracking my flights, and I should send you my flight numbers and status updates myself? Got it," Paisley concluded.

Trinity laughed and said, "Want to talk to me for the next hour or so?"

"I board in about forty-five," the woman replied.

"So, for the next forty-five, then?" Trinity asked.

"As long as you're okay with the frequent announcements in the background," Paisley told her.

"I have a feeling that's going to be our new normal," Trinity said. "Wait. You were supposed to be in the air by now."

"Delayed. Weather in Chicago. They said we should only arrive an hour late."

"Don't you sit in one of the fancy lounges where they don't make the annoying announcements?"

Paisley chuckled and said, "No, I book economy flights because I don't want my clients to have to pay for me to fly in first, and I don't want to pay for it myself."

Trinity smiled and said, "You're so different than you were in school, bragging about your custom skis made by some popular ski maker. Is that what they're called? Ski makers? I always rented when I had to."

Paisley laughed and replied, "I still have skis. We could go sometime."

"No, *you* can go. I'll stay in the lodge," Trinity told her.

"If you're in the lodge, then I'm in the lodge with you," Paisley said.

An announcement for a flight came from Paisley's side of the phone.

"Where is this lodge?" Trinity asked.

"Pick a place. I'll take you one day," Paisley replied.

And Trinity liked the sound of the words *one day.*

CHAPTER 31

Paisley arrived in Chicago only an hour and a half behind schedule, picking up her rental car that she'd only reserved because the company she was working with this week wasn't actually in the city itself. The office was in the burbs, and Paisley liked having a car whenever she could. She didn't mind public transportation, but she preferred to be able to control when she left and arrived places as much as possible when she wasn't in a city. She got to the hotel around nine, starving, so she ordered food up to her room from the restaurant. The menu selection wasn't great, and she'd likely be eating rubbery chicken and an undercooked baked potato, but it was better than nothing. Thankfully, she had a granola bar in her bag, so she ate that while she waited and pulled out her computer to get some last-minute prep done prior to her first meeting the next day.

By ten-thirty, she had eaten, finished her work, and was more than ready for bed. While she and Trinity hadn't stayed up late making love on their last night together, Paisley still hadn't slept well. She kept thinking about how she could fit a relationship into her work schedule. She already felt stretched thin with work, missed her friends, and had her mom on her back for being gone so much she couldn't have dinner with her parents regularly. Now, she also had a girlfriend who would require a lot of her time. It was time Paisley *wanted* to devote to their relationship, but there were only so many hours in the day. At eleven, she brushed her teeth and readied herself for bed. She was asleep the moment her head hit the pillow.

Awaking at the sound of her alarm, Paisley hit the stop button on her phone with pinpoint accuracy and rolled onto her back. She stretched, and when she did, she recognized that she'd woken up very ready for something.

"Oh, come on," Paisley muttered to herself.

She clenched her thighs and knew she'd be changing her underwear before work because they were soaked through. Paisley couldn't remember her dream, but it must have been a good one. She stared at the ceiling of the hotel room that looked exactly like all the rest and sighed. She reached for her phone on the table to check the time, even though she knew what time it was, and noticed she had three texts from Trinity that she'd missed, along with a call.

<u>Trinity Pascal:</u> I thought you'd call before sleep.

<u>Trinity Pascal:</u> Okay. Good night, babe.

<u>Trinity Pascal:</u> Are you up yet?

Paisley growled at herself because she'd forgotten to put her girlfriend on her favorites list so that Trinity's notifications would come through regardless of her do-not-disturb settings. She quickly remedied that and dialed.

"Hey, did I wake you?" Trinity asked.

"No, my alarm did. I'm sorry, I fell asleep last night without calling. I thought I'd read on my phone or something, but I was out."

"It's okay. This is new for both of us," Trinity said. "So, meetings all day?"

"Yeah, with the owner and his operations team," Paisley replied. "What about you?"

"I'm running behind; tired and moving slower than usual."

Paisley smiled to herself and asked, "Where are you now?"

"My kitchen, making coffee. Why?"

"Because I'm in bed, and I woke up in quite a state."

"Quite a state? Who *are* you sometimes?" Trinity laughed.

"Trin, did you catch my meaning?"

"You woke up... needing something?"

"Yes, I did," Paisley confirmed.

"Did you *do* something?" Trinity asked her.

"Not yet," she replied.

"Not yet... You want to?"

"I don't think I can get through the day if I don't," Paisley stated.

"Fuck," Trinity said, and Paisley heard sounds coming from Trinity's side of the phone.

"What was that?" she asked.

Trinity replied, "Me putting my bowl of cereal down while simultaneously trying to get my jeans unbuttoned."

Paisley laughed and said, "I love how you just told me that. Most people might be embarrassed to admit that."

"Well, they're idiots. What did you sleep in?"

"Tank top and panties."

"What color?" Trinity asked.

"White and black."

"Bikinis?"

"Yes, babe," Paisley said. "Are you going to get off standing up in your kitchen?"

"No, I'm moving to the couch."

Paisley's smile went wider as she slipped her hand between her legs and said, "I don't have much time."

"That's okay; neither do I. What are you doing?"

"I woke up really wet, so I'm sliding around my clit with two fingers."

"Did you bring your vibrator?" Trinity asked.

"No," Paisley said. "Short trip."

"Next time, bring it. I want to hear it through the phone as you come."

Paisley bit her lower lip and started stroking faster.

"Are you..."

"Yes," Trinity said.

"I miss you," Paisley said, meaning it in more than just this way.

"I miss you, too," Trinity said. "Pais, it won't take me long."

"Me neither," Paisley said.

"Go inside for me, baby."

Paisley lowered her hand and moved two fingers inside herself, curling them how she liked.

"Did you?"

"Yes," Paisley said, lifting her hips off the bed for better access. "It feels good, babe."

"I want to be inside you," Trinity told her.

"You are, baby. You are," she replied, picturing Trinity on top of her, rocking into her.

"God, I'm going to–"

Trinity went silent, and Paisley knew she was coming. Knowing that was enough to get herself there, Paisley pulled out her fingers and rubbed her clit hard and fast until she came hard, probably biting her lip hard enough to draw blood, but she didn't care.

"Oh," she said, rocking her hips into her hand, drawing out the orgasm. "God, yes."

"We can do this, Pais," Trinity said a moment later.

"Yeah," Paisley said, still slowly stroking until she could come down all the way.

"I'll text you later when I'm done working," Trinity promised. "We can do this again if you want, but maybe on video this time," she suggested.

Paisley smiled as she settled her hand between her legs and finally got her breathing under control.

"You have to wear a T-shirt and nothing else," Paisley said. "The green one that matches your eyes."

"What will you wear for me?" Trinity asked playfully.

"What do you *want* me to wear for you?"

"Nothing," Trinity replied.

Paisley grunted because while phone sex was good and video sex would be better, real sex was what she wanted with her girlfriend, and it had only been a day since she'd last seen Trinity naked and gotten to touch her and be touched *by* her.

After hanging up, Paisley took a quick shower, dressed for work, and left for the office she'd be in today and tomorrow. The owner was a kind man in his sixties who'd started the company with his brother thirty years ago. After his brother passed away, though, his nephew took over the business operations, but he hadn't done the best job, and they were now losing money. Any time Paisley worked with family-owned businesses, things got tricky, but she liked the challenge. The nephew, it turned out, was a complete idiot who had spent their entire annual marketing budget in one month and had bought a software system to operate the business that came with lackluster support, so no one in the company understood how to use it as a result.

"I know we only have you here for two days, but is it possible for you to stay on the full week?" the owner asked her after their final meeting of the day. "Next week as well, if you're not onto your next client? Tim means well, and it's my fault for not giving him more oversight."

"Tim is forty years old," Paisley remarked, trying not to sound harsh. "And he went to business school and grew up in the company. The decisions he's making aren't just unwise – they're bad. You're hemorrhaging money, and unless you replace him, based on the numbers you have shown me, I don't see the company surviving any longer than eighteen months, assuming you lay off some of the administrative staff and cut back in other areas, too."

The man sighed and said, "I can't just let him go."

"I'd suggest something in sales, then," Paisley replied. "A commissioned rep. You could use another one anyway, and he wouldn't have decision-making authority. Plus, he'd be rewarded for his hard work with commissions, and if he underperforms, he's still a part-owner, so once you're making a profit again, he'd get a decent paycheck. If that doesn't work out, though, you might have to think about him being a silent partner, at most."

"His father had such an eye for the right decisions. I thought it would get passed down, but it must have skipped a generation."

"Tim's daughter?" Paisley asked, smiling.

"He had her out of wedlock to the embarrassment of his mother." The man laughed. "He was only nineteen at the time. She's young, but she's talented."

"If you want my opinion, she's the one to take over the marketing team."

"She's still in college," he argued.

"From what I've seen today, she's the best you've got unless you hire from outside the family," Paisley noted. "She's going to school for marketing, and she may be young, but she understands digital marketing better than Tim. When I asked her some questions about where she'd spend money, she had the right answers."

"I hadn't thought about promoting her. She's an admin right now. We thought she'd work here until she graduates and then leave us."

"Give her the marketing job now, and I bet she'll stay in the family business," Paisley said. "She's bored in her current role."

"I'll think about that tonight." The man nodded. "And what about for the rest of the week and next week?"

"Can I take a look tonight and get back to you?"

"Of course," he said, smiling at Paisley. "Now, you're in my city. How would you like to join us for dinner at one of our favorite local places?"

"I'd love to, but I actually have plans," Paisley replied.

"You know someone in town?" he asked.

"No, but I'm in a long-distance relationship, and we're going to talk about our days and eat together."

"Well, that sounds nice. I'll leave you to it," he said, standing up.

Paisley left out the part about the possible video sex with her girlfriend, shook his hand, grabbed her stuff, headed to the first diner she saw to pick up something fatty for dinner, and made her way back to her hotel. When she got there, she texted Trinity that she was ready. Ten minutes went by before Trinity texted that she was still at the office. There had been a problem with the assembly line they were testing, and she and Will had stayed back to try to fix it before running a full test with the actual product on it tomorrow.

Paisley ate dinner on the bed while doing some work and waited. Another two hours went by, so she decided to keep working, and when nine o'clock came around, she texted Trinity again; surely, she was home by now. But the woman didn't answer. Paisley turned on the TV to CNN, hoping the news of the world would take her mind off of Trinity not calling or texting back. It was around ten when her phone finally rang.

"Hey," she said. "Did you *just* get home now?"

"Yeah, but I left the office a while ago," Trinity replied.

"I don't–"

"I'm going to tell you something that sounds worse than it is, so just let me start with the fact that I'm okay. I'm fine."

Paisley shot up in bed and said, "What happened?"

"I was in a car accident on the way home, but, babe, I'm fine. I promise, I'm fine."

"You were–"

"I was rear-ended on the way home. The roads were slippery. We weren't going that fast, but my airbag went off, so the guy that hit me called the cops and an ambulance."

"Ambulance? Trinity!"

"They didn't even take me to the hospital; they just checked me out. I don't even have a scratch on me, babe. They suggested I go to my doctor tomorrow to have him double-check everything, but I'm good."

"Do you have a sore neck or back?"

"A little, but they checked me for a concussion, and I passed the test, so I'll do the appointment tomorrow, but I'm okay."

"Fuck, Trinity," Paisley said, standing up and pacing.

"I'm okay."

"Babe, I can't get to you," Paisley said, realizing it at the same time.

"You don't have to. Vidal is here with me right now. She's going to sleep on the couch just in case, but she's being overprotective. I really am okay. Babe, I promise, okay? You don't have to worry. I'm just sorry I missed our evening plans."

"Trin, not the time," Paisley replied, pacing holes in the patterned carpet now. "Babe, I can't–"

"Let me put Vidal on the phone for you."

"What? Why?"

"Because she can help. Hold on," Trinity told her.

"No, I–"

"Paisley?" Vidal said.

"Is she really okay? Be honest with me."

"She's fine," Vidal replied. "She called me right after it happened. I was there when they told her that she was okay and to check in with her doctor. Her car is messed up in the back, but it's drivable, so I had Will pick it up for her. We'll get it to the mechanic for the estimate for her tomorrow, too. Will's brother has a shop."

"But she's okay?" Paisley asked again, sitting on the edge of the bed, staring at her luggage.

"She's good. She wasn't hungry, but I'm making her some soup. And I'll be here all night, okay?"

"Thank you," Paisley said, sighing. "Thank you. I wish…"

"I know. Let me put her back on for you, okay?"

"Yeah. Thanks."

"Hey," Trinity said. "Satisfied?"

"No," Paisley replied. "I want to see for myself."

"I'm about to eat whatever Vidal is making for me. Want me to FaceTime you when I'm in bed?"

"Yes," Paisley said instantly.

"Okay. Give me a bit. I need to shower, too."

"Can you take a bath, please, and leave the door open a crack?"

"What? Why?" Trinity asked.

"Because I don't want to worry about you falling in the

shower and you having the door locked so Vidal couldn't get to you."

"Babe, I won't fall. I'm okay."

"Trin…"

"Okay; quick bath it is. But if Vidal sees the goods, that's on you."

"I don't care. I just want you safe," Paisley replied.

"Pais, I'm okay. I'll still be able to come see you this weekend. I'll rent a car if mine is too messed up to–"

"Not tonight, okay? We'll figure out that part later. Just get some rest."

"Okay. Give me about a half-hour."

"Okay. Bye." Paisley had been about to say something she shouldn't say over the phone for the first time.

"Bye," Trinity replied.

When the phone went dead, Paisley tossed it onto the bed next to her and continued to stare at her luggage. Her heart was racing. She could have lost her tonight. She didn't, but now she was states away and unable to take care of her girlfriend. Paisley wanted to be the one to make Trinity soup and sit on the edge of the tub, making sure the woman was okay while she bathed. Paisley opened her computer, went to the browser, ignoring the emails she hadn't yet responded to, and made her decision.

CHAPTER 32

"I left you in your bed this morning," Vidal said.

"Hey, watch it… People will talk, and I have a girl-friend," Trinity teased.

"You're not supposed to be here," Vidal argued in response.

"I'm fine," Trinity said, moving behind her desk.

"I told you to take the day off."

"And you're not the boss of me," Trinity replied.

"Technically, I am – I'm the CEO."

"Because *I* didn't want the job," Trinity remarked.

"Well, either way, I'm sending you home," Vidal said.

"Come on. I'm fine."

"What does Paisley think about you working the day after a major car accident?"

"*Major* is a stretch," Trinity said, opening her laptop. "And I didn't tell her."

"I heard you on the phone with her before I left."

"I told her I'm fine. I did *not* tell her I was coming into the office."

"Trin, at least work from home today. You're going to the doctor this afternoon anyway. How did you even get here?"

"Took an Uber."

"Why?"

"Because I couldn't just stay at home alone; I need to be distracted."

"From?"

"Thinking about Paisley," Trinity stated. "The long-distance thing is brand-new, and I'm struggling."

"So, you're using work as a distraction from your relationship?" Vidal asked.

"Yes," Trinity said, opening her email.

"Isn't it normally the other way around for people?"

"Couldn't tell you," Trinity said.

"Trin, you've been weird since you got back. Is it really just because you miss Paisley?"

Trinity looked over at her friend and asked, "How's what's-his-name?"

"Nice try. *That's* over. Back to my question."

"It's over?"

"Well, we might still hook up if we're both single, but I told him that was all I'd be interested in. He seemed okay with that."

"Of course, he did," Trinity said, laughing and then feeling the small headache at the back of her skull get a little more painful.

"Trinity, you've been weird since Paisley left the first time, if I'm being honest. Distant, I guess. Like, I'm making all the decisions, and you're just agreeing with me or helping Will out front."

"I miss her," Trinity said. "It's been hard. But yeah, I'll do better."

"That's not what I'm saying," Vidal replied. "I'm checking on you. We're friends first; partners second."

Trinity closed her laptop and turned to Vidal.

"I'm sorry. I'm not being fair to you."

"What's there to be fair about?"

"Boss, that lady is outside," Will said from the open door of the office. "Sorry to interrupt, but I wasn't sure if I should let her back. I thought she was done."

"Will, this is ridiculous," the female voice argued. "I'm coming back there."

"Pais?" Trinity said, standing quickly and walking around her desk.

By the time she got to the open door of the office, Paisley was standing in the alcove, with her roller bag next to her.

"What are you doing here?" Trinity asked.

"What are *you* doing here? I went to your apartment because I expected you to be home," Paisley replied.

"I have work," Trinity said.

Paisley left the roller where it was and walked over to her. She looked Trinity up and down, making no attempt to touch her at first. Satisfied that Trinity was in one piece, Paisley pulled her in for a hug. Trinity hugged her back hard, breathing her in and smiling. They'd only really been apart a couple of days, but it had felt so much longer, especially when she'd been rear-ended and worried she was near death for that split second when the air bag came for her face.

"I needed to see you," Paisley whispered.

"I'm okay. I promise, Pais," Trinity said, squeezing her a little tighter.

"When's your appointment?"

"One," she said.

"Why are you here? I thought you'd stay home."

"I wanted to work," Trinity lied.

Paisley pulled back to take a look at her and said, "I'm taking you home."

"Yes, please," Vidal said, coming out of the office. "I swear, when I left her, she was in bed. I did *not* tell her to come to work."

Paisley looked over Trinity's shoulder, smiled at the woman, and said, "Thank you for taking care of her."

"She's not that bad," Vidal replied. "She didn't demand I give her a bell to ring whenever she wanted something."

"I guess that's a good sign for when she has the flu," Paisley said, pressing her forehead to Trinity's shoulder.

"Hey, I'm okay," Trinity told her once again, knowing that Paisley must be really worried, based on her reaction.

Paisley wasn't the kind of person to show this kind of emotion in front of relative strangers. That was especially true given the fact that Vidal and Will were now her former clients.

"Can we go home, please?" Paisley said.

"Yeah, sure. Let me get my stuff." She kissed Paisley's forehead.

Trinity grabbed her things from the office, gave Vidal a look that she hoped said she was apologetic for coming in only to leave again, and walked back out to Paisley, who took Trinity's bag from her shoulder and then took Trinity's hand. Paisley also wouldn't let her wheel her roller bag for her, which was overkill, but the woman seemed to need to remain in control right now, so Trinity would let her.

"Where's your car?"

"Babe, my car is at home," Paisley replied. "I flew straight here from Chicago."

"I just talked to you this morning," Trinity said.

"I was standing outside, waiting for the shuttle to take me to the rental car place," Paisley explained. "We're here." She nodded toward a red SUV.

"Not really your style," Trinity noted.

"It was the first car in the aisle; I was trying to get here as quickly as possible. I would have taken the red-eye, but the only one available came with a layover and would've gotten me here at the same time as the later direct one."

"Pais, you were on a job..." Trinity said as Paisley opened the car door for her.

"And *you* were in an accident." Paisley stood in front of Trinity as Trinity sat in the passenger seat. "I had to get to you to make sure you were okay."

"I video-chatted with you. I showed–"

"It's not the same." Paisley leaned down and kissed her lips.

She closed the door for Trinity, and within minutes, they were at Trinity's apartment. Paisley had Trinity back in bed and was making her an early lunch. Trinity had something on the TV, but she wasn't paying attention; she was listening in on Paisley's call.

"Thank you so much for understanding," Paisley said and paused. "I don't know yet. I can do some work from here until I can get back." Another pause followed. "I think it's a good idea, sir." Pause. "I'll get you those software recommendations by the end of business today. I have three that I think you should take a look at that come with training and better support than what you have now." Pause. "Great. I'm glad to hear that. I'll take a look at the email after I get back." Pause. "Okay. Thank you. Bye."

Paisley walked back into the bedroom with a sandwich on a plate.

"You're missing work."

"Here. Eat this for me," she said, handing Trinity the plate and walking around to the other side of the bed.

"Pais…"

"My client was very understanding. I'm going to do some work from here after your doctor's appointment."

"Babe, I'm so happy you're here, but you–"

"Trinity, I'm here. We're eating now, and we're going to the doctor. Then, I'll figure it out, okay?"

"Yeah, okay." Trinity smiled.

They ate in relative silence, and then Paisley drove her to her doctor's appointment. Sitting in the lobby with Paisley holding her hand made Trinity feel like the pounding in her head wasn't nearly as bad. And she knew Paisley was right to want her to get checked out, but it just seemed unnecessary – she'd be fine in a few days, at most, and Paisley would have made this trip for nothing and risked losing a client just because some guy couldn't control his car on the road.

"Trinity Pascal," a nurse said when she opened the door leading to the back.

"That's me," Trinity replied.

When she stood, Paisley let go of her hand.

"I'll be right here, okay?"

"Can she come back with me?" Trinity asked the nurse.

"Sure. If you want her to."

"Come back with me, Pais," Trinity requested.

"Are you sure?" Paisley asked.

"Yeah, I'm sure. Come on."

Paisley stood and took Trinity's hand again. They waited for the doctor in the exam room for another fifteen minutes after they'd taken Trinity's X-rays. When he came back in, he nodded, turned to the computer, and opened her scans.

"Well, I don't see anything here to be concerned about. Just the headache?"

"Yeah, it's at the base of my skull."

"Has it gotten worse? Better?"

"A little better."

"What did you take for it?" the doctor asked.

"Nothing," she replied.

"Nothing? Babe…" Paisley said.

"What? I was coming to the doctor. I didn't know what I should take for it."

The doctor examined her neck and upper back again before returning to review the scans again. Trinity watched as Paisley squinted her eyes toward the pictures on the big screen.

"I bet you wish you went to med school about now, huh?" Trinity said.

"Shut up," Paisley told her, but she smiled as well.

Trinity stared at her. Paisley had dropped everything and had flown to her to make sure Trinity was okay. She hadn't needed to, but she'd done it anyway.

"Well," the doctor began, "I think I'd like you to take some ibuprofen for the headache for now. If it hasn't gone away in a day or so, call the office – we might want to get some more scans."

"In twenty-four hours, or do we wait two days?" Paisley asked.

"If it's worse, call tomorrow. If it's subsiding but not gone, the day after. If you're at all worried, though, I can schedule the–"

"Yes," Paisley interrupted.

"Paisley…"

"Trinity…" Paisley glared at her, and it wasn't playful, either.

"You can just schedule whatever you think I need," Trinity told the doctor after that brief interaction.

"Thank you," Paisley mouthed to her.

Trinity nodded, felt a little pain, and squinted through it. Paisley stood from the chair and moved over to Trinity on the table, rubbing her back over the gown they'd made her wear for no reason.

"Pain?"

"Just a little," she said.

Paisley's hand went under the backless gown. Her lips went to Trinity's temple. She kissed her and pressed her forehead to the spot gently as if she thought she could take the pain away.

"Okay. I'll have the nurse come back in, and we'll write you a script. I'll give you a muscle relaxer to help you sleep in case you need it. If you don't, you don't have to take it. She'll get you the paperwork for the CT scan. You'll have to call them for the next appointment, but I'll write down that I want it tomorrow or the day after, at the latest."

"Thank you," Trinity said.

"Should we be worried?" Paisley asked him.

"I don't think there's anything to worry about, but the CT will help me make sure. Right now, just rest."

"So, no work?"

"I would say, not until we get the CT results."

"Thank you," Paisley said.

"I'll let you get dressed and send in the nurse," the doctor said.

He left them after a quick smile and a nod, closing the door behind him.

"It's just a headache," Trinity spoke.

"Maybe, but I want to make sure," Paisley said. "Sorry, I kind of took over, didn't I?"

"I liked it," Trinity replied, getting off the table as gracefully as she could in a hospital gown.

"You *liked* it?" Paisley asked, moving Trinity to turn away from her so that she could undo the strings of the gown for her.

"Yeah, I like having you here," Trinity told her.

"I wish I wasn't here under these circumstances." Paisley slipped Trinity's gown off and handed Trinity her T-shirt.

"Me too." Trinity slipped on her shirt and turned to see Paisley sitting down in the chair, holding Trinity's jeans out as if she wanted Trinity to climb into them as she did so. "I can dress myself. I've been doing it for a while now."

"Bending over will aggravate your headache. Just–"

"Okay." Trinity laughed but stepped into the jeans all the same.

She buttoned and zipped them just in time for the nurse to walk into the room after a quick knock. Paisley stood, motioning for Trinity to sit in the chair, and Trinity listened as Paisley talked to the nurse about the prescription and the scan. Paisley's hand was on the back of her neck, just resting there. Trinity leaned back against it and closed her eyes for a second. As much as she didn't want to be in pain, have her car in the shop, or worry Paisley, she was so happy to have her standing next to her, touching her again, that it was almost worth it.

CHAPTER 33

"Hey," Trinity greeted, wiping her eyes and looking adorable to Paisley in her pajama pants, a T-shirt, and with a tired expression.

"Hi. Did I wake you with my typing?" Paisley asked.

"No, I woke up when I rolled over, and you weren't there," the woman replied, sitting down next to Paisley on the couch.

"Sorry. I wanted to get a little work done while you were asleep."

"It's okay; you ran out on a client for me."

Paisley turned to her and asked, "How's your head? Oh, and don't lie."

Trinity smiled before replying, "Better. I feel better."

"Not lying to me just so I stop asking?" Paisley wanted to make sure.

"No, I'm not lying. I wasn't lying before, either. I am fine. I really don't think any more tests are necessary. I'm doing them for you, you know?"

"Yes, thank you. Also, I want to kill the asshole that hit you."

"Pais, the roads were bad. It's not really his fault. He helped me right after it happened."

"He was too close to your car," Paisley muttered.

"Hey, babe?"

"Yeah?" Paisley asked.

"Can we just be together right now and forget the reason?"

Paisley nodded and said, "Are you hungry? I can try to cook something from whatever is in your fridge, but I think we're better off ordering."

"Whatever you want is fine," Trinity replied. "I feel a little sweaty since someone decided to wrap me up in three blankets, thinking a bedroom sweat lodge would help with a headache, so I'd like to take a quick shower."

"Bath? Please? For me?"

"Order food and join me in the shower to make sure I don't fall," Trinity suggested. "No funny business, I swear." She held up her hands in supplication. "Just a shower."

Paisley closed her laptop and said, "Okay. Let me just order from that pizza place you said you liked."

"Great. Pineapple, please." Trinity stood.

"I'm not ordering pineapple on my pizza," Paisley said, laughing as she reached for her phone.

"Then, get it on mine. I'm starving."

"Pineapple doesn't go on pizza," Paisley argued.

"Is this one of those ridiculous couple arguments we're going to have?" Trinity pulled her shirt over her head as she walked into the bedroom.

"Probably." Paisley looked at Trinity's bare back. "God, she's gorgeous," she whispered to herself.

"What?"

"Nothing!" she half-yelled for Trinity to hear in the other room. "Be there in a second. Don't get in without me!"

"You're smothering me," Trinity said playfully as she stuck her head in the doorway.

"You love it," Paisley replied.

"I do," Trinity agreed.

Paisley ordered two medium pizzas, figuring they could have the leftovers later, and made her way into Trinity's room, where she disrobed and met her in the bathroom.

"I've got it," Paisley told her, moving in front of her to turn on the water.

"Oh, I'm having some very nice flashbacks right about

now," Trinity replied, pressing her front to Paisley's ass while Paisley was bent over.

"Babe!" Paisley stood up and turned around, facing her.

"What?" Trinity laughed, wrapped her arms around Paisley, and pulled Paisley into her. "I've missed this."

"I miss it, too, but I want to make sure your head is okay." Paisley ran a hand over Trinity's cheek.

"What if I just touch you and slowly, so it's not too strenuous?"

"I hardly think that's fair."

"Not really concerned about fair," Trinity said, kissing Paisley's neck.

"Will you just get in the shower?" Paisley asked, laughing lightly.

"Fine. Now, *I* want to kill the guy who rear-ended me. Little did he know, he's also blocking me."

Paisley laughed a little harder and climbed in after her.

"I wouldn't be here," she reasoned.

"Yeah," Trinity agreed. "But he made me miss our video-sex appointment last night, and now you're standing right in front of me here, looking sexy and naked, and I can't do anything about it because you're worried about my headache."

"We should report him to the authorities," Paisley said, giving her a playful puppy-dog face as the water began to rush over Trinity's skin.

"You're mocking me," Trinity replied, giving her a glare back.

"Yes, I am. Now, let me wash you."

"What base is it if your girlfriend washes you in the shower but doesn't actually touch you anywhere that counts?"

"I think that's just called the batter's box, babe."

After their quick shower, Paisley returned to her laptop on the couch while Trinity grabbed the pizza at the door. She brought it over to them along with two beers.

Paisley wanted to object to her drinking alcohol, but Trinity had had a rough few days. If she wanted a beer, she could have a beer.

"So, what are you working on?" Trinity asked.

"This family-owned business. Brother died a few years ago. His son was left in charge along with the other brother who started the business decades ago. Son's name is Tim, and he's blowing it."

"Are they done for?"

"The owner is receptive to my ideas. I guess that's why he hired me. He's got a chance at making it, but I need to figure out their customer service department."

"What's wrong with it?" Trinity asked, biting into her pineapple pizza.

"They've hired out. They use a contractor instead of having it in-house, and there's no quality control or measurements that show whether they're any good at their jobs or not, which probably means—"

"They've contracted with a bad company," Trinity finished for her.

"Yeah. I've listened to a few of the phone calls, and they offer email support, so I've checked some of those at random, and I can't say that I'm impressed. When I looked into everything before I got there, a lot of their complaints were with the service. Who they've hired is cheap, and I think they're getting what they paid for."

"Can they afford to change it up?" Trinity asked.

"Not really. I'd have to suggest they cut something, and it would be a big something. They'd need twenty-four-seven support and at least a team of six."

"Can I..." Trinity nodded toward the laptop.

"Sure." Paisley handed it to her and reached for the plate with a slice of her own pizza Trinity had laid out for her.

She sat there and ate it, finishing the last bite while watching Trinity stare at spreadsheets and read a report she'd been working on.

"They're promoting someone?" Trinity asked after some time.

"The granddaughter. She's an admin now, but they're going to put her on marketing and make Tim a commissioned sales rep."

"Will those costs balance out?"

"No. She's entry-level, so they'll start her low, and Tim was making a VP's salary before. He'll be one hundred percent commissioned now since he's a part-owner, too."

Trinity stared at the spreadsheet some more and said, "Well, that's one person right there, then; entry-level support rep, at least. It looks like they have three admins outside of the one they just promoted."

"Yeah."

"I'd have two of them switch to support during the day shift. The company is way too small to have that many admins. I mean, Vidal and I aren't thinking about hiring admins for a long time, and they're not much bigger than us. Have two of them cover support and help with admin on the side if no calls are coming in. That gives you three."

Paisley smiled and asked, "And where do the other three come from? We'd need a manager and two reps."

"Not really," Trinity replied. "If that Tim guy is going to sales, are you recommending they hire a new ops person?"

"Yes, and at a lower level since Tim was handling marketing, too, and that's now covered." Paisley took a sip of her beer.

"So, have the new ops manager manage this team, too. It's only five more people, and if they get to a better place, they can add a front-line manager in the middle."

"And the other two reps?" Paisley asked.

"What's the budget for hiring for the rest of the year look like?" Trinity checked.

"Tab two," Paisley said.

Trinity went to the second tab on the spreadsheet and read through it for a minute while Paisley set another piece of pineapple pizza on Trinity's plate and took another one of her own.

"Oh, here," Trinity said.

"Where?" Paisley leaned in.

"You've got two owners here." Trinity pointed.

"Yeah, that's the wife of the owner and his daughter," Paisley said.

"But they're pulling salaries without positions listed here," Trinity argued.

"They don't work there day-to-day, no," Paisley said.

"But they're pulling actual salaries, not just profits or shares," Trinity continued with her point.

"I guess that's how they wanted it," Paisley replied.

"Babe, if you can get them to halve their salaries, you have your two more entry-level reps. If they can agree to stop taking salaries, considering they don't work there, you can hire two more people on top of that."

"It's his wife and daughter…"

"He just demoted his nephew, right?" Trinity said. "I mean, he's trying to save his company… Up to you, though. It's your client."

"What would you do if it were yours?" Paisley asked.

"Tell him to drop the salaries unless they want to go to work. They'll also get back whatever they don't spend on this vendor they're using now, but I think you still ask them to drop the salaries and use that money elsewhere."

"The company isn't profitable right now, so they wouldn't make anything until it is," Paisley told her.

"That's what it means to own a small business, though," Trinity replied, taking a drink of her beer. "Plus, my guess is at least the daughter has a day job. Am I right?"

"I don't know," Paisley replied. "I haven't asked. I was going to dive into this stuff with them today."

"And then I got into a car accident," Trinity said. "Sorry."

"I hate that you got into an accident, but you don't have to be sorry, Trin. I came here because I was terrified."

"I didn't mean to scare you," Trinity said.

"Honey, you didn't mean to get rear-ended because of bad roads in winter, either," Paisley said, closing the computer in Trinity's lap and moving into her side. "I hated that I couldn't get to you. My heart wouldn't stop racing all night. Even after we got off FaceTime and I'd seen your face, I still needed to be here. This morning, when we talked, I almost told you I was on my way here, but I knew you'd stay awake or make me coffee or something, and I wanted you to stay in bed and rest until I could get here to help. Little did I know, you were a rebel and decided to go to work."

"I didn't know you were coming, or I would have stayed home so that I wouldn't get in trouble." Trinity wrapped her arm around Paisley. She kissed the top of her head and asked, "When do you have to leave again?"

"I'm staying through the weekend," Paisley said.

"You are?" Trinity asked, knowing how happy she sounded.

"Your scan is tomorrow, and the results will take a couple of days – I want to be here when you get them, if that's okay."

"Of course, it's okay," Trinity replied. "What about work?"

"I'm going to finish up my recommendations for them remotely and offer to come back next week for a day to deliver them in person, and then spend an extra day if they need me to for free since I ran out on them."

"You're a good person, Paisley Jane."

"At least you're not calling me PJ anymore," Paisley joked.

"I changed you in my phone," Trinity said.

"To what? Should I even ask?"

"You're Paisley Hill now. But I *did* add a heart before *and* after your name just for fun."

Paisley laughed a little and reached her hand up under Trinity's shirt to place it over her heart.

"I thought you said no–"

"I just wanted to feel your heart," Paisley said.

"I'm going to be fine, Pais," Trinity told her.

"I know," Paisley replied softly. "Now, tell me more about how I should tell this man to fire his wife and daughter."

Trinity laughed.

CHAPTER 34

Trinity hated the doctor's office. She'd been here three times now in three days. Technically, this was only the second time at this particular office since she'd had the CT scan the day before elsewhere, but it was still too much for her. Paisley had made all the calls to set things up and, somehow, managed to get the test results sent to the doctor faster than usual. Why results still took this long to send when everything was digital these days was beyond Trinity, but normally, it was days of waiting. Paisley had managed to get the results escalated. Trinity wondered if she'd cried or something, convincing the staff that she was worried about her girlfriend having a brain tumor, but she hadn't asked. In the end, it didn't matter anyway. Trinity was sitting in the chair this time since reading the results shouldn't require an exam. Paisley was pacing in the small space between the tiny computer desk and the chair.

"Is this something I should know about you?"

"Huh?" Paisley asked, looking at her without stopping her pacing.

"The pacing, babe." She pointed to the floor beneath Paisley's moving feet.

"Oh, yeah. I pace a lot."

Trinity smiled and said, "When you're nervous?"

"When I'm nervous; when I'm working; when I'm deep in thought. It just depends."

"Hello," the doctor said, walking briskly into the room and sitting at the desk after pumping some hand sanitizer into his hands and rubbing them together.

Paisley stopped pacing and moved beside Trinity.

"Okay. Let me just pull these up again. I've had a look at them already, but we'll pull them up together."

Trinity swallowed.

"How's the headache been?" he asked.

"Gone," she said. "Yesterday, even before the scan."

"That's good," he replied. "Any other symptoms pop up?"

"No, I slept a lot after I came here the other day."

"A two-hour nap, and she slept the night through, too," Paisley added.

"That's good. The body needs to recover from the shock of an accident sometimes." He pulled images up on the screen. "Okay. Well, I don't see anything here to be concerned about."

"No?" Paisley asked.

"No. It's possible the headache was due to the shock or very mild whiplash. Have you had any neck pain at all?"

"Initial soreness from the airbag, but it went away by morning," Trinity said.

The doctor continued to stare at the screen and said, "Whiplash is tricky. It can appear that you're fine, but it can sneak up on you later. It can also hit you right away."

"You think she has whiplash?" Paisley asked.

"No. Like I said, if the headache is gone, and there's no soreness, I wouldn't worry. But since this was a car accident, and the person who hit you is likely paying for all this, I'd recommend going to see a physical therapist to check the full range of motion on that neck."

"A physical therapist, really? Is that necessary?" Trinity asked.

"It's precautionary, really, but if the headache comes back later, or if you end up having neck pain in the next few weeks, it helps the medical claim process with insurance to start treatment as soon after the accident as possible." He finally turned around to face them.

"Treatment for something I might not have?" Trinity asked.

"I've had patients feel fine the first few days, and then their neck tenses up on them. While it's not too late to get them feeling better, it's harder to get the insurance companies to pay for accident-related injuries if you don't seek treatment right away."

"God, what a system," Paisley said, shaking her head.

"So, let me have my staff give you a list of PTs we recommend and work with. You should set up the first consultation as soon as you can. They'll check the range of motion and work with you if there are any issues. Think of it like this: worse thing that happens is you get a few neck massages."

Trinity smiled at his lame attempt at a joke.

***

Ten minutes later, they had a piece of paper with the names of physical therapists on it and were on the way to Trinity's apartment.

"I don't need physical therapy. I feel fine."

"Babe, I think it's a good idea to go for at least an appointment."

"There was nothing on the scan."

"Yeah, but just because it didn't show up, doesn't mean it might not cause problems for you, like he said."

"Seems silly. I can move my neck just fine, and the headache is gone."

"One appointment? For me?" Paisley asked.

Trinity turned to the woman, who was looking at her with a concerned expression.

"Fine. For you."

"Thank you," Paisley replied and turned back to see that the light had changed from red to green.

"I want to go back to work tomorrow, Pais," Trinity said. "And you have to get back to Chicago."

"I'm here through the weekend. I'll deal with Chicago later."

"I'm going to go to the office tomorrow, though. I want to talk to Vidal, and I need to do it in person."

"Everything okay?" Paisley asked.

"We were talking about work stuff when you showed up the other day, and I was about to tell her that I'm unhappy."

"Oh," Paisley said. "I thought you weren't going to do that."

"She deserves to know. It's her company, too. Really, it's *her* company. She's been making all the decisions as of late, including hiring you – which I'm grateful for, by the way." Trinity looked over and caught Paisley's shy smile. "But I think we need to change it up. Maybe me focusing on new products, like you suggested, is a good idea."

"Could you do that while she takes care of everything else, or would she need to hire someone?" Paisley asked.

"I don't know. We hadn't planned on hiring anyone else in a leadership role for a while, and I think that's what she'd need to carry the load, but I need to talk to her about it first."

"Do you want me to get a flight out tonight?" Paisley asked. "I can go back to Chicago, and you can focus on–"

"What? No way," Trinity interrupted, placing her hand on Paisley's thigh. "I'd love it if you stayed through the weekend. We were supposed to have the weekend together, remember?"

"I know, but I don't want to get in your way," Paisley replied.

"You're not, and you won't. I just need you to let me go into the office tomorrow. I love protective-girlfriend-Paisley, but I need to–"

Paisley chuckled and said, "No, I get it. I've been a little too *involved* for our relationship still being so new, I know. I just don't know how to be anything else… I've never been with someone who was in an accident when I was in another city. I just couldn't focus on anything other than getting to you. It was all I could think about: get to Trinity."

Trinity smiled as she watched Paisley focus so intently

on driving. It was like Paisley wanted to make sure Trinity got home safely, given recent events.

"I love that you're here," Trinity said. "Having you there, at the doctor's office, and knowing you were waiting for me after they scanned my brain to make sure it was still there, has made this a lot easier."

"I think your brain is still in there," Paisley said, smiling now.

A few minutes later, they were back in Trinity's apartment. Trinity went into the bedroom to change into some sweats while Paisley was already in the living room, laptop open and working. Trinity stood in the open doorway of her bedroom, arms crossed over her chest, watching Paisley work with a smile on her face.

"I know that this news will be hard to deliver, but I think this is the best option for the business," Paisley said into her phone. "Yes, I'm moving some things around on my end. I should be able to confirm a new date soon. I appreciate your patience. I just needed to be here." There was another pause. "If you use the money from the contractors to pay for one of the new software systems I recommended, you'll actually be able to afford to keep your current software running until the new one is completely implemented." Paisley paused again. "I think it's best to make sure the staff is trained on the new software before you turn off the old one, especially because you'll be hiring some new people soon." There was a longer pause this time. "And I can help with that, yes." Short pause. "Okay. I'll send the email over and be in touch soon." Paisley disconnected and typed something on her computer.

"I love watching you work," Trinity said, walking up behind the couch.

"You do?" Paisley asked, laughing. "It's a bunch of boring phone calls and emails. You *hate* emails."

"No, I don't. I told you that," Trinity said, wrapping her arms around Paisley's neck as she leaned down over her. "Is he going to essentially let his wife and daughter go?"

"Yes. They both have actual jobs, it turns out, so he thinks telling them they won't be making something for nothing, given the business is at stake, should be fine. He's wanted to do it for a while but needed the push, I guess."

Trinity looked down into Paisley's shirt and said, "I have a very nice view right now."

"Oh, yeah?" Paisley chuckled at her.

"Can I have an even better one if you're able to take a break?"

"I don't know, Trin. You–"

"I'll say it a thousand more times if you need me to; I'll even buy a shirt that says it if that makes you feel better – *I'm fine.*"

"I just don't want to risk anything," Paisley replied.

"You risk me having to take care of things myself while you're sitting right out here."

Paisley looked up at her and said, "You wouldn't?"

"I would," Trinity stated. "You can either sit out here and know what I'm doing in there, come in and watch, or come in and *participate.*" Trinity stood upright and walked toward the bedroom without waiting for a response.

"Wait," Paisley said.

Trinity smirked.

***

"Welcome back," Vidal greeted her. "How are you feeling?"

"Good. Much better after yesterday, in fact."

"Test results came back okay?" Vidal asked.

"Sure. That, too," Trinity said, sitting at her desk and thinking about the agonizingly slow sex she'd had with Paisley the day before.

It was agonizingly perfect and lasted for hours because Paisley hadn't wanted anything too *acrobatic*, as she'd put it.

"Ah… I see," Vidal said, laughing as she closed her computer. "Paisley's still here."

"Until Sunday."

"You got some, didn't you?"

"I did," Trinity replied with a smile.

"So, why aren't you at home, still getting some?"

"Because she has work to do, too. She basically fled a client in need and came here to take care of me."

"Were you surprised?" Vidal asked.

"Yeah, honestly," Trinity replied. "I told her I was okay. I didn't think she'd fly here."

"She loves you," Vidal stated.

"She likes me. We're–"

"No, she loves you," Vidal repeated. "Trinity, I saw the look on Paisley's face when she came through that door and saw you looking unscathed. The sigh that woman let out was silent yet, somehow, still audible. You don't do that when you just *like* someone. If you're in a new relationship, and you like them, you call and text and check up on them and see each other this weekend like you two had originally planned."

"She's kind of intense about a lot of things, so I think it's just who she is," Trinity said in denial.

"Okay. Whatever you say… But I've liked a lot of people, and I wouldn't have flown across the country to check on them when they kept telling me they were okay. Maybe *I'm* the asshole," Vidal said.

Trinity hadn't come into the office today to talk about Paisley, but hearing that Vidal thought Paisley loved her *did* make her smile.

"When's your next meeting?" Trinity asked, changing the topic.

"I pushed off the meetings from today until next week since I didn't think you'd want anything too crazy today," Vidal told her.

"I'm okay," Trinity argued.

"I know. Still, I thought it would be best to just finish up everything else we're working on and start fresh on Monday. Plus, I have a sneaking suspicion that you want to talk to me about something, so I thought it best that we not have guests in the office today."

"How did you know?" Trinity asked.

"Well, I'm the best friend," Vidal said in explanation. "I know all your faces, tones, and on top of that, before Paisley showed up, you were about to tell me something. So, out with it." Vidal closed her laptop.

CHAPTER 35

"I'd love it if we can talk about a three-year agreement for that one-year price," Paisley said.

"I'd have to get approval for that. We normally do the two-year for the one-year price," the sales rep replied.

"I'm sure your boss would love to know that you've got a growing company locked in for three years," Paisley negotiated. "There are probably some nice co-marketing opportunities for both of us here, and we're going to pay for the professional services package as well, so I think if we can get that twenty percent over three years instead of the five percent on the first year and seven on year two, it'll balance out for you guys."

"Let me check, and I'll get back to you by the end of the day," the guy said.

"Thank you," Paisley replied.

And the Zoom meeting ended shortly after that.

"Twenty percent off three years? That would be a big help," the owner said, running a hand through his short white hair.

"They'll come back with fifteen for two, which is what I really wanted anyway. Plus, they'll probably throw in a discount on the professional services package if you offer to give a customer testimonial or something."

"It's better than *I* would have gotten," the man replied.

"You need to find the best negotiator you have on staff and have them handle deals like this. At least, make sure they're involved at the end, if not all the way through. And Tim is clearly not that guy, either, given his past performance."

"I'm not sure who that is," he said.

"If we get this one locked down for you before I leave,

251

have a few people help with the next deal and see how they do; who comes out on top. You'll figure it out for the near future and, eventually, you can hire someone if needed. Maybe the new operations manager is the person for the job. You can interview for that," Paisley suggested.

"I haven't been involved in an interview in years," he replied.

"It's time to get involved," Paisley said. "It's *your* company. I recommend being involved in every interview for a while. Once things have stabilized, you can step back and interview management positions only if you'd like."

"Okay," he said, taking notes on a yellow legal pad.

"And a friend of mine – the one in the accident – overheard us talking while I was taking care of her. She noticed you have two videoconference software systems, and you're paying for three different cloud storage systems as well."

"We are?" the man asked.

"Yes. My guess is that Tim had one he liked, someone else had one they liked, and so on. That's usually how it happens. I went ahead and reviewed all the software you guys use in-depth after she noticed that." Paisley pulled the spreadsheet up on the TV so that he could see it as well. She couldn't believe she had missed it in the first place, but with a new relationship and then Trinity's accident, her focus hadn't been on this company as much as it should've been, unfortunately. "I made recommendations based mainly on cost and on features offered. It's not much, but you can switch from a few monthly plans to annual ones, saving a little there. Those four I've highlighted in red you can drop entirely – it adds up to about fourteen grand a year."

He pushed his glasses up higher on his nose and shook his head.

"It seems I've let a lot of things get away from me."

"The good news is that it's all fixable," Paisley replied.

The owner smiled warmly at her and said, "I believe you turned me down the last time I asked, but I'd love it if you let my family take you out to dinner tonight. The work you've put in, even with the family emergency you're going through, is going to save this business, which is my family's life's work. The least we can do is buy you a nice meal before you leave."

Paisley wanted to turn him down again because her flight was at nine o'clock tonight and a dinner like this sounded like a long one, but she'd already packed and checked out of her hotel, so it was either dinner alone at the airport or a nice meal with a good family and then heading to the airport, so she accepted.

***

"Did he like the software thing?" Trinity asked over video chat later.

"Hi, one of us had a physical therapy appointment today, and the other wants to know how it went," Paisley told her.

"Fine. They don't even think I need to go back, but they suggested one more appointment next week just to be sure. Now, tell me about–"

"Babe," Paisley interrupted her and then yawned. "It's late. Can I tell you about my day tomorrow?"

"I'm just curious how it went."

"He took every single one of our suggestions," Paisley replied, closing her eyes.

"Yeah?"

"Yes," she said, still with her eyes closed.

"That's great. Is it going to help?"

"It should," Paisley said softly.

"Are you going to fall asleep?" Trinity asked.

"Yes," Paisley replied. "How are you this awake right now?"

"I waited up to talk to you," Trinity said.

"But you're all fired up, and I'm ready to sleep for ten hours," Paisley noted. "I hope you weren't expecting video sex tonight," she added.

"What? No. I just wanted to hear how it went."

"It went well. I think they'll survive," Paisley said.

"That's great," Trinity commented before deciding to ask, "Did you tell him about–"

"Yes."

"You don't even know what I was going to say," Trinity said, laughing.

"Told him everything. Tired now," Paisley mumbled in response.

"You're really cute when you're sleepy," Trinity said.

"So, I must be *adorable* right now," Paisley replied. "I have to be up early tomorrow and on the road for three hours to get to my next client after moving things around so I could still give them a full day. Can we maybe say goodnight?"

"Yeah," Trinity said. "Hey, Pais?"

"Huh?"

"I wanted to–" She stopped.

Paisley reluctantly opened her eyes and looked into Trinity's through the small phone screen she had resting against a pillow.

"Never mind," Trinity said.

"What is it?"

"Nothing. I'll tell you tomorrow night."

"Are you sure?" Paisley asked.

"Yeah, I'm sure. And my car isn't as bad as they initially thought, so it should be done soon, thanks to Will's brother. I can come this weekend instead of you coming here."

"Okay," Paisley said, nodding off again.

***

After she had left that Sunday and had flown straight to Chicago, Paisley had rearranged her entire December schedule, making calls to her clients to apologize for any changes and offering to work remotely for now until she

254

could get there in person. She had a trip this week for three days that was a drive instead of a flight, which was nice – it was just three hours in the opposite direction of Trinity… She had managed to make it so that they could spend another weekend together and had planned to drive to Trinity this time. When she heard Trinity say she'd be driving to Paisley instead, Paisley had agreed because she'd basically been asleep already. Waking up the next morning, though, she texted Trinity that she could still go to her.

Trinity Pascal: You're worried about me driving, aren't you? He hit me; it wasn't my fault. I will be okay. I'll see you Friday night.

Paisley grunted in frustration, but she had to let this one go – Trinity was a grown woman and would need to drive to see her at some point.

She got ready and drove to her next client, which was a mid-sized healthcare company that manufactured surgical instruments. They'd wanted her to take a look at their organization structure, mainly to see if there could be any cost savings there. That usually meant one thing: they were hoping she'd come in and tell them to make cuts. Paisley hated being even partly responsible for someone possibly losing their job, but it came with the territory. Initial boring meetings over, she went back to her hotel, ordered dinner, and got to work on reviewing her takeaways from the conversation she'd had.

"Hey, how bored are you right now?" she asked Trinity after she'd eaten dinner.

"Have something in mind?" Trinity asked with mischief in her voice.

"Not that," Paisley said, laughing.

"Oh. Then, I'm only a normal amount of bored and not an excessive amount. What's up?"

"Want to help me come up with some ideas for my client?"

"Yeah? Okay."

"Are you sure? You worked all day."

"I'm sure. Want to FaceTime, though?"

"Yeah. Let me just get set up over here; I want to be able to share my screen."

"So professional," Trinity teased.

"Shut up."

"Hey, if I help, can I get a prize later?"

"Depends on the prize," Paisley teased and liked where this was going.

"You; naked on camera."

"That could be arranged," Paisley replied. "As long as you'll *also* be naked on camera."

"Let's get to work," Trinity said quickly.

***

"You're really good at this," Paisley said.

"I'm even better in person. Take them off, babe," Trinity replied.

"That's not what I meant," Paisley said, stepping out of her plaid pajama pants.

"What did you mean, then?" Trinity asked.

Paisley lay back down on the bed, wearing only her panties, and watched as Trinity took off her T-shirt. Paisley swallowed and wished she was with her girlfriend instead of in this hotel that had a weird smell throughout.

"You're good at making recommendations," she replied.

"Oh, talk dirty to me, baby," Trinity joked.

Paisley laughed and moved the computer so that it rested between her legs after she spread them.

"Shit," Trinity said, moving her computer until it was in the same position as Paisley's.

"Show me," Paisley asked her softly.

Trinity's hand moved into her purple underwear.

"Like this?" she said.

"Yes," Paisley replied in a whisper and watched.

"I miss you," Trinity said.

"You have no idea," Paisley replied, sliding her own hand into her panties.

"Then, show me," Trinity replied.

"I will. This weekend."

"Yeah?" Trinity said. "What will you do?"

"Let you do whatever you want to me," Paisley replied, stroking her clit.

"What if I—"

"Whatever you want," she repeated, interrupting Trinity.

Trinity gasped, and Paisley could see the woman's fingers moving beneath the fabric of her underwear, and she wanted to see more but loved not being able to see it at the same time.

"A couple of days from now, I'm going to have you— " Trinity stopped. "Fuck. I'm so close already."

Paisley gasped and watched as Trinity's fingers sped up. She wasn't that far behind her, and minutes later, they were both slowly stroking themselves to come back down from their orgasms.

"Want to fall asleep together?" Trinity asked.

"I'd love that," Paisley said.

As nice as this was – the video sex, the talking all the time, being able to include in that talking stuff about work that Paisley hadn't been able to share with any past relationship – she missed her. Paisley really missed her, and she wanted to fall asleep next to her girlfriend, not next to a screen with her beautiful face on it.

CHAPTER 36

"Are you sure you can't stay longer?" Paisley asked.

"You act like I'm leaving right now; I just got here last night," Trinity replied, buttoning her shirt.

"Why are you getting dressed up?" Paisley asked, lying naked in bed and watching Trinity walk around her room, putting on a button-down shirt and a pair of slacks.

"We're going to a nice place."

"We are?"

"I made a reservation," Trinity replied.

"I thought we were going to have sex all weekend," Paisley said.

"We've been having sex since I got here," Trinity responded, turning around and lifting her left eyebrow when she noticed Paisley hadn't bothered putting on a single item of clothing yet. "It's a date, Paisley. I wanted to take you on a date. We haven't actually done that yet. I think when you're long-distance, it's easy to just stay in bed or around the house all weekend when you get to see each other because you just want to be naked, but I want to take you out. I want a date."

"So, I have to dress up, too?" Paisley asked.

"You can wear whatever you want, but I'd highly encourage you to wear a dress or a skirt," Trinity told her.

"Oh, yeah? Why?"

"Because I love looking at your legs."

Paisley got out of bed, walked to Trinity, and kissed her, giving Trinity a great view of those legs.

"Give me thirty minutes," she said.

***

Thirty minutes later, Trinity was finished getting ready

and had gone downstairs to wait for Paisley. She decided to text Kelly while she was waiting and got a reply shortly after.

<u>Kelly Stein:</u> Tonight's the night?

Trinity messaged back that indeed, it was. She was tired of waiting. Now that the accident was behind her, she had a clean bill of health from her doctor and her physical therapist, and they were finally together in person again, she was ready to put it all out on the table. Trinity hoped the night ended with them making love and not awkwardly falling asleep next to one another for the few days they had together, but only time would tell.

With Paisley ready and looking unbelievably gorgeous in a dark-green dress with a skinny white belt and white heels, Trinity held her breath for a moment before she finally smiled, pushed her nervousness aside, and took Paisley's hand as they left the house. She drove them and didn't let go of Paisley's hand the entire drive. It took only about twenty minutes to get there, another five to get the parking in order with the valet, and another couple to get where they were going.

"Trin, what are we doing here?" Paisley asked.

"I thought we'd have drinks first. Our dinner reservation in the restaurant isn't for another half an hour," Trinity replied.

"Why did you rush me out of the house then?" Paisley asked.

"I recall sitting on the sofa, waiting patiently for you," Trinity said, pulling her into the hotel's piano bar. "Besides, this place, apparently, has amazing martinis. I looked it up; they're known for it."

"Do you even *drink* martinis?" Paisley asked.

"No," Trinity replied. "But I thought I might try one with *you* tonight if they're so good."

"Aren't you full of surprises?" Paisley said playfully.

Trinity cleared her throat and, with her head on a swivel, looked for a place for them to sit. Most of the bar was still empty, with a smattering of booths filled with businessmen and women and one by a woman who was by herself, watching the man play the piano in the corner. The bar itself was dimmer than Trinity had expected it to be, but it was late evening, so it made sense. The booths were made out of dark leather and had ornate chandeliers hanging over each one. Paisley followed her to one of the booths in the back, away from the main grouping of businesspeople. Paisley moved into the booth, and Trinity sat on the same side, which normally she wouldn't do, but she wanted to be as close to Paisley as possible this weekend. Well, all the time, but this weekend even more than usual.

"Good evening. Would you like to hear about our drink specials?" a waiter dressed in a white shirt, blue tie, and black vest asked after placing drink napkins down in front of them.

"I hear you're good with martinis," Paisley said.

"Yes. We have a selection of those you can pick from the menu at the end of the table, but if you're interested in a recommendation, I'd suggest the cucumber or the Hawaiian. Those are two of our best sellers."

"Oh, the Hawaiian sounds good to me," Paisley said.

"And I guess I'll try the cucumber," Trinity spoke.

"Great. I'll have those out in just a minute. Are you staying at the hotel?"

"No, just drinks and dinner tonight," Trinity said.

"Very well," he said, walking off with a smile.

"So," Paisley began, turning into her. "What exactly are we doing in a piano bar downtown?"

"It seemed like something nice to do before dinner. I figured if we beat traffic, we could have a drink here and then make our reservation. And if not, just dinner and maybe a walk afterward. This hotel is on the water."

"You really did your research, didn't you?" Paisley asked.

"I did, yes," Trinity replied. "So, how did it go with the healthcare people? We fell asleep last night, and well, we were *busy* today, so we haven't talked about it."

"Busy, huh?" Paisley teased. "You woke me up by making me come."

"Complaining?"

"Not at all," she said, placing her hand on Trinity's thigh.

Trinity wrapped her arm around the back of the booth and moved in a little closer.

"Here we are," the waiter said, approaching with two drinks.

He took them off the tray one by one, placed them on their appropriate napkins, and then added a bowl of what looked like trail mix between them.

"Would you like me to let the restaurant know you're in the bar?"

"That would be great. Reservation for Pascal," Trinity replied.

"If you need anything else, please let me know." He left the check and walked off.

"Want to try and trade?" Paisley asked.

A woman in a red dress caught Trinity's eye, and Trinity nodded for Paisley to look. The woman walked onto the small stage, where the pianist was playing, and stood behind a microphone. The song changed on the piano a few seconds later, and the woman's sultry voice joined the instrument. Trinity hadn't known they'd have someone singing tonight, but it added to the ambiance, which made her feel like this was the perfect night to tell Paisley how she felt. Before she did that, though, she had other plans.

"It's good. Try it," Paisley said.

"I will," Trinity replied, turning into Paisley a bit more. "Do you remember what you told me a while ago?"

"I've told you a lot of things since we met. Can you be more specific?"

"I know you said in the fantasy, you were getting *her* off and going upstairs, but I was hoping…" Trinity slid her hand up the inside of Paisley's thigh as she leaned into her ear. "You'd let me instead."

"Trin, we're in public."

"No one can see us," Trinity replied. "The lights are low, and there's a piano playing and a woman singing." She ran her thumb over Paisley's panties. "You look gorgeous. I'm blocking anyone from seeing behind me, and the table blocks everything else."

"Trin, we can't." Paisley looked at her.

"Let me, please," Trinity said, hovering her lips over Paisley's.

When Paisley didn't push Trinity's hand away, Trinity moved aside the panel of Paisley's panties and ran a fingertip over her clit. Paisley hissed quietly against Trinity's lips.

"This is crazy," Paisley whispered.

"It's your fantasy."

"Yes, a *fantasy*, and *I* was touching *you*," Paisley argued.

"Well, I had the idea to bring us here, so I guess it's a little of my fantasy, too, now," Trinity replied. "Should I stop?"

"No," Paisley whispered.

Trinity pressed their lips together and kissed Paisley as she stroked her clit slowly, building her up while music played around them, businesspeople laughed and talked, the waiter continued to drop drinks to other tables, and the bartender worked on cleaning glasses. After a moment, Trinity kissed Paisley deeper, letting their tongues dance together in an attempt to remind the woman of what she'd done with that tongue earlier that day. Paisley let out a soft moan. Trinity stroked a bit faster. She wanted to go inside, but at this angle, it wouldn't work. When Paisley spread her legs wider for her, though, it was even more tempting.

"Pais?"

"Yes?" Paisley said as her eyes closed and her head went back against Trinity's arm.

"Baby?"

"Yes," Paisley said.

"Come for me," Trinity whispered into her ear.

"Yes," Paisley said. "Yes. Yes." Her hips moved against Trinity's hand, thankfully covered up by the table.

"You're so sexy, baby," Trinity whispered as Paisley tried to catch her breathing.

"I can't believe… we just did… that," Paisley managed out as she began to come down.

"Says the woman who fantasized about it," Trinity replied.

"You do know what a fantasy is, right?" Paisley chuckled softly.

"Did you forget that I've had about a million of them about *you*?" Trinity said.

"Most of those took place at our old high school, so I can't help you there," Paisley remarked.

Trinity wiped her hand on an extra napkin. Paisley gave her a look.

"What? You were wet," Trinity said. "I'll wash my hands before we eat."

"Can we just go home?" Paisley asked, moving a hand to Trinity's thigh now. "I can cook us something, or we can order in. I just want to be alone with you this weekend."

"Aren't we hanging out with your friends tomorrow?"

"I'll cancel," Paisley said.

"No, don't. I like your friends."

"You like me more, though, right?" Paisley asked, joking.

But this was it; this was Trinity's moment. She swallowed and decided to put it out there and be brave.

"No, Paisley." Trinity paused. "I love you."

Paisley didn't say anything at first, and as Trinity's face and neck warmed with embarrassment, she prepared to say that it was okay if Paisley wasn't there yet. She'd tell her that they would be fine, and they would just finish their drinks and go to dinner. Trinity would drive home tomorrow afternoon, cry a little in the car and at home because she doubted she could prevent the tears, and eventually, Paisley would say it back.

"I love you, too," Paisley said.

"Sorry?" Trinity asked.

"I said, I love you, too," Paisley replied, smiling at her.

"You did? Sorry, I wasn't sure I'd heard you correctly."

"Trinity Pascal?"

"Yes?"

Paisley paused to look into her eyes and said, "Baby, I love you."

Trinity smiled, cupped Paisley's cheek, and kissed her quickly.

"Pardon me for interrupting… The restaurant said your table is ready now if you'd like to take your drinks with you," the waiter told them.

"Oh," Trinity said.

She couldn't really think about dinner and drinks right now. Paisley had just told her she loved her, and it was all Trinity could think about.

"Can you give us just a minute? We'll run to the restroom and head to the restaurant."

"Of course. I'll let them know you're on your way," the waiter replied and walked away.

"You okay?" Paisley asked her.

"I didn't think you'd say it back," Trinity admitted.

"Why not?" Paisley turned more toward her.

"I don't know. I just thought you'd get there later."

"Trin, I've been here for a while now," Paisley replied. "I don't think I was ready to say it until now, though."

"Me neither," Trinity replied.

"Did you plan this romantic night to tell me?"

"Yes," Trinity said.

Paisley smiled at her and said, "I love you. I want to work through all the hard stuff with you. I've never wanted that with anyone before."

"Me neither," Trinity said.

"So, what do you say about maybe going to Vermont to ski next winter and visit our old campus," Paisley suggested while wiggling her eyebrows.

Trinity laughed. She loved this woman, and she had told her. Paisley loved her back. Trinity wasn't sure how it had all happened. She could still picture dropping that tray in the cafeteria and Paisley giving her that glare. Only now, there was something more in the look than she'd previously remembered. Paisley had been going through things, too. Now that Trinity knew her, she understood what that look was really saying on that day. It was saying that Paisley didn't know what to do, how to intervene, how to be brave and stand up to their classmates.

Trinity leaned in, kissed her again, and said, "Next winter?"

"Yeah," Paisley said, laughing a little.

"I'd like that a lot," Trinity replied, standing up and holding out her hand for Paisley to take.

CHAPTER 37

"So, you are officially in love?" Weston asked.

"I am," Paisley said, smiling. "Crazy, huh?"

"How is it going to work? Long-distance for a while?"

"Yeah, it's the only option for now."

"But what happens when you want more?" Aria asked.

"I want more already," Paisley replied. "If I could, I'd have her here right now, but her business is there, and my home base is *here*."

"You'd be the one that would have to move," Talon said, sounding sad.

"We haven't even *begun* to have those conversations," Paisley said.

"Yeah, but her business has an actual office – you travel all the time. It would be a lot easier for you to sell your house and move there."

"I guess, but that's a long way away," Paisley said.

"Is it?" Aria asked. "You two are already in love."

Paisley took a sip of her coffee and said, "Is that a *bad* thing?"

"No, of course not," Aria said.

"I think Aria and Talon aren't expressing themselves very clearly," Weston said. "They're worried about what happens when you move."

"When I move?"

"You *are* moving?" Talon asked.

"What? No." Paisley laughed. "I'm not moving."

"Anytime soon," Talon added.

"They're worried that you're leaving," Weston said.

"We hardly see you as is," Talon said. "We got lucky that you moved things around to be with Trinity this month. I half-expected you to spend the two days you're here with her instead."

"She's busy working, too. They have some stuff going

on there," Paisley said. "I told her I'd stay away to let them sort it out. Something about suppliers, parts, hiring, and burning the midnight oil to get it all together."

"And if this works out with you two – which, to be clear, we hope it does," Aria said. "You'll be gone. We've managed to make it this far in our lives still living close and spending time together when most groups of friends are spread out by now either by busy work or family schedules, or they've moved away."

"Yeah, but that's not us," Paisley said.

"Isn't it?" Eleanor said. "Weston already spends most weekends and a whole lot of weeks at the cabin with Annie. We're all expecting her to just tell us they're moving there permanently."

"We wouldn't move there permanently until we expand it," Weston argued. "Annie and I don't even live together officially yet."

"Yes, you do," Aria and Talon said at the same time.

"She still has her–"

"Just because she still has a lease, doesn't mean you two aren't living together," Eleanor said. "And I give it maybe another year before you two are in that cabin full-time. I can see you starting work on the cabin as soon as spring hits."

"I mean, we've talked about it, yes," Weston replied. "But it's only an hour and a half away. We came back to meet Trinity. We like the drive."

"But how long will you make it every time we want to hang out?" Talon asked. "Soon, it'll be every other time, and then, every third time. Then, Annie's pregnant, and we're only seeing you for the baby shower and to take turns holding the kid."

"Annie's pregnant already? Are you guys not coming to the wedding? I'd had plans for you to be involved a bit," Weston joked. "Not like I can expect my brothers to stand up next to me without giggling."

"You get what I mean," Talon said.

"Where's Scarlet right now?" Aria asked.

"Probably with Dakota. I texted her, but she didn't reply," Paisley shared.

"See?" Talon replied. "Even Scarlet is hooking up."

"I don't think Scarlet *hooks up* with anyone," Weston remarked. "She's dating someone finally, and that's great."

"But she's not here, and Paisley texted her – she always replies to Paisley," Talon argued.

"Let's give her this one, okay?" Paisley said. "She's waited forever for this."

"Dakota *is* hot," Talon stated.

"Agreed," Weston replied, taking a drink of her coffee.

"Who's hot?" Carmen asked, approaching the table with a cupcake for Eleanor.

"Okay… I need a gym membership. Anyone have a guest pass I can use?"

Carmen laughed, setting the plate down in front of her girlfriend, and said, "You do *not* need a gym membership. Eat it, or don't. I made it for you."

"How can I not eat it when you made it just for me?"

"There's probably another eleven of them in the back, so I don't think she made them *just* for you," Aria noted.

"London has a red velvet with your name on it in the back," Carmen told her.

"Oh," Aria stood, and with that, she was gone.

Carmen took her chair and pulled it close to Eleanor.

"I have a confession," Talon said.

"You do?" Paisley asked.

"I'm worried about what happens when we all start to spread out."

"Not a confession; we got that already," Paisley replied.

"I'm worried because Emerson and I are looking at houses up to an hour away from here."

"What? Why?" Paisley asked, surprised.

"Because we can't find what we want close to the office, and we can work from home a few days a week if we want anyway, so we figured the commute would be okay. We'd drive together, obviously, and take the carpool lane, so it wouldn't be *that* bad."

"You're giving *me* a hard time about the cabin?" Weston said.

"I know… I just don't know what to do. We've been looking, but nothing within our price range comes up close enough to the city, so we're expanding the search."

"Talon, you're allowed to move an hour away if it's what you and Emerson want," Paisley began. "Wes is allowed to move to the cabin. Scar can spend whatever time she wants with Dakota. Aria and London are allowed to go to Italy for as long as they want. I'm allowed to move wherever if and when Trinity and I get to that point. Ellie is—" She turned to her friend. "What do you two have going on?"

"Nothing right now," Eleanor replied. "*I'm* the good friend."

Paisley laughed and said, "Well, whenever you have something, you're allowed to have it. We all love each other. And we love the people we're with; we want lives with them. We'll make sure we keep up some of our friend traditions; others might change to include more people, and then maybe one day, they'll include kids, too. It'll be harder, sure, but I think something I've learned this year in particular, is that it's all worth it. I want to put in the effort. It's not just all about work. I love you all so much, and I don't want to miss things, but it's a reality."

Everyone gave her forced smiles because they all realized it was true. A lot of things were about to change for them. With Paisley spending time with Trinity, that left less for her friends. With Talon and Emerson possibly moving an hour outside of the city, they wouldn't be available as often. Weston and Annie already weren't. Eleanor and Carmen would have something come up one day, and Aria and London could go anywhere, thanks to Aria's money.

London owned the bakery with Carmen and Mariah, but everyone knew that the three women wanted to expand.

It could be that they did that, and London ended up man-
aging one of the bakeries on the other side of the country,
or at least, the state. Hell, Eleanor and Carmen could end
up doing the same thing if Eleanor would move with her.
For the first time, Paisley wasn't jealous of her friends having girlfriends or that they got to spend time together when
she didn't because she just knew it would all work out. She
wasn't sure how, but she did, and that meant everything to
her.

***

"Hi, Mom," Paisley said into the phone as she left the
bakery.

"Hi, honey. How are you?"

"I'm good. You?"

"Will we see you on Sunday?"

"No, not this–"

"Fine. Fine. No need to make an excuse," her mother
said and sighed dramatically.

"I'm not making an excuse, Mom." Paisley laughed as
she climbed into her car.

"Well, I need to start planning Christmas. So, will we
see you, or will you be spending the holiday in some dingy
hotel in–"

"I'm not spending it working," Paisley said, starting
the car.

"That's good. Will you be with your friends?"

"Mom, I'm coming to Christmas dinner."

"You are?" the woman asked.

"Yes, I am. I'm doing Christmas Eve with my friends,
though."

"But Christmas Day?"

"I'll be there. Well, *we'll* be there."

"We?" Paisley's mother asked.

"Yes, Mother. Trinity and I will be there. And I'd really
love it if you could invite her mom as well."

"Her mom?"

"Yes, Sharon."

"She's joining us?"

"If you invite her," Paisley said, laughing as she entered traffic.

"Have you met her yet?"

"No, but we're going to do that next weekend," Paisley said. "Just a lunch with the three of us."

"And you're sure you want me to invite her to Christmas dinner? What if you mess it up?"

"Thanks for the vote of confidence, Mom."

"Have you even met a parent before? A parent of someone you're dating, that is."

"It'll be fine, Mother."

"I don't want to invite the woman if there's–"

"Invite her," Paisley requested. "She'll be there. Trinity and I will be there."

"And Trinity will be there as…"

"My girlfriend. Yes, she'll be there as my girlfriend. Sharon will be there as the mother of my girlfriend. No, Trinity and I aren't living together yet. There's also no engagement announcement. The wedding is a long way off, and if you talk to Sharon about grandchildren on Christmas, I will take Trinity away, and you'll never see her again because *you* can't have nice things."

Her mother laughed and said, "Oh, honey. You're in love, aren't you?"

Paisley smiled as she sat at the stoplight and said, "Yes, I am."

"That's great. I'm very happy for you. I will be on my best behavior, okay?" her mother promised.

"Thank you. Oh, will Grandpa be there?"

"I don't know yet. He might spend the day with your uncle since he was with *us* for Thanksgiving. Why?"

"Trinity really liked him. I think she was looking forward to catching up with him."

"He liked her as well. He said as much at Sunday dinner last week."

"He did?" Paisley asked.

"Yes."

"Because she brought him bourbon?"

"Because she talked to him," her mom replied. "He's old, sweetie. Most people bring him a drink, say hello, and walk away. She stayed and talked to him."

Paisley's smile went wide, and she said, "That's my girl."

"Yes, and we like her, too, so don't mess it up," her mom replied.

Paisley laughed again and said, "I'll do my best."

EPILOGUE

Trinity sat in her car, which was in the driveway. She waited a minute, and the garage door opened. Paisley walked out, motioning for Trinity to move her car inside. It might seem like a small thing to others, but the fact that Paisley had cleaned out the other half of the two-car garage, when she was already as busy as she was, just so Trinity could park inside the garage and not have to scrape the ice off her windshield or warm her car up whenever she visited, meant a lot to Trinity. After parking and turning the car off, she climbed out and pulled Paisley into a long hug.

"Hi, babe," Paisley said. "Maybe we can continue this inside? Not a lot of space between the cars here."

"Nope. I'm hugging you here."

Paisley laughed, but she didn't pull out of the hug. Trinity finally let go and kissed her quickly before moving to the trunk of her repaired car. Thankfully, the guy who hit her had insurance, so it covered the repairs; and while her medical claim was still being processed, her own insurance company said it should be fine. That gave her one less thing to worry about, which was good because she had a lot on her plate right now. First, there was the friend hangout on Christmas Eve with Paisley's friends, and then Christmas dinner with Paisley's family, where Paisley would meet her mom for the first time. There was also something important she needed to talk to Paisley about, and not knowing how the woman would take it was giving Trinity mild anxiety.

"So, tonight is our night," Paisley said. "Whatever you want to do. Tomorrow day is ours, too, but Weston and Annie wanted to know if we wanted to join them at the cabin. I told them I thought it was a little silly to drive all the way there in the morning and drive back in the afternoon to get ready for dinner at Aria's place, but they still offered. It's beautiful out there, and cell phones barely work most of the time, so we'd be able to disconnect for a few hours. Then, we have Christmas dinner the next day obviously, and–"

"Pais?" Trinity said, stopping her girlfriend's adorable rambling.

"Yeah?"

"Babe, can we talk about something?"

"Oh," Paisley said, sitting down on the sofa. "Is everything okay?"

"Everything's great," Trinity replied, taking a seat next to her.

Paisley looked over her shoulder and noted, "You have three bags."

"One is my backpack; doesn't count," Trinity said.

"Still, it's two big bags. I know you didn't get me *that* many Christmas presents. We talked about this – no big gifts."

"Can you focus for a second?" Trinity asked, laughing. "I got you two gifts. One is bigger than the other, but not in size."

"Trinity Pascal…" Paisley squinted at her.

"I'm not proposing on Christmas, Pais." Trinity laughed. "You'll get your gift on the day like everyone else, but I was hoping I could maybe stay here through New Year's Day."

Paisley smiled and said, "The whole week?"

"Yeah. You said you only have that client two hours away that you'll be with overnight, right?"

"I leave Tuesday morning; back on Wednesday night."

"Can I go with you?"

"You want to work from the hotel?" the woman asked.

"No, I was hoping I could go *with* you," Trinity replied.

Paisley looked confused and said, "With the client? Wait. What about work?"

"I talked to Vidal," Trinity said. "That's why we've been so busy – we've been working things out."

"What things?" Paisley asked, leaning back a little.

"She's buying me out," Trinity said.

"What?" Paisley asked.

"We've been talking to the bank and the investors, and it's the right call. My heart's not in it, and hers is. She wants this stuff – the day-to-day decisions and building the company with hires and products. I told you, the most excited I've been in a long time was working with you. That's not just with my company but also helping you with the other clients you worked with. I know I didn't do much, but I loved it, Pais. I liked helping one company problem-solve and move on to the next one with you."

"What are you saying, Trin?"

"I'll work for free at first until I can, I don't know, prove myself. Then, maybe I–"

"Trinity, you want to work with me?"

"Well, *for* you. It's your company," she replied.

"Babe, we can't work together," Paisley said.

"Why not?" Trinity asked.

"We're in a relationship."

"So?"

"So, I love you. I don't want to risk that," Paisley told her.

"Paisley, we've been working together in one way or another this whole time."

"Not the same thing," Paisley argued, standing up.

"Ah, here's where I predicted the pacing would start. Good to know I got that part right," Trinity teased as Paisley began pacing in her living room.

"You actually want to do what I do?"

"Yes, I do."

"It's traveling a lot. You've seen the hotels I stay in."

"And they bother *you*, not me, snob. I don't mind a shampoo and conditioner combo," Trinity joked.

Paisley gave her a playful glare and said, "How would

that even work? You'd be in one place; I'd be in another."

"I've thought about that a little," Trinity said. "So, I'd move closer to here; maybe get an apartment in the city or something."

"You're moving now?" Paisley asked.

"I don't need to be there if I'm working for you," Trinity reasoned.

"*With* me," Paisley said again.

"Anyway, I'd move close by so that we could see each other whenever we're both home. We can take jobs that require both of us sometimes, so we'd travel together and save on expenses since we'll share hotel rooms." Trinity winked at Paisley, who rolled her eyes in return. "And yeah, there will be trips that I'm on my own, and you're on your own, but we can schedule them so they're not back-to-back, and the time apart will make us appreciate the time together even more; kind of like it does now."

"You're serious about this?" Paisley asked.

"You're going to hire anyway, right?"

"Two people, yeah."

"So, hire me and hire one more," Trinity said.

"I'd need to see a resume and at least three references," Paisley teased as she sat back down.

"I'll have Vidal call you. Then, you can see my mom on Christmas and ask her. And, well…" She pointed to Paisley. "*You* can be my third."

"I don't think I can give you a job reference because you do that thing with your tongue that I like," Paisley joked.

Trinity laughed and said, "Pais, I want this with you. I know it's scary, and we've only really known each other for a couple of months, at most, but I think I'll be good at this. Vidal and I have been working through all of the logistics, so if you say no, that's okay. I'm still leaving the company; I'll just have to figure out another step."

"I can't believe this," Paisley said, smiling. "Really? This is what you want?"

Trinity shrugged a shoulder, nodded, and said, "Yes. I'd want it even if we weren't dating. Honestly, I might have asked you about it sooner had we not been together, but I think we can make this work. I mean, Weston and Annie share a profession *and* an office. So do Talon and Emerson, right?"

"Right," Paisley said, laughing. "But I don't have an office for us. We can share mine, I guess, but I'm hardly ever in it."

"If there's a third person, we need a real space."

"I was going to get a VA," Paisley said.

"Virtual assistant?"

"Book travel, set up meetings, respond to those emails you hate."

"I don't hate emails," Trinity said, laughing.

"They can work from wherever. And if I was hiring another consultant, I was going to get a small office for us in one of the co-working spaces, but if that consultant is you, I don't really have to do that, do I?"

"No?" Trinity asked.

"No. We can work out of my home office when we're both here, and you can use it when I'm not," Paisley replied.

"Then, I should find an apartment close by to reduce my commute," Trinity said.

"You know I'd ask you to move in here, but it's–"

"I'm not ready for that yet, either," Trinity interrupted. "Especially if we're doing this."

"I've said this many times already, but... Trinity, you're really sure about this, right?" Paisley took her hand. "I think you'll be great at it, but I've never worked with any-one before, and you're my girlfriend... I doubt I'm good at asking for help or delegating, and I have no idea if I'm going to be an asshole boss to this poor VA."

"Maybe one day, it'll be our company," Trinity said. "Like, far down the line."

Paisley smiled and said, "I've been alone in this."

"I know," Trinity said.

"And that was important to me."

"I know. It was just a comment. I didn't–"

"That *was* important to me." Paisley cupped Trinity's cheek. "I've loved working with you recently – watching you look at that spreadsheet and see stuff I missed, helping that company – it was nice."

"Yeah?"

"I'd love for us to work together," Paisley confirmed.

"I know it's really early, but can I have this week off, then? I'd really like to spend it with my girlfriend."

"Your girlfriend is still working, remember?" Paisley laughed.

Trinity moved until Paisley was lying down on the couch and said, "Well, then I guess I should ask another question instead. Can I start this week?"

Paisley smiled up at her, wrapped her arms around Trinity's neck, nodded, and said, "But, Trin? We come first." She placed a hand over Trinity's heart. "*This* is the most important thing."

Trinity nodded and said, "Agreed."

"How much does Vidal hate me right now?" Paisley checked.

"Actually, she's pretty happy about the whole thing. She had a little – or, really, *a lot* – of resentment that had been kind of waiting to boil over. She had a five-minute vent session about how I wasn't carrying my own weight and was more concerned with helping Will in the front instead of helping her lead the company. Then, we got down to brass tacks."

"Brass tacks," Paisley said. "I love when you talk busi-ness."

Trinity laughed and said, "There were a lot of brass tacks." She lowered herself until she was kissing Paisley's neck. "And many meetings."

"Tell me more," Paisley said.

"Budget spreadsheets all over the place; just… all over the office."

"This is really working for me," Paisley chuckled.

"Wait until I tell you about the investors' meeting where we had to present the hiring forecast."

Paisley reached down, undid Trinity's jeans, and said, "Keep going."

Trinity laughed and said, "Do you want me to spoil your Christmas gift?"

"Yes," Paisley replied.

"I got *myself* a pair of new skis," she said, kissing Paisley's throat. "For next winter." She kissed her jaw.

Paisley laughed and pushed Trinity's pants down her thighs.

"There's still plenty of winter left... We can go *this* winter," she said.

"Music to my ears," Trinity said, lifting Paisley's shirt up in order to feel skin.

"So, what did you get *me*?" Paisley asked.

Trinity looked down at her, saying, "Oh, I'm not actually going to tell you."

"What?" Paisley laughed and gave Trinity's now bare ass a light smack.

"How did you get my underwear down without—"

"Just kiss me," Paisley requested. "You're here. *You're* my gift."

Trinity smiled and went to ask, "Should I take what I got you back or—"

Paisley kissed her hard then, and Trinity forgot her question.

Made in the USA
Las Vegas, NV
04 December 2022

61124316R00173